MW01027887

THE SNOW RAVEN

OTHER TITLES BY CONNIE DIAL

The Third Hell

JOSIE CORSINO MYSTERIES

Fallen Angels

Dead Wrong

Unnatural Murder

Set the Night on Fire

Warning Shots

DETECTIVE MIKE TURNER MYSTERIES

Internal Affairs

The Broken Blue Line

A JOSIE CORSINO MYSTERY

THE SNOW RAVEN

CONNIE DIAL

The Permanent Press
Sag Harbor, NY 11963

For information, address:
The Permanent Press
4170 Noyac Road
Sag Harbor, NY 11963
www.thepermanentpress.com

Library of Congress Cataloging-in-Publication Data

Dial, Connie, author.
Title: The snow raven / Connie Dial.
Description: Sag Harbor, NY: The Permanent Press, [2020]
Series: A Josie Corsino mystery
ISBN: 978-1-57962-589-4 (cloth)
ISBN: 978-1-57962-638-9 (ebook)
1. Mystery fiction. 2. Suspense fiction.

PS3604.I126 S66 2020
813'.6—dc23 2020030207

Printed in the United States of America

"To the dedicated men and women of the LAPD who chose narcotics enforcement and to those who paid the ultimate price in that endeavor."

~ ONE ~

Los Angeles, CA. 1981

Josie lost sight of her partner but heard rummaging behind the apartment building's massive air-conditioning unit. The moonlight wasn't bright enough to navigate this rooftop without tripping over an assortment of junk or stepping on deposits of what smelled like shit. She hit her ankle on a venting pipe protruding from the tar paper and swore before kicking and knocking it over.

"Go away, Corsino. I can't piss with you standing there," Detective Larry Tomic said, peering at her from under a dim security light.

"It's disgusting enough up here without your contribution," she said, rubbing her ankle.

"Sorry, can't hold it. Wait by the fire escape. That's how he comes up."

This was her life now, she thought, waiting for a junkie snitch in the toilet he called home. She figured there must be something seriously wrong with her because she loved it. Although she was the only woman in a squad of seasoned Hollywood narcotics detectives, it usually didn't bother Tomic that his partner was a girl. Some of the other detectives complained at first about her invasion into their all-male world, but he'd always treated her like one of the guys, except when he had to pee.

Josie understood the primary reason for his acceptance. After she'd joined the squad three years ago, he'd quickly discovered that she could buy drugs from anyone. She'd been promoted to detective and transferred to Narcotics from Newton patrol, but had worked undercover intelligence before that, so she knew how to look and behave like someone who lived on the fringes.

She was almost six feet tall and slender and although she'd trimmed her dark unruly hair for uniformed patrol, she'd let it grow out again and wondered with all the spider webs she just walked through how many of the eight-legged creatures were nesting among her split ends. Boots and worn jeans were her favorite wardrobe so fitting into the druggie lifestyle had come easy. It helped that none of the local gangs or dealers had ever seen or expected to find a woman dope cop working LAPD street enforcement. From her first day, she and Tomic made more arrests than any of the other teams. Higher stats meant their entire squad looked good so most of the guys were slowly adapting and learning to live with "a girl" sharing their space.

She located the fire escape and looked over the side of a three-foot retaining wall. She could see four stories down to the alley; there was no sign of the snitch.

"Maybe your strange visitor from another planet had second thoughts," she said as Tomic stood near her now, zipping up his pants and peering over the edge. He was a little shorter than she was, not muscular but strong. His light brown hair needed a trim and he hadn't shaved for a couple of days—the uniformed look of most dope cops; except, Tomic always wore cowboy boots. Josie figured it was male ego, to give himself the extra height.

"Not Superman . . . he's too stupid to be afraid . . . unless dickhead believes you've got kryptonite in your pocket," Tomic said.

Clark Kent was the name of her partner's snitch, his real name. He was tall and muscular so Tomic started calling him Superman. It was a joke, but with an IQ slightly higher than a cocker spaniel's, Kent began to act as if he believed he was the comic book hero, even wearing dark-rimmed eyeglass frames . . . without glass.

Kent admitted to smoking grass, shooting a little speed, and snorting or smoking coke when he could afford it. He was a natural busybody and seemed to know everything that happened on Hollywood's streets including the name of every active drug dealer, so Tomic fed his fantasy "to fight the never-ending battle for truth, justice, and the American way" and got a lot of useful information in return.

It was cold, and the wind was picking up on the roof. Josie zipped up her leather jacket and brushed off the top of the wall with her gloved hand before sitting where she could watch the ladder. Twenty minutes later she saw a figure moving around the dumpster in the alley. Whoever it was pulled down the fire escape steps and started to climb up.

Bundled in his parka, Tomic was sitting on a short stack of wooden pallets and leaning against her leg. She figured he'd probably heard the noisy ladder moving but tapped him on the head anyway and he grunted while getting to his feet. Like most older street cops, his body had been abused not only by police work but by hard living.

"Finally," he said a few seconds later, helping the bigger man pull himself up and onto the roof. "Where've you been? Ten means ten not ten thirty or eleven."

"Sorry, Detective Tomic, you know I got so much freakin' shit to deal with, sir," Kent said in his surprisingly high voice while brushing dirt off his pants and smiling at Josie. He shook his head and, leaning closer to her, whispered, "Still can't freakin' believe you're no lady cop." The temperature had dropped enough that she could see puffs of cold air as he spoke, but all he wore were Levi's and a tight, short-sleeved T-shirt which she knew was intended to show off his bulging biceps. His acne-scarred complexion and tiny voice told her he owed most of his muscle mass to steroids.

"What've you got for us?" she asked, as the snitch sat beside her on the wall. Her partner was looking at his watch and clearly ready to go. Josie was tired, too, but lately the prospect of a dope arrest seemed to trump everything else in her world.

"I wouldn't a drug you up here unless I got something big," Kent mumbled with a manufactured East Coast accent he'd picked up in some gangster movie. He was born and raised in Southern California.

"Okay, so what the fuck you got?" Tomic asked impatiently.

"It's what you got that's fucked . . ." he said, pausing for dramatic effect before adding, "Bunch a cops dealing crack." He began rubbing his arms as if he'd suddenly felt the cold.

"What cops?" Josie asked, sliding off the wall. He had her attention.

"Don't know no freakin' names but I can take you to a guy who does for fifty bucks . . . thirty's mine, twenty for him."

"Let's go," Tomic ordered, grabbing Kent's massive arm with both hands and attempting to drag him off the wall.

Kent pulled away nearly knocking Tomic over and said, "Not now, boss. He ain't gonna be there 'til tomorrow . . . won't tell me where there is yet."

"Who is this guy?" Josie asked.

"Can't say. I'll call you in the morning, but for now I gotta go."

"Can't or won't?"

Kent climbed back over the side and onto the ladder.

"Can't . . . promised, but you'll understand when you meet him," he said, winking at her and disappearing below the wall.

~ TWO ~

By the time Tomic drove Josie the few blocks back to the narcotics office parking lot it was nearly midnight and the building was dark and locked. She was tempted to walk across Wilcox to the Hollywood police station and sleep in the officers' cot room, but she had promised her son she'd be home for breakfast. It was the first day of school and she wanted to be with him when the bus got there. He'd been complaining they didn't spend enough time together anymore.

David was only seven but old enough to realize his mother was different from other moms. None of those women made lunch with a 9mm semiauto Beretta strapped on her hip. Her husband was good about filling in and his mother lived close enough to help, but the boy wanted her, and she knew not being there enough was making him unhappy.

She could smell the stench from the roof that had saturated her clothes and hair, but the narco building didn't have a shower. They were lucky to have a sink and toilet. It was a rundown city facility behind the Hollywood division gas pumps and housed two of the four West Bureau narcotics squads—Hollywood and Venice—with more than a dozen scruffy men and two females, her and the secretary. They had to pick up after themselves because the city's maintenance crew frequently refused to clean the mouse-infested "pigpen."

After Tomic dropped her off and drove away, she stood by the door for a few minutes but decided not to go inside. There was paperwork to do but it could wait until morning. She unlocked an old Dodge sedan and rolled down all the windows before heading toward Pasadena. The plan was to air herself out before she got home.

It was late but she knew Jake would be up. Her husband was a supervising attorney in the Los Angeles District Attorney's Office downtown and worked as hard as she did. The difference was he could bring his work home. He'd always been indulgent about her long hours, but Josie saw a change in him after she got promoted again to Narcotics Detective II supervisor a few months ago. He liked the extra money but still told her it was too dangerous and not appropriate work for any woman with a small child. She disagreed.

Before David was born they had rarely argued. Jake supported her when she was one of the first women to work in an LAPD black-and-white patrol car. As a couple, they worked hard, played hard, and laughed a lot, but about a year ago all that seemed to change. Their lovemaking was still frequent and pleasurable, but increasingly he acted as if he resented her desire to be a street cop. He said he was afraid of losing her, but she didn't believe that was the real reason. Her work was exciting and challenging and she was good at it. She hated that he made her feel guilty.

She suspected Jake's mother, or *Nonna*, as David called her—grandma in Italian—was the primary source of his discontent. The older woman was first-generation Italian but embraced the old country's ways. She was good at babysitting David but had never warmed to Josie as her son's wife. On more than one occasion, she preached how a woman should stay home to take care of her family. Josie ignored her. Jake pretended not to hear.

"Hi, hon," she said, finding him at the kitchen table with stacks of case files. "It's cold in here. Did the furnace break down again?" she asked, leaning over to kiss him.

They'd bought this three-story home in Pasadena, just north of downtown Los Angeles, shortly after David was born. It was old and still needed work, but she'd fallen in love with the big rooms, all the crown molding, original fireplaces, big backyard, and large front porch, but was growing impatient with the antiquated plumbing and furnace.

"No," he said, not looking up until he closed the file. "Mom doesn't like the heat on when she sleeps."

"She's staying over again?" Josie asked, not trying to hide her disappointment.

"It got late. I didn't want her to drive. Where'd you park that oil-leaking piece of crap they make you drive? Not in our driveway I hope."

"I put it as close to your Porsche as I could," she said and waited for his loud sigh before adding, "Just kidding, it's in the street in front of the neighbor's house. He'll probably have it towed as soon as he gets up."

"Perfect."

"Snob."

She took a bottle of brandy off the credenza in the dining room and poured herself a full snifter. "Want one?" she asked. He nodded. She put it in front of him and sat across the table.

"Love you," he said, raising the glass before taking a sip. "You look tired."

"Long day," she said, took a big swallow, and waited for that wonderful warming sensation.

"How come you never talk about what you and Tomic do?" he asked with a forced smile after a few seconds of silence. She usually loved his smile . . . and everything else about him, but she knew where this conversation was going and was too tired to have it. Jake was older than she was, with gray hair, and like his mother had some old-fashioned ideas, but he was intelligent and handsome with a great sense of humor too. She'd loved him almost from the first time they'd met but his obsession with getting her into a less dangerous, more "appropriate" assignment was becoming tiresome.

"Because most of the time what we do is boring," she said, lying. "I probably have as much paperwork as you . . . maybe more. Tonight we sat on the filthy roof of the anything-but Paradise Apartments with a family of raccoon-sized rats and waited for Tomic's snitch."

"Oh, so that's the reason. I wasn't going to mention it, my dear, but you are a bit odoriferous this evening," he said with a smirk that told her he was resigned to the fact she wouldn't allow him to fully share that part of her life.

"Sorry about that . . . although, I do clean up nicely."

"That's true. I'm willing to conduct a personal inspection in bed in about . . . oh, say half an hour or so . . . okay?" he asked, looking at his watch and grinning.

She was beyond tired but didn't turn him down because she always slept better after their lovemaking.

"Are you just getting home?" The question came from behind her, but Josie didn't need to turn around to know her mother-in-law was standing in the dining room doorway, probably bundled in her chenille bathrobe and fuzzy slippers and wearing a hairnet to cover her heavily sprayed helmet of perfectly coifed white hair. "Are you drinking wine at this hour? You'll never get up in the morning."

"Hi, Mom, sorry if we woke you," Josie said, not turning but smiling sweetly at Jake who grimaced.

"Go back to bed, Mom. We'll talk in the morning," he said.

"I'm thirsty," she announced and shuffled to the sink, got a glass of water, and shot a disapproving glance at Josie before slowly leaving the kitchen. She was a stocky, relatively healthy old woman but Josie could hear her groaning as she climbed the stairs toward her bedroom on the second floor.

She and Jake stared silently at each other until the grunting stopped.

"Thus, the price we pay for a loving, trusted, grandma babysitter," he said.

"Am I complaining?" she asked, getting up with her empty glass and picking up the bottle.

"No, that was me. Meet you in the bedroom."

A SHOWER and twenty minutes of passionate lovemaking were the perfect formula for a good night's sleep. Jake was already up by the time she woke the next morning. After another shower, she dressed quickly and was downstairs before Grandma Corsino had David dressed and at the kitchen table.

The young boy ran and jumped on Josie's lap as soon as he saw her. He couldn't stop chattering and she realized how long it had been since they'd sat at the breakfast table together. She pushed his hair back away from his handsome face. Unlike her or Jake, David had a pale complexion, thin light brown almost blond hair, but he had inherited her height and slender frame. When he was in kindergarten, his teacher discovered his talent for drawing and music and found him a piano teacher. He would have an advanced art class this year, also, but Jake said he worried his introverted little boy was being encouraged to do things that would further isolate him from other kids his age.

"Are you excited about first grade?" Josie asked, as Jake's mother pushed a bowl of cereal in front of them.

"Feed the baby so he don't miss the bus," Grandma Corsino demanded.

"He's a big boy, Nonna. He can feed himself," Josie said, sliding him onto the chair next to hers.

David started eating, but stopped and with his mouth full shouted, "I'm so excited, Mom!" spitting corn flakes on the table and on his uniform shirt and laughing as the milk dripped down the sides of his mouth.

Josie laughed, but Jake and his mother looked at her as if she'd just started the boy on the road to becoming a sociopath. She wiped his face and cleaned the front of his shirt with a dish towel and said, "Lighten up guys; that was funny . . . in an *Animal House* sort of way."

She walked her son to the school bus, hugged and kissed him before he climbed onboard. Josie waved until the bus was out of sight but felt pangs of guilt knowing it was probably one of the rare mornings when she'd be able to do this and how unhappy her son would be on all those other days.

HER MOTHER-IN-LAW wanted to make breakfast for her, too, but Josie made a feeble excuse why she couldn't wait. Jake gave Josie a long kiss before he left for work and she knew if Nonna hadn't been there, they would've been naked on the kitchen floor and late for work again. Instead she got into her car to go to work, stopping at the Winchell's donut shop near the Pasadena Freeway and got their biggest cup of coffee and a bear claw to eat on the way to Hollywood.

Tomic had been subpoenaed to testify in court so she got to the narcotics office before him. The Venice squad was serving a search warrant that morning, so their side of the building was empty, but the chubby secretary, Dolores, was in the reception area. The radio base station was on her desk and she had the microphone in her hand talking to Lieutenant Randy Watts, West Bureau's officer in charge. He was telling her he was on his way to downtown LA and wouldn't be at the office until later that afternoon. Dolores jumped up and did a little Snoopy happy dance before signing off.

"Why's the lieutenant downtown?" Josie asked, writing her name on the check-in sheet.

"Don't know, don't care . . . he drives me crazy . . . needs to stay there and bother the captain . . . leave me alone," Dolores whined. "I've got such a headache."

"Did Donny bring PCP in the office again?" Josie asked. Last week, the detective had confiscated a bottle of the hallucinogenic drug and left it on his desk while he finished reports. It wasn't sealed tightly, and the fumes made everyone in the building dizzy and confused.

"No, but his partner is living in our interview room. His wife threw him out again last night and he moved in . . . brought all his stuff. I can't work, can't get to the case files or anything," she said, moaning and dramatically dropping onto her chair.

The Hollywood squad room was on the other side of the building at the end of a long hallway lined with steel lockers. Josie had to pass the interview/stock room on the way to her desk, so she banged on the door with her fist and shouted, "Curtis, get up."

Curtis Flowers was one of the few black men in the division and one of the best narcotics detectives in the city, but his personal life was a bad soap opera. His illegal immigrant wife, Sofia, either threatened to kill him or threw him out of their house at least once a month and he lived in his car or the office until she forgave him. The door finally opened, and he stood in front of her with his closely cropped afro, dressed only in boxer shorts.

"Morning, Josie, want something?" he mumbled, looking around as if he couldn't remember why he was there.

"No, Dolores needs to get to her files."

He nodded, stepped back inside, and closed the door. She knew Curtis still hadn't quite accepted her into his world. She thought he liked her but in a lot of subtle ways he made it clear he didn't think any woman belonged in narcotics street enforcement. Tomic told her Curtis had argued vigorously to keep her out of their squad and once she got there, he constantly complained about her tactics. That didn't surprise her since her "get the drugs at any cost" tactics mimicked Tomic's and although her partner liked Curtis, they were very competitive.

The Hollywood squad room was already humming with activity. Josie checked the board for messages but there was nothing from Kent. She retrieved Kent's informant package from the file cabinet in the lieutenant's office and filled in their brief contact last night.

There were two long wooden tables in the squad room with enough space for four detectives at each table, two on each side. Squad leader Detective III Red Behan's desk was in the corner by a window that faced Wilcox Avenue. She and Tomic; Curtis Flowers and Donny Roberts; Tony "Too Tall" Gilbert and Art Friedman were the three Hollywood teams. The lieutenant kept promising to find them two more detectives but despite a flood of cocaine and heroin hitting Hollywood's streets during the last few months, it hadn't happened.

"Josie, you gotta hear this," Art said, sitting beside her with a tape recorder. He was a fastidious, serious man and she never understood why he was working street enforcement. He'd spent most of his career at a desk job in the conventional boring environment of Parker Center, the police administration building, as an adjutant but had transferred here about the same time she did. He kept his hair short and trim, was clean shaven, wore pressed slacks instead of Levi's, and claimed he didn't mind the crazy impulsiveness of this job while everything about him said he should. He was clearly out of his element and was the only detective in the Hollywood squad who hadn't been promoted to the rank of Detective II supervisor.

He turned on the tape recorder and the original theme song from the *Howdy Doody* television show played. Everyone, including her, laughed. Lieutenant Watts was skinny, redheaded, and freckled, a dead-ringer for the popular kids' puppet, and they all knew Art in his quiet unassuming way would find the most inappropriate time to play the recording.

"Fuck me!" Donny shouted and fell backward off his chair. He had been sitting with his feet on the table in front of her but was scrambling on the floor on hands and knees now to get to the other side of the room as quickly as he could.

"What the hell's wrong with you?" Art asked, getting up to help while his partner, Too Tall, wearing his tinted glasses, never looked up from the sports page of the *LA Times*.

Donny pointed at the table as a foot-long, shiny, red-tinged snake slithered out from the hole where the telephone lines came through. It was Curtis's pet Rosy Boa, Rosie. Josie remembered the tiny reptile from his owner's last stay in the interview room and she figured it must've gotten out of its cardboard box during the night. She picked it up and tried to show Donny it was harmless, but he scooted on his butt into a corner to get away from her.

"Throw the damn thing outside and shoot it!" Donny shouted, scrambling to his feet.

Curtis, dressed now, came into the room and gently took the snake from Josie. He looked at his partner, shook his head, turned around, and went back toward the interview room whispering something to Rosie.

"I hate fuckin' snakes," Donny yelled, brushing off his pants.

"We figured," Art said, picking up the chair. "Come on, Too Tall. Let's get outta here before Behan gets back."

Tony Gilbert folded the paper and took one last gulp of coffee. He was about six foot four, slender with shoulder-length black hair and a day-old beard, and rarely was seen without tinted glasses that supposedly helped with his migraines. At some point in his life he'd gotten tired of telling people how tall he was, so when anyone asked, he'd always say, "too tall," and his nickname was born.

The door to the holding cell was closed, but someone started pounding and kicking at it from the inside. The space was an oversized closet with a dim light and a bench. Most of the time, especially in the summer, the door was kept open to keep arrestees from suffocating.

Too Tall opened the door and Billie stepped out, followed by a wave of pungent body odor. She was almost Josie's height but very overweight and wore pink tights, ballerina slippers, and a low-cut pink halter top. Her dyed blondish-orange hair was in two sloppy ponytails sticking straight up.

"Motherfucker," she said, rubbing her eyes. "You fucking shitheads said a couple a fucking minutes. Detective Corsino, help me out here. These fuckers kidnapped me."

"Morning, Billie . . . hustling kind of early," Josie said.

"No, I swear. These pricks got me outside the Shack. I was gettin' my damn breakfast."

Josie didn't have a chance to respond. Too Tall grabbed Billie's arm and escorted her toward the hallway. This was one of those rare occasions when Josie believed Billie. Art and his partner were smart enough to be good cops, but they were lazy. Billie was a heroin addict who had a baby and she didn't want to go to jail. Every cop in Hollywood knew she'd give up information on her drug contacts if you caught her using or selling heroin. But these guys never bothered to catch her dirty. It was easier for them to make up some phony charge and then force her to snitch or go to jail.

When Josie first got to Hollywood, Behan had told her the most important rule in working with snitches was to be fair. He said, "If they know you won't bullshit or cheat them and you keep your word they'll make you look good." He was right. She'd made a lot of important cases with informants, including Billie. Art and Too Tall rarely got more than dime-bag dealers.

Behan came into the squad room with a mug of coffee as Billie was being pulled down the hallway, and she pleaded with him to free her from his two "asshole dicks."

"Nice outfit," Behan mumbled as Billie disappeared out the door. "Pink is definitely your color."

The tall lanky Hollywood squad leader sat at his desk and stared into the coffee mug. He was another redhead but without freckles and, unlike Watts, was highly respected among his subordinates.

"You okay?" Josie asked.

"Where's your partner and why aren't you in the field catching bad guys?" he asked, holding his head with both hands.

It was a familiar scene. Behan would be miserable until late morning when he'd disappear for an hour, then come back refreshed, smelling of breath mints and ready to do his job. His drinking wasn't a problem . . . not for her.

"He's in court," she said.

"Then go out with Art and Too Tall. Keep Billie from making them look stupid again."

"No, thanks," she said, and he turned to glare at her but didn't make it an order. She knew he didn't like the way that team worked either.

"Okay then, where's Curtis?" he asked.

"In his bedroom," she said, pointing at the interview room. Josie enjoyed working with Curtis, even though he watched and critiqued her every move. He and Tomic had taught her a lot. Curtis's partner, Donny, was a nice guy, but he'd rather sit in the office, make phone calls, and do paperwork than work the streets. "I'm waiting for Tomic's snitch to call for a meet this morning."

"Did Sofia throw Curtis out or stab him again?" Behan asked.

Donny shrugged and said, "I got paperwork, but Josie can partner up with Curtis until Tomic gets back."

"No, you and your partner get out of here. You can do paperwork later," Behan ordered.

He finished the mug of coffee and glanced up as a locker slammed shut in the hallway.

"Curtis, if that's you, I'm serving your eviction notice. Get your shit out of my interview room before the lieutenant gets back," Behan shouted.

"No problem, boss," Curtis said and went back into the room to retrieve a couple of boxes. He got Donny to help carry them out to his city car and load them into the trunk.

"Shut up," Behan said when he noticed Josie staring at him. "As bad as my life gets, I never moved into a police station."

She didn't say anything but they both knew he'd been divorced several times and he should've been a little more sympathetic about Curtis's situation. Josie guessed he didn't want to deal with the lieutenant. Watts was politicking for a cushy lieutenant's job downtown and was terrified any controversy in West Bureau would derail his chances. He wouldn't allow anything that was risky or had the least chance to turn out badly, so she and most of the other detectives had stopped getting his permission. They were willing to take responsibility for the outcome of their cases and Watts was willing to let them.

There was another, louder bang in the hallway as if a hammer had been smashed into one of the lockers. Josie and Behan jumped up and ran out of the squad room to find Tomic leaning against the wall. His locker had a huge dent at the bottom where he'd apparently kicked it.

"What the hell is wrong with you?" Behan asked, rubbing his aching temples and staring at the mangled locker door.

"Superman's dead."

~ THREE ~

It was Tomic's routine to stop across the street every morning and talk to homicide and burglary detectives before coming to the narcotics office. He had been assigned to Hollywood so long the division's table detectives used him as a reliable resource to help locate their witnesses or suspects, and in turn, he pumped them for information to pin down crime patterns related to drugs. Tomic always knew where parolees stayed and who was likely to have stolen guns or contraband. He rarely shared that information with other narcotics detectives, except Josie and Behan.

"It's a waste of a good clue to give anything to the rest of these guys," he'd tell her. She was certain he didn't include Curtis in that group, but she also knew he wasn't about to make Curtis look good either.

This morning the homicide detectives had encountered Tomic on their way out of the squad room and told him Clark Kent's body had been discovered wrapped in a Persian carpet behind the Paradise Apartments. They said an anonymous woman had called 911 and said she found the bludgeoned man, identified him, but refused to give her name before hanging up.

"Maybe it's not him," Josie said, getting into the passenger side of Tomic's Ford. Behan had decided to go with them and climbed into the back seat.

"He's so stupid he tells everybody he's snitching," Tomic said to no one in particular as he made a northbound turn on Wilcox toward Hollywood Boulevard. He was silent the rest of the way, but Josie guessed from his white-knuckled death grip on the steering wheel that he was seething inside.

Tomic always behaved as if he didn't care what happened to Kent but Josie knew different. She had seen her partner take money out of his pocket when he thought she wasn't watching and give it to the snitch for food or rent. She found out he had managed to get Kent into a detox program last winter when the man had crashed at the end of a week-long alcohol and meth binge. The two men used each other to survive in their very different worlds, and that familiarity had created a bond.

Kent's body was on the ground in the alley in front of a dumpster and close to the fire escape that he had used the night before. The ladder had been pulled down. He was lying on top of a ten-by-ten-foot Persian rug spotted with pools of blood and other dark stains. Josie thought the rug looked expensive or had been at one time, with faded blue and yellow designs on a deep red background. It was worn and frayed now but must have been gorgeous in its prime.

He was on his stomach with his arms secured together behind his back with duct tape wrapped around from his wrists to his elbows. The back of his head was a bloody mass of bone and hair. She got closer and could see his face was just as badly damaged, unrecognizable, but it was Superman's body still wearing the same T-shirt and jeans from the night before.

One of the homicide detectives was hovering over a wooden baseball bat on the ground near the corpse. It was covered with blood.

"This isn't where it happened," Behan said, looking up toward the roof. "I'm betting they attacked him up there, rolled his body in the rug, and dumped him over the side, head first. Actually, the fall probably killed him." The homicide detectives hadn't told him anything, but the big redhead had worked homicides before coming to Narcotics and Behan had been promised by the Hollywood captain that the supervisor's spot on that table would be his as soon as the bureau chief allowed him to fill the position. Josie would miss him but was happy he'd have an opportunity to go back to a detective table. She hoped it would provide a touch more stability in his life.

"What makes you think it didn't happen right here?" Tomic asked, looking anywhere but at the mangled body in front of him. Josie had worked with him long enough to know his temper was about to explode.

"See there about halfway up the ladder . . . on the left side," Behan said, pointing.

Josie saw it right away; there appeared to be a bloody clump of dark human hair stuck to a bolt near the rung where the ladder extended to reach the ground.

"That's nasty," she said.

Tomic turned away, swore and shook his head. "I'm going up on the roof," he said, walking quickly toward the front of the apartment building with Josie and Behan following.

They climbed four flights of stairs to the roof and found a team of homicide detectives wearing disposable latex gloves carefully searching the tarpapered trash heap. A sea of evidence markers, folded index cards with numbers, covered the surface.

"Is this where they jumped him?" Tomic asked the detective lieutenant standing by the access door. Her partner was breathing normally, but Josie had to catch her breath after trying to keep up with his record-breaking sprint up the stairs. She could see the burst of physical activity had calmed him a little. Behan was smart enough to climb at his own pace and arrived a few minutes later.

"Yep, there's blood splattered everywhere. He put up a pretty good fight before they took him down," the lieutenant said.

"Strong as an ox . . . not nearly as smart," Tomic mumbled. "Have you found anything helpful yet?"

"Looks like there was a party, some heavy-duty drinking . . . drugs," he said, pointing at a small glass bong sitting on an upside-down plastic bucket. "We'll catalog and print everything, but with all this filth I'm not expecting much. He was your snitch, Larry. Who'd want him dead?"

Tomic snorted a laugh. "Every asshole dealer and dime-bag junkie he gave up."

"What was he working on?"

"Nothing for me," Tomic said quickly, avoiding Josie's stare. "I haven't used him for a while. Did you search his room?"

"He has a room?" the lieutenant asked. "I thought he lived up here."

"He's got a cot in the basement when it gets too cold. Let's get outta here, Corsino," Tomic said, tapping her arm and walking away.

She followed her partner back down the stairs but couldn't stop thinking about the entry she'd made in Kent's informant package documenting their meeting with him on this roof about twelve hours ago. Luckily, they hadn't officially paid him anything out of the bureau's Secret Service fund, so the promised fifty dollars didn't have to be accounted for, but by updating the informant package she might've made her partner a liar.

When they were alone on the stairwell she told Tomic what she'd done.

He stopped and asked, "Did you write anything other than we met with him?"

"No," she said. "I figured we could be dealing with a dirty cop investigation, so I just said we talked to him here at the Paradise."

"Okay, good. That doesn't mean we're working with him."

"Why don't you want them to know?"

"Because we aren't sure who Kent was going to give up. We'll just talk to Behan on this for now . . . he's the only one I completely trust. Besides he'll probably be on Hollywood's homicide table in a few days, so it should be easy to coordinate."

If Behan was involved, Josie was comfortable keeping Kent's information quiet. They had to find the man Kent was going to introduce them to, but she wasn't sure how that would happen without the informant's help.

The door to the basement room was secured but Josie picked the flimsy lock. She guessed they didn't have long before the homicide lieutenant sent detectives down to check out Tomic's tip. She knew he wouldn't allow his guys to search without a warrant, but she and Tomic didn't have a homicide to solve and weren't as concerned with legal formalities.

"What am I looking for?" she asked, using her foot to turn over a filthy crate Kent had probably used as a table.

"Names, numbers . . . I don't know, but be careful, he's got used syringes stashed everywhere in this dump . . . it's a hepatitis petri dish."

"Between the steroids and the meth, his body must look like a pin cushion," Josie said.

She stood in the middle of the junk-filled room and looked around for a place to start searching. The man was a pack rat. An army cot was covered with a dirty blanket and surrounded by stacks of homosexual porno magazines, empty food containers, old clothes, exercise equipment, broken pieces of furniture, bicycle parts. The room smelled worse than the dumpster in the alley.

"Bingo," Tomic said, removing a small spiral notebook from a portable unplugged refrigerator sitting in the corner with a lantern on top. "Let's get out of here."

She hadn't started to search and was pleased to forgo digging into the garbage heap. They left the room and locked the door again. When she and Tomic got back to the lobby, Josie noticed the elevator light indicating it was headed down toward the basement. She guessed they had barely avoided running into homicide detectives.

Behan had gone back to the alley and they found him talking to uniformed officers who were keeping the curious neighbors and the media away from the crime scene.

"Where'd you two go?" Behan asked, when they were back in the car headed toward the office.

Josie looked at Tomic. When he didn't answer, she said, "The basement."

"Find anything?"

Tomic pulled the notebook out of his pocket and, without taking his attention off the road, tossed it over the seat to Behan.

"Does the Hollywood lieutenant know you have this?"

"Not yet," Tomic said. "I need it to find a guy Kent told us about last night." He repeated the information.

"What do you think, Corsino?" Behan asked, handing her the notebook after briefly glancing at it.

She didn't need to see more than a couple of pages to know Tomic's snitch was keeping a ledger for drug sales. Based on the prices and amounts, she figured it was cocaine, mostly quarter- and half-gram sales.

"Superman was a paper boy," she said. "This looks like he had a regular delivery route, but the last week seems pretty erratic and busier than usual."

She didn't explain because they all knew paper boys were paid to deliver drugs so dealers didn't have to worry about getting caught. Kent was the perfect candidate for that job. He wasn't smart enough to rip off the dealer or realize the risks, and he probably worked cheap. Everyone expected him to take a little product off the top as his tip for providing the service. If he distributed enough of the white powder or rock, he could stay high most of the time without spending a dime.

All the customers in the notebook were coded with bird names: Blackhawk/ half gram; Sparrow/quarter gram; Robin/ half gram; Crow/half ounce, etc. An aviary of drug users filled every page with dates and amounts purchased. Some paid cash. Others had a running account that got settled at the end of the month.

"Maybe Kent wasn't as stupid as we thought," Josie said, giving the notebook back to Tomic, and adding, "There are a couple phone numbers inside the back cover we can check out, but we're shit outta luck if the key to those code names was stored in the gooey mess that used to be his brain."

"Drop me off in front of the station and I'll see if the homicide guys get any match on the prints they lifted from the Paradise," Behan said as they approached the police building. Tomic did and then drove around the block to park across the street in the narcotics lot behind the gas pumps.

Too Tall and Art were in the office finishing reports on the marijuana dealer Billie had been coerced into giving them. Josie recognized the arrestee's name. He sold dime baggies on Hollywood Boulevard, mostly to tourists who didn't realize what they had purchased was oregano. It was a desperation arrest, a felony that would get tossed out as soon as the lab report came back, but Too Tall and Art had produced a number and that would keep Behan off their backs for a day. She knew they wouldn't leave the office again unless another team had a search warrant or needed assistance. Tomic was right; they were lazy, but it didn't bother her because that left more dealers out there for her to catch.

"Sorry to hear about Superman," Too Tall said as soon as Tomic sat at the table.

"How'd you know?" Tomic asked.

"They were talking about it across the street when I booked my arrestee. Got any suspects?" he asked, but Tomic was concentrating on the pages of the spiral notebook and didn't respond.

Josie went into the lieutenant's office to get Kent's informant file again, not realizing Lieutenant Watts had returned. He was sitting behind his desk talking on the telephone, so she started to back out of the room, but he held up his hand and indicated he wanted her to stay. While he finished his conversation, she opened the file cabinet and looked for Kent's package, but it was gone. She searched the entire drawer thinking she might've misfiled it that morning before they left in a hurry, but she hadn't.

Watts hung up the phone and when she turned to say something, Josie saw Kent's package sitting on his desk.

"You done with that, boss?" Josie asked, pointing at the package.

"Why did you and Tomic meet with him last night?" Watts asked, handing it to her.

"Routine . . . nothing special," she said, lying. "Behan knows."

"So you have no idea why he might've been beaten to death the same night he's been with the two of you?"

"Not a clue," she said, tucking the bulky file under her arm and walking back into the squad room.

She sat beside Tomic and he looked up to ask, "What'd Howdy Doody want?"

She told him. He nodded and went back to examining the notebook. They both knew Watts wouldn't pursue it. Josie opened the informant file and searched for names of Kent's associates, his prior arrests, and anyone who might've had a reason to want him dead. His picture was stapled to the inside cover. It must've been taken pre-steroids because his handsome face was tanned and clear. His mop of black hair was combed straight back, and she thought the photo could've been a model's portfolio shot featuring Kent's large blue eyes and movie star smile which she tried not to picture as gore splattered all over the Persian carpet.

Most of the big dealers he'd snitched on were still in prison but there were a few who weren't in custody and had plenty of reasons to kill him. He'd also had several boyfriends who used steroids and drugs. Josie knew it wouldn't be the first time in Hollywood's homosexual community that a love spat had turned to "Roid Rage" and death. The only next of kin Kent listed was an older sister in the city of Torrance, a few miles south of LA.

When Behan got to the narcotics office, she told him about the sister, but he said the Hollywood homicide detectives had already located and notified her about her brother's death.

"There's nothing in here to tell us the real names of all his feathery friends, so I'm guessing someone he trusted is keeping the code or he hid it somewhere," Tomic said after almost half an hour of studying the notebook. "Dude wasn't smart enough to keep all that information in his head."

"Boyfriend . . . sister?" Josie asked. "Who do we talk to first?"

"I'd say his sister," Behan said and gave her a slip of paper with an address in Torrance. "I borrowed it from my homicide guys."

"When will they officially move you across the street?" Josie asked, knowing Lieutenant Watts had to be fighting Behan's transfer. Red was a respected squad leader and a good narcotics detective. Watts needed to keep him to make himself look good.

"It's already done. I'm just helping out until they can promote somebody and move another squad leader in here."

"Good riddance," Tomic said with a straight face.

"He'll miss you," Josie said. "When are you buying drinks to celebrate your new job?"

"Tonight, Nora's."

"That's special," she said sarcastically.

Nora's was a shabby restaurant and bar across the street on Sunset Boulevard. It was a hangout for Hollywood officers and detectives. Few lieutenants or any rank above them would venture into the place. Josie figured most of the brass didn't like to socialize with their rowdy underlings and the rest didn't want to be able to see or know what went on there. She made a promise to herself that if she ever promoted to a management position she'd never worry about her career more than the people who worked for her. Morphing into a Randy Watts-type leader was her worse nightmare.

KENT'S SISTER lived in an area known as Old Torrance which bordered on a narrow strip of land called Harbor Gateway. The landlocked city of Los Angeles had annexed the strip to allow its direct and only access to the harbor in San Pedro. The gerrymandered community was inconvenient for any LAPD division to police, so crime flourished and trickled over into the nicer city of Torrance.

The houses in that eastern part of Torrance were primarily small craftsman-style cottages surrounding a dated downtown area. As Tomic drove through the narrow tree-lined streets, Josie thought it had a small town feel with a single mom-and-pop market, hardware store, small restaurants, several antique stores, and a turn-of-the-century post office.

People sat at outside tables, bundled in heavy coats drinking coffee, talking, and apparently not caring or unaware that most serious shoppers had shifted loyalties and were spending their money in the bigger, better-stocked malls.

The sister's house was on a street backed up against railroad tracks. It was a working line and Tomic was forced to wait impatiently at Western Avenue for a long freight train to pass before he could turn onto the street. Josie had called ahead, and Beverly Kent was sitting on the porch steps when they arrived.

She had large blue eyes like her brother, but her dark hair had strands of gray, and her complexion was pale and clear. Beverly was a handsome middle-aged woman but when she stood to meet them, Josie noticed it was difficult for her to balance her thin body. After the introductions, Beverly invited them into the house. She had to use the railing to help climb the steps and she walked slowly and carefully.

She offered to make coffee and was moving toward the kitchen, but Tomic insisted she sit and he would do it, so she told him where the cups and instant coffee were.

"Does he know what he's doing?" Beverly whispered when she and Josie were alone. She had a soft, pleasant voice.

"Most of the time," Josie said and added, "I'm sorry about your brother and I apologize for bothering you today, but we really want to find who killed him."

"It's okay. I know Detective Tomic was his friend. Clark always talked about him," she said, staring at the floor. She was wearing a bulky sweater and sweatpants with tennis shoes, but her hands trembled as if she were cold.

"Can I get you another sweater, maybe turn up the heat a little?" Josie asked, looking around for a thermostat.

"Hmm, oh no, I'm not cold," she said, smiling and holding up her hands. "Young-onset Parkinson's. Actually, I'm not that young but under fifty is unusual for this, poor me," she said without a hint of self-pity.

Tomic carried mugs of steaming instant coffee out to the living room and sat on the couch beside Josie.

"How involved were you in your brother's life?" he asked after Beverly took a dainty sip.

"Not very," she said. "He did tell me he enjoyed working with you. And by the way he didn't really believe he was Superman, but thought it was funny to pretend."

"Have you ever been to his place?"

"In Hollywood, no."

"Did he have another place?" Josie asked.

"I kept his room for him after our mother died."

"Can we see it?" Tomic asked.

"Why not, he won't object, will he?" Beverly asked and put the coffee mug on the glass table in front of her. She got up slowly. Josie guessed it wasn't just physical pain that affected her movement this time. There seemed to be a sadness that weighed on her limbs, a wound that went deeper than Parkinson's. The fragile woman hesitated a moment and then added, "You know his first name was really William, William C. Kent Jr. Our father was a pilot in WWII, shot down, killed. When Mother died a few years ago, Clark changed. He became terrified of dying. I think the drugs made him feel invincible."

It was clarification for their benefit. She didn't wait to discuss the information and slowly led them to the back of the house. There were three bedrooms and her brother's was the smallest, at the end of the hallway.

"Did he ever talk about his life in Hollywood . . . anyone who was close to him? Someone he trusted or worked with or maybe was afraid of?" Josie asked as they stood in the cramped room. It was a younger man's space with movie posters from *The Empire Strikes Back* and several martial arts movies Josie didn't recognize. The bed was made but there were clothes scattered on the dresser and chair and boxes stacked in the corner.

"No," Beverly said and backed into the hallway. "Look as long as you like and take anything you want except family pictures."

She didn't wait for a response and left them alone in the bedroom.

Josie looked through a pile of magazines on the floor. There weren't any of the raunchy porno rags she'd seen in Hollywood. These featured and would probably appeal mostly to weight lifters and body builders. So, he kept that side of his personality away from the family home.

They needed more than an hour to go through all the drawers, boxes, and the closet. Josie had nearly given up when she found a slip of paper in the pocket of a wool blazer that had been left on the closet floor. The note was printed and said, "Pick up eight-track. Deliver to club," and was signed "Raven."

"Another bird peddling cocaine," Josie said, showing the note to Tomic, then folding it again, hoping Raven's prints might still be there.

"Sounds like rock. I didn't get a close look at that bong on the roof. He might've been basing . . . that would account for the killer being able to jump him."

"South end gangs are staking out corners on the boulevard near the theaters . . . Curtis caught a guy yesterday with a pocket full of baggies . . . probably six, seven hundred dollars' worth of rock cocaine," she said, then asked, "You think this Raven might be Kent's snitch?"

"More likely his dealer. Kent was the bouncer at The Carnival, that club on Melrose. I'm guessing that's the club he means. We'll check it out first," Tomic said.

They spent a few minutes with Beverly after finishing the search in her brother's room, but Josie could see the woman was tired and struggling to get comfortable, so she thanked her and got Tomic out of the house. Clark's sister leaned on the porch rail watching as Tomic drove away from the bungalow, but she didn't wave or smile or pretend their visit had been anything other than what it was, an intrusion into her family's life . . . polite and friendly but nonetheless an intrusion.

"Will there be anyone at the club this early?" Josie asked as Tomic drove onto the northbound Harbor Freeway.

"The owner lives in an apartment over the club. She's usually there."

"She?"

Josie was surprised. She hadn't met a woman who owned one of the popular clubs in Hollywood. It was a man's world.

"Abby Morrison, her old man is Guy Testa. Rumor is he gave her The Carnival as a wedding present."

"Is he the Gaetano Testa?" Josie asked, emphasizing the "the" and thinking of the organized crime figure who lived in Las Vegas.

"Yep, Abby's his only kid. She got married last year . . . husband's gone but she still has the club."

"Gone?"

"Disappeared. She filed a missing person's report six months after the wedding, but he's vanished without a trace."

"Have they dredged the bottom of Lake Tahoe . . . or one of the mob's other forwarding addresses?"

Tomic wrinkled his forehead as if he had a sudden headache and said, "I wouldn't make Mafia jokes in front of her. She's sensitive about her heritage."

Before they got off the freeway, Josie had recited every Italian Mafia joke she could remember. Being Sicilian, she'd heard dozens of them, mostly from her brother, Mick, or Jake's relatives.

"Okay, got that out of your system?" Tomic asked, as he parked the car in front of the club.

"Pretty much," she said, staring at the front of the building. She usually came here at night and never paid much attention to how shabby it looked, basically a warehouse with a cheap painted wooden facade resembling a carnival tent around the front door. Several strings of lights were strung from the roof to spikes in the asphalt.

The entrance was chained and padlocked, and steel grates covered the side windows. Tomic led her through an alley to the back of the building where metal steps led to a narrow landing and another reinforced door. He pushed a buzzer and a woman's voice came from the box below it.

"Yeah," she said, clearly annoyed.

"Abby, it's me, Larry Tomic. Open the door," he demanded, looking up at a camera pointed in their direction.

The door clicked, and Josie pushed it open. They stepped into a well-lighted foyer and were facing a wall covered with original oil paintings. Most of it was contemporary art, shapes and colors, not Josie's taste but she thought it worked with the commercial feel of this space. They walked around the wall and into a huge open living area and Josie could see someone had spent a lot of time and money decorating. The only thing out of place in the trendy, pricey loft was Abby Morrison.

The woman was short, fat, and had hair identical to Nonna's sprayed bouffant except it had been dyed blonde. Her eyebrows were brown over dark eye shadow. She stood in the middle of the room holding what looked to be a martini and wearing a striped colorful caftan and sandals that revealed sparkly purple toenail polish.

"Thirsty?" she asked, holding up her glass but not waiting for an answer before taking a long drink and leaving a half-circle of dark red lipstick on the rim.

"Hear about Clark Kent?" Tomic asked.

"I heard he won't be coming to work . . . or going anywhere else," Abby said, squatting on the nearest chair. She was stoic. If she had any feelings about her bouncer's fate, Abby wasn't sharing them.

"How long had he worked here?" Josie asked.

"Who are you?" Abby asked with the first indication of any interest in their conversation.

"Sorry, Detective Josie Corsino," Tomic answered, pointing at Josie.

"A woman narc . . . ain't that a new one . . . he's been here off and on, long as me, about a year."

"Know any reason somebody would use his head for a piñata?" Josie asked.

Abby laughed and said, "Yeah, sweetie, lotsa reasons . . . lotsa somebodies. Snitches ain't exactly popular."

"How about you? You want him dead?" Tomic asked.

"Nah, I kinda liked the kid . . . not too bright but he did whatever he was told."

"Like dealing drugs in your club?"

"No way," Abby said, trying not to smile. "Not in my place. I run a drug-free establishment."

"Sure, you do," Tomic said. "Has he had a problem with anyone during the last week or so?"

"The only one I know about is . . . Butch . . . Brian Thomas. He and Clark had a lovers' spat; Brian got drunk in the club, and Clark tossed him out on the sidewalk. Butch swore Clark would be sorry."

"Anybody else see it?" Josie asked.

Abby thought for a few seconds. "Bartender, parking lot attendant, probably one or two waitresses," she said, grinning at Josie. "Come back tonight and ask them yourself . . . drinks on me." The invitation was directed at Josie. Abby poked under her hair with one finger scratching her scalp. Her long fingernails had the same purple polish as her toes, and she wore three large diamond rings on her left hand. "Okay, we done?" she asked, putting the martini glass on the marble floor and struggling to get out of the chair.

Tomic offered his hand and she allowed him to help her stand. She tugged at the caftan where it had hung up over flabby mounds of flesh until it was straight again, then held out her hand to Josie.

"Pleasure to meet a lady detective, come back anytime," Abby said.

They shook hands and Josie was surprised by the woman's firm grip that held on just a little too long.

"SHE'S TRYING really hard to be scary with that whole Queen of Hearts imitation," Josie said when they were in the car.

Tomic didn't look away from the road but said, "It's smart to be afraid of her. Abby is the female Gaetano. Except for the dyed hair and layers of makeup, she even looks like him, and don't let her dumpy housedress fool you. She's meaner and smarter than her father."

"She seems to like you."

"She lets me boss her around because I don't hassle her club business. If Clark pissed in her backyard, she could turn his head into a bloody hamburger without blinking."

"So you think she might've killed him?"

"No, doubt it. She always treated him like her special needs little brother. She could've; I just don't believe she would."

"How about Butch?" Josie asked. "Do you know him?"

"No, probably some bum-boy Kent picked up hustling on Santa Monica Boulevard. When we get to the office, if you go across the street to Vice and see if they got a file on Brian Thomas, I'll run him. If he's been hanging with Kent, odds are he's got a rap sheet."

Josie agreed to check out Kent's boyfriend, but she figured Abby's death grip was meant to convey a message and despite Tomic's usually reliable instincts, she suspected Gaetano's daughter knew a lot more about Superman's murder than she was sharing.

~ FOUR ~

The Vice office was on the second floor of the Hollywood station. Josie had a good working relationship with most of the officers in that unit since many of her snitches were whores and addicts and she was frequently privy to information that helped with prostitution enforcement. She'd never arrested anyone for pimping, whoring, gambling, or any other vice-related crime. Her tolerance for that type of violation was higher than most cops unless drugs were involved.

The Prostitution Enforcement Detail or the PED officers were leaving to work Santa Monica Boulevard when Josie got there. She looked in the lieutenant's office, but he was gone too.

"What do you need?" a woman asked from behind her in the hallway.

Josie recognized the voice and turned to see Marge Bailey standing in the doorway. The tall gorgeous blonde was wearing worn Levi's, boots, and a pullover sweater and looked more like a Vogue model than a cop.

"What are you doing here?" Josie asked.

"Working, what the fuck do you think I'm doing."

"Vice again?"

"Got promoted to sergeant and the bastards sent me back here. I asked for Newton patrol . . . assholes."

Josie smiled because she thought Marge's language and looks always seemed weirdly out of sync. They had worked together at Newton as two of the first women in patrol and had become friends, but after they passed probation and got transferred to different divisions, they'd lost touch.

"It's your fault . . . your fame as a decoy hooker is legendary."

Marge held up her middle finger and sat behind the desk near the lieutenant's office.

"No, actually this is LAPD's diversity stupidity syndrome, DSS, in action. Did you need something or just come up here to annoy me?" she asked.

Josie didn't ask what she meant because she'd heard Marge's DSS theory too many times, i.e., the department brass selected women or minorities to do jobs even when they weren't ready, so they could point to the numbers to prove they weren't discriminating, and diversity was thriving. The inevitable failures were confirmation and proof women and minorities probably shouldn't be doing those jobs.

"Need to check your logs for a name, Brian 'Butch' Thomas."

"Doesn't sound familiar but I've only been here a couple of days and the cast of characters changes daily," Marge said, pulling a large ledger off the shelf behind her.

The name was there with a picture. Brian Thomas aka Brad Thomas, Brian Terry, and Butch Terry was a regular customer of Hollywood Vice, mostly for selling his body on Santa Monica Boulevard. He was blond with streaks of blue and had a metal stud implanted under his lower lip.

"Handsome devil," Marge said, retrieving a file from a nearby cabinet and putting it in front of Josie. "This is everything we have on him."

It contained a rap sheet showing that Butch had been arrested dozens of times for prostitution or being under the influence of opiates. He had two burglary arrests and one assault charge. He was twenty-one years old, much younger than Kent, and gave his current address as the Paradise Apartments.

"What's the little turd been up to?" Marge asked, dropping the log book back onto the shelf.

Josie explained his connection to their murdered snitch and added, "Don't know if he had anything to do with Kent's death, but they did have a pretty nasty fight at The Carnival according to the owner."

"Guy Testa's daughter isn't what I'd call a reliable source."

"She says there're other witnesses."

"Who'd swear on a Bible to any lie she told."

"Probably, but it's worth a chat. Wanna help me find him?"

Marge took her jacket off the back of the chair and picked up a hand-held radio.

"Shouldn't be difficult. According to the file, he's either hustling on Santa Monica or blowing some asshole behind the chicken shack," Marge said, taking her car keys off the desk.

It took longer for Marge to drive to Santa Monica Boulevard than it did to locate Butch. As she stopped in front of the fried chicken stand, Butch was coming out of the alley following an Asian man in a business suit who hurried away from the location as if someone were chasing him. Butch waited until the man was a block away, then sat on the steps of a nearby T-shirt shop and took a wad of cash out of his shirt pocket. He didn't seem to notice the unmarked police car parked at the curb a few yards from where he was perched.

They got out and were standing on the sidewalk in front of him before he looked up and realized what was happening. He stuffed the money back into his pocket and stood. The thought of running might have entered his mind but the two women standing on either side of him were taller than he was, wore guns, and had badges clipped to their belts.

"What's wrong?" he asked innocently, backing up to lean against the wall. He had a pale boyish face and large blue eyes. His blond hair was still streaked with blue but had been shaved up the sides giving him a cartoonish skunk appearance and he'd added another stud above his left eyebrow to match the one under his lower lip. "I ain't done nothing," he said, trying not to make eye contact.

Josie ordered him to turn around and handcuffed him behind his back to search for weapons. She put on her black leather gloves but asked if he had any needles in his pockets before starting. She'd been stuck too many times by a dirty needle sticking out of some hype's kit or cut with a razor blade and didn't want a trip to Central Receiving to get another gamma globulin shot for hepatitis. He didn't have the kit on him, but she pulled up his left sleeve and saw a fresh puncture wound over the vein on his inner arm still oozing a pinkish fluid.

Okay, she thought. I have some leverage. He talks to me or goes to jail for ninety days and has to detox cold turkey. She was certain from the age of the hole in his arm his urine would likely test positive for opiates and he'd need another fix in a few hours.

"When's the last time you shot up, Butch?" she asked, opening the back door of Marge's car.

"That's my cat done them marks. She scratched me bad this morning. I ain't done no tar for weeks . . . those tracks are real old," he whined, sliding onto the seat while trying to show her his inner arm.

Josie shut the door and grinned at Marge.

"He's dirty."

"Yeah, whata shock," Marge said, opening the driver's door. "I'll take you and shithead back. I've got to check on my PED guys."

When they arrived at the narcotics office, Marge helped Butch get out of the car and stood beside him while Josie pulled out the back seat to search for anything the young man might've tried to discard. She wasn't disappointed. Two tiny uninflated red balloons, each rolled to the size of a large pea, were directly behind the seat where Butch had been sitting, a common way to package a dose of heroin for sale.

"This is just not your day," Josie said, showing him the balloons in the palm of her hand.

"Those ain't mine."

"We both know they weren't there before you got in my car . . . I checked," Marge said, glaring at Butch who slumped and groaned.

Tomic and Behan were in the office with Too Tall when Josie ordered Butch to sit on the bench in the holding room.

"Will one of you strip search him?" she asked, sitting with her back to the holding room. "He dropped a couple of balloons in the car."

"I'll do it," Too Tall said, starting to get up.

"Never mind, Gilbert," Tomic said, putting his hand on Too Tall's shoulder before he could stand. He removed the handcuffs, told Butch to take off all his clothes, and did a thorough search. As soon as Butch was dressed again, Tomic secured the young man's right wrist to the bench with Josie's handcuffs and closed the door. "Have you talked to him?" Tomic asked, sitting beside her.

"No, but he's primed to make a deal. His pupils are pinned, and now I got him on possession or even possession for sale if I really want to screw with him." She said the "sales" part louder hoping Butch could hear.

As soon as Gilbert made a run to the fried chicken place to pick up dinner, Tomic had Butch out of the holding closet and sitting in the cramped space of their interview room, aka Curtis's home away from home. With the cot and file boxes, there was barely enough room for a card table and two chairs, so Josie and Behan watched and listened from the two-way mirror in the lieutenant's office. She asked Tomic to interview him since it was obvious he didn't like her.

"Do I get my money back?" Butch asked as soon as Tomic sat across from him. "My old man sent it to me."

"Depends."

"Huh?" The young man seemed confused, then a smirk, and finally a look of resignation covered his face.

Tomic knew immediately what he was thinking and said, “No, asshole, I don’t want a blow job. It depends on whether you tell me the truth.”

“I don’t know nothing.”

“Then I guess your money gets booked and you go to jail for possession of heroin for sale and being under the influence. Good luck with detox,” Tomic said, standing.

“No, wait,” Butch whined, scratching at his arms and face. “What’d you wanna know?”

“When did you last see Clark Kent?”

Even from the other side of the mirror, Josie could see the blood drain from the young man’s face.

“I didn’t kill him. I swear to God.”

“Did I say you killed him? Where were you last night?”

“I ain’t seen him since he kicked my ass . . . couple days ago.”

“Weren’t you staying with him at the Paradise?”

“No . . . fuck no,” Butch said, looking down at the table. The scratching on his arms accelerated and Josie thought he was going to make them bleed. Tomic grabbed his dirty hands and held them still.

“Stop,” Tomic said, forcing his hands down on the table. “Just chill out and tell me what happened between you and Kent.”

Butch folded his arms, tucking his hands under his armpits. “He said I stole his shit.”

“Speak English, what shit?”

“Crack.”

“Did you?”

“He left it with me. What’d he expect,” Butch said matter-of-factly.

“So, you sold his coke to get your smack and your lover beat the crap outta you. Is that basically what happened?” Butch nodded and Tomic asked, “Whose stash was he holding?”

Butch shrugged. “Never tells me nothing . . . jus’ do this, do that. I was glad to get away from him . . . never did fuckin’ shit for me.”

“Who killed him, Butch?”

"Dunno . . . he told me that fat bitch at The Carnival was gonna rip off his balls for losing the crack. But lots a people hated him . . . I wasn't the only one . . . stupid fuck thought he was the biggest meanest dude on the street . . . guess he weren't." Butch whispered the last few words and swallowed a laugh. "Can I go now?" he asked as Tomic got up and left the room.

Josie and Behan met Tomic in the squad room.

"He's too scared to tell me much . . . rather go cold turkey than get a snitch jacket," Tomic said, sitting at the table. "He's your arrestee, Corsino. What do you want to do with him?" he asked, looking at her.

"Book him and try to keep him alive a little longer," she said.

"He might be afraid to say anything because he knows there's a cop involved," Behan said. "See if the men's jail can keep him isolated, use detox as an excuse."

Too Tall came back into the squad room, carrying a greasy bag of chicken, and glanced into the holding room before sitting at his squad table. "Where's your guy?" he asked.

"Where's Art?" Behan asked. "Why aren't you two working?"

The big detective shrugged indifferently and said, "He had to go to Central to pick up some reports. I was hungry so I took a break to eat."

Behan's face turned almost as red as his hair. He knew Too Tall and his partner had made one arrest and were done working for the day. Behan made no secret of the fact he hated slackers but before he could say anything, Curtis and Donny came down the hall herding three older men in handcuffs and shoved them into the empty holding room.

"Stay," Curtis shouted at the men and held up his right hand like a traffic cop. "*Comprende*?"

The men didn't answer but sat shoulder-to-shoulder on the narrow bench in the cramped closet and tried to get comfortable.

"The Aloha?" Behan asked.

They all knew he was referring to the Aloha Hotel on Las Palmas just blocks from the police station. It was a hotbed of marijuana sales and the original Hollywood farmers' market for street drugs. Every illegal immigrant who came across the border knew by word of mouth that he could set up shop in front of the Aloha and make a lucrative day's wages. The down side was eventual incarceration, but most of them were out of jail and back on the street before the arresting officers could finish the paperwork.

"Of course," Donny said. "Curtis went hand-to-hand, bought from all of them, and we found their stash hidden in the bushes . . . about a half pound of pretty decent weed."

While the others talked, Josie slipped into the interview room, handcuffed Butch, and told him to follow her across the street to Hollywood jail. She had him printed and booked and put her card with the narcotics office phone number in his plastic property bag. Josie continued questioning him, but the young man insisted Kent hadn't told him anything and seemed resigned to endure the discomforts of heroin withdrawal from behind bars. They both knew it probably wouldn't be that bad because the quality of the street drug was so poor he couldn't get much of the opiate in his system. She was certain he was hiding something but nothing she said seemed to convince him he could trust her.

Curtis was finishing the paperwork on his arrestees by the time she got back to the office. His partner had passed her walking the three marijuana dealers across the street to the Hollywood jail and Tomic and Behan had already gone to the bar at Nora's to get a head start on Behan's promotion party.

It was late. Josie knew her son would have already eaten dinner and was probably asleep, but she called home and talked to her mother-in-law. Jake wasn't home yet, so it looked like another late night and sleepover for Nonna. There wasn't any good reason Josie could think of to hurry home now. Spending quality time with her husband's mother was unlikely, so without giving it much thought she locked up the drawer in her table and headed to Nora's.

~ FIVE ~

The bar was dark and smelled of stale beer. It was hot and crowded with a mix of Hollywood detectives, a few off-duty, uniformed officers in their Metro Tux—white T-shirts, uniform pants, and polished black boots. Local street people and blue-collar workers from the surrounding shops and businesses made up the remainder of the clientele.

There was nowhere else Josie would rather be. These cops who daily experienced the depths of human depravity came here to talk about the ugliness and hopefully push it out of their thoughts and dreams for a while. They needed this place to share stories among kindred warrior souls. She figured it was a better idea to do it here rather than take those tales home to terrify the spouse and kiddies.

She immediately found Tomic and Behan at the bar drinking with the Hollywood homicide detectives. The big redhead was laughing, something he rarely did during work hours. Josie liked and respected her boss, but worried Behan needed to keep his alcohol intake at a certain level to function. She felt guilty because most likely the accommodation would eventually lead to his destruction, but like everyone else in the squad, she needed him at his best and hundred-proof rye whiskey was how he got there.

The men made room for her at the bar and Tomic set a shot of whiskey in front of her. She raised the glass to Behan and drank.

"Good luck, boss. You'll miss us," she said, putting the empty glass on the bar. Josie expected a sarcastic remark from Behan, but he turned and tapped on the granite for another drink.

She ordered another drink, too, and swiveled the stool to rest her back against the bar. Glassy-eyed Dolores was sitting at a table in front of Josie drinking shooters with detectives from the Venice squad. The bureau secretary was laughing and seemed to be having a good time, but Josie knew no amount of alcohol consumption would result in the compromise of her virtue. She was young, naive, and not very attractive, usually an easy target for these men, but they treated Dolores like a little sister . . . an unwritten office rule—tease, annoy, and protect the chubby girl who made coffee and ran interference for them with Lieutenant Randy Watts, but never ever screw her.

The crowd was thinning out. Most of the civilians had been replaced by a few cops who increased the rowdiness and noise level. Curtis and Donny finally arrived and joined them at the bar, but Too Tall and Art were sitting at a table in the corner talking to a thin, clean-cut young man that Josie recognized immediately. He was an Internal Affairs sergeant she'd met last month at a Board of Rights hearing when she'd testified as a character witness for an accused officer. The three men were huddled close, in what looked like an intense conversation, and the IA sergeant kept looking around as if he feared someone might sneak up and overhear them.

Interesting, she thought, and started to say something to Tomic, but he was already fixated on the same table.

"What the hell's that about?" Tomic asked, rubbing his day-old beard.

"You know he's IA, right?" she asked.

"Pete Adair, nice guy, lousy investigator. Looks intense . . . wonder who Too Tall's ratting out this time."

She knew it was never proven but widely believed among most detectives in the division that Gilbert had gone to IA to report a fellow detective for cheating on his overtime. The other detective had embarrassed Gilbert at a narcotics training day and Too Tall was notorious for his thin skin and fondness for retaliation.

"Maybe you, for the ledger we took out of Superman's place?" she asked.

"Could be . . . fuck him."

"Did we keep it or give it up to the homicide guys?" she asked, knowing if her partner went down she would too.

"Behan gave it to them after I made a copy."

"I'll be back," Josie said, sliding off the stool. She walked directly to the corner table and stood in front of the sergeant. "Hi, Pete, Josie Corsino, remember me?"

The young man stood and smiled. He seemed genuinely happy to see her.

"Of course, I do. You did a really great job testifying at that board. The captains were very impressed. Sorry your friend didn't fare better."

"He made some bad choices," she said, pulling a chair from another table and then sitting uninvited, asked, "Mind if I join you? You're a little out of your territory, aren't you, Pete? Something going on I should know about?"

The three men at the table exchanged nervous glances before Art said, "Pete's a friend and I wanted to discuss something personal with him. That okay with you, Josie?" His tone was nasty, and he had difficulty looking at her.

Mission accomplished, she thought. Art's rattled.

"I'll let you guys get back to business, just wanted to say hello," she said, shaking hands with the IA sergeant. And then, grinning at Art, added before walking away, "Let me know if I can help with anything."

"Well?" Tomic asked as soon as she settled in next to him.

"Who knows. They're all acting weird, but then again it is Too Tall and Art," she said and laughed to herself. "Art's such an insecure mess; I'll make him tell me eventually. Let it play out. We've got nothing to hide . . . do we?" she asked, studying his face for a sign of disagreement.

"I'm wondering if somehow they got the same info we did about a dirty cop."

"Maybe," she said, but was certain the two men didn't have a snitch capable of giving them that information . . . unless Billie knew and had let it slip when they captured her that morning.

As soon as she had that thought, Tomic said, "Billie."

"We've been working together too long."

"Tomorrow we'll track her down," Tomic said, emptying his glass and getting up, steadying himself before adding, "She and Superman traveled with the same street trash, so she could've heard the same rumblings or rumors he did."

He turned and headed straight for the front door and out to the parking lot without another word to anyone. Tomic wasn't by nature a social animal and didn't care much what other cops thought of him. She knew most of the narcotics detectives thought he was arrogant and self-centered. They were right; he was, but his instincts were sharp, and she could handle his personality. Besides, he treated her like an equal, a partner not a woman foisted on him like some affirmative action social experiment.

She was certain he wasn't stumbling home to the wife and kids. On her route to the Hollywood Freeway, Josie expected to see his city car parked at a rundown dive they called the "Freeway." The bar was a hundred yards from the onramp and probably had another name, but she never knew it. More importantly, the bartender was Tomic's twenty-two-year-old lover. Sue Ann, or the cheerleader, as she'd come to be known among the squad, was the antithesis of Tomic. Outgoing and fun-loving, she talked too loud with the husky voice of a chain-smoker and savored life only a little less than the considerable gin and vodka she consumed. They were opposites, but she seemed to distract the man, make him happy in some peculiar way. Josie liked her and despite some serious moral objections to the pairing, chose not to judge her partner's indiscretion.

The house was dark when she got home. It was after two A.M., but she was still surprised Jake had gone to bed. He usually waited up, so they could talk or snuggle in bed before falling asleep either with or without the benefit of sex. Josie didn't like the feeling of coming into a cold, dark, empty kitchen. Although she'd always prided herself on being an independent woman, being alone wasn't something she wanted or enjoyed. She poured a glass of brandy and sat at the kitchen table unable to ignore a nagging sensation that everything she did, needed, or wanted lately seemed to be pushing away the people she loved most.

~ SIX ~

Jake and Nonna were gone by the time Josie woke the next morning. David's clean cereal bowl was sitting in the dish drainer, and his book bag was no longer propped against the wall by the door, so she was alone. Her phantom family had started its day the way it ended yesterday, without her.

There was an easy solution to the problem; maybe not so easy because police work was an addiction. But she'd decided to let it go a little while longer and then try to find a position where she could be home more, repair the damage done these last few years. It would be difficult turning off the adrenaline drip, but she knew if her family was going to survive, she'd probably have to give up something she was good at and that made her happy. The plan was sketchy, but it let her rationalize and pretend there might be a resolution that could work.

As soon as she walked into the narcotics office, any thought of weaning herself from this life evaporated. Tomic was waiting and she gulped half a mug of coffee before they started the search for Billie.

"Do you ever eat anything except donuts and fried chicken?" Tomic asked as they drove eastbound on Sunset Boulevard toward Billie's favorite breakfast place. "Maybe if you ate real food you could gain a few pounds."

She was finishing a cream-filled éclair from Winchell's and swallowed the last bite before saying, "I eat all the time. It's my metabolism. I come from tall thin Sicilian genes. Jake and his mother are good cooks, but I'm never home long enough to eat."

"You will be. They'll promote you again. You'll get a cushy job and be home every night."

"Boooring."

"Live with it. Everybody knows you're headed like a fuckin' rocket for a staff job."

"Not ready for that."

"Get ready so you don't turn into another empty suit. You're smart. People like you and they'll follow your lead. Pay attention now so you don't fuck it up when you get there."

There it was. Tomic had given her his words of wisdom and more importantly his stamp of approval. He never offered praise or encouragement, so he might actually believe she was a good cop. A crappy day that had started with doubt and disappointment suddenly was looking good. Maybe she wouldn't have to worry about leaving street enforcement. The problem would resolve itself when she got promoted. Good news, bad news.

Billie was in the parking lot at the Shack but ducked behind the building when Tomic drove around the corner. She must have realized they'd seen her because she came out of the alley and tried to pretend she wasn't hiding. She waved and walked to the rear door of the restaurant where Stella, her skinny lesbian roommate/lover, was standing, gently rocking a rickety baby carriage. Billie was wearing a frilly yellow housedress over tight red leotards, and her orange hair had streaks of red now—Pippi Longstocking on acid, Josie thought.

Rolling down his window, Tomic drove as close as he could to her and the other woman and asked, "Who the hell dresses you, woman?"

"Hi, Officer Tomic," Billie said sweetly, while awkwardly lifting a baby out of the carriage.

Josie got out and walked around the back of the car. She worried about Billie's baby. It was small and sickly pale. Thanks to Stella, the little girl was always clean, meticulously dressed in warm clothes, and smelled of baby powder, but she was clearly not healthy. The carriage was falling apart, but a new fluffy white blanket covered the inside, providing a protective nest. Stella tried to be a surrogate mother, but she was a hype, too, and the damage had been done. The baby was born addicted to her mother's heroin and had suffered withdrawal and seizures from birth. She was struggling to survive but Josie had seen it too many times and knew the odds weren't in her favor.

She took the baby from Billie and held her close, inhaling that sweet pleasant odor of a newborn.

"How's Ashley doing?" she asked, as the tiny blue eyes stared back at her. There was no crying or baby noises, no movement.

"Still won't fucking eat nothing," Billie said indifferently, glancing at the other woman. "Stella's been trying different formulas but the kid ain't interested."

Stella, who could easily pass as a little Mexican boy, had lived with Billie on and off for years. She rarely got arrested and when she did, refused to snitch or even say much. She lived in the shadows, but Josie was certain she had dozens of contacts and knew a lot more about Hollywood dealers than Billie, who had burned so many bridges as an informant that very few of the established drug dealers would sell to her any longer. Josie surmised a lot of the information that Billie peddled to get herself out of jail came from Stella.

"I'm gonna bring the kid home now," Stella said, holding out her hands to Josie and taking the baby.

"We need to talk to Billie a few minutes. You wanna stay. You might be able to help us and make a few bucks," Tomic said.

"Nah, I ain't got nothing to say to you," Stella said, gently laying the baby back in the carriage and pushing it away from the restaurant.

"Fucking retard," Billie whispered, watching her lover walk away. "Bitch's got so much fucking shit to sell. Don't know why I don't throw her stubborn wetback ass out."

"Because you and your kid would starve and die from withdrawal," Josie said.

Billie crossed her arms and didn't say anything, but they both knew Josie was right. Stella's place was a dump, but her generosity was the only reason Billie and her baby weren't living on the street eating garbage.

"You need me for something or what?" Billie asked, leaning against the wall, scowling.

They went inside the restaurant and Tomic found a booth by the kitchen door away from the front window. This particular snitch never cared if she was seen talking to the police, but Josie did. She and her partner had already lost one careless informant that week.

"What do you know about Clark Kent's death?" Tomic asked, after the waitress left three cups, a pot of coffee, and a basket of chili fries on the table.

"Me? How would I fucking know?" Billie asked, grabbing a handful of fries and stuffing them into her mouth.

"He was your friend," Josie said, knowing Billie was probably the only real friend Kent had in Hollywood.

"Yeah, so I ain't gonna kill the dumb fucker, right?"

"But you know who did."

The big woman squirmed, pulling on the lace ruffles decorating the housedress and nervously scratching at her face with both hands.

"Well?" Tomic asked after a lengthy silence.

"I hear shit, you know . . . bullshit mostly."

"What did you tell Too Tall . . . Detective Gilbert?" Josie asked.

Billie stopped fidgeting, slumped back, and stared at her.

"Fuck." She sighed but quickly recovered, leaning over the table again. "Word is a cop did him. Sonofabitch got in the middle of something big and got his crazy roid ass killed. That's it. That's all I told Gilbert."

"Word from who?" Tomic asked.

"You know . . . everybody."

"Stella?" Josie asked.

"Fuck no! She don't say nothing about nothing. You know that," she said, looking away.

"What else did you tell Gilbert?"

"Nothing, I fucking swear on my baby's life . . . ain't gonna give that scary mothafucker shit I don't hafta . . . besides, there ain't nothing else to tell."

"Keep your eyes and ears open. I want to know who killed Kent . . . and there's a lot of money in it for whoever gives me that name," Tomic said.

"How much?" Billie asked, sitting up, suddenly interested.

"Too much even for you and Stella to flush down your veins. This is fed money and there's a lot of it."

A few minutes later, they left Billie in the restaurant, having planted the dollar seed in her greedy mind. Josie hoped their informant could work her magic on Stella, convince the other woman to dig up some useful information for a lot of cash, but knew the odds weren't good the cautious Mexican would help.

Tomic had fabricated the fed money, but Josie knew he'd find some cash if Billie could point them in the direction of Kent's killer or the corrupt cop. The asset forfeiture laws had flooded the division with money, a lucrative side effect of seizing expensive cars, houses, and those huge bank accounts from drug dealers. The difficult part was convincing the narcotics captain that street enforcement detectives should share any of it. His major-violator squads downtown gave him bigger seizures and headlines, so they got the cash and new toys, but a lot of their leads came from street detectives like her and Tomic.

As soon as they were back in Tomic's car, Dolores was broadcasting a message from the lieutenant telling them to come back to the station. Curtis needed help serving a search warrant. When

Tomic drove into the lot, he groaned. Their captain's new car was parked in front of the door beside Lieutenant Watts's shiny new Buick. It was a sore point with Hollywood detectives that they never saw a new car and got the broken hand-me-downs from Major Violators. Granted that section's drug and property seizures were the primary reason for the large asset forfeiture fund, but Josie always thought working detectives should at least get better equipment than command and staff officers.

Captain Clark was sitting in Lieutenant Watts's office and glared at them through the open door as Josie and Tomic sat at their squad table. The six Hollywood narcotic detectives were joined by one team from Venice and two uniformed officers who stood at the back of the room. The uniforms would go in the front door with the entry team, so the crooks couldn't claim they didn't know it was the police when the door went down.

"Vern," Josie said, turning and acknowledging the older patrol officer. He nodded back and reached over to shake hands with her and Tomic.

Vernon Fisher was a veteran uniformed training officer who probably made more narcotics arrests than any plainclothes detective in West Bureau. He'd never been assigned to narcotics but had an uncanny ability to find heroin and cocaine dealers. From the look of her unfaded uniform, his partner was a probationary officer. Josie thought the small nervous woman seemed very young and gave the impression she'd rather be anywhere than in this cramped grimy squad room. Josie figured it was her first search warrant and any new officer with any sense, looking around this room, should've been nervous. The collection of long hair, beards, messy clothes, and aura of chaos had to be culture shock after six months in the structured safe environment of the police academy—like going from Saint Mary's church to a Hell's Angels rally.

The noise level in the room dropped noticeably when the captain and lieutenant finally came out of Watts's office and stood near Behan's desk. Captain Clark cleared his throat and waited until everyone stopped writing or talking, put down the phone, and looked up at him before he spoke. He was a big man, and the only guy she knew who could possibly consume more alcohol than Red Behan. Josie figured his knowledge of narcotics operations and success in bringing hundreds of thousands of dollars into the department through asset forfeiture laws had to be the only reason the chief was willing to ignore all the episodes involving Clark's car crashes, weekend binges, and other alcohol-related indiscretions including one she had personally witnessed.

She suspected he'd only had a few drinks today since he seemed to be in a moderately bad mood. On those rare occasions when she'd seen him sober, he was usually nasty and demeaning, so it wasn't too difficult to know when he'd been drinking heavily—he was a happier asshole.

"Men," he said and grinned at Josie, adding, "and woman."

Josie knew her attempt at a smile was probably more like a sneer, but she didn't care. She had never shown him much respect and knew he didn't like her either. Clark had warned her when she was transferred to field enforcement that he expected her to leave after a few months because in his words, "This isn't the sort of work a woman should like or can handle very well. I'm anticipating your request for a transfer so don't feel bad when it happens."

He told her the assignment was an experiment to prove women couldn't handle the stress and when she failed it would be a long time before another woman would have the opportunity to work the Narcotics Field Enforcement division. Over three years later, it was clear she wasn't going to fail. She was still in the division, had been promoted, and was thriving. That seemed to annoy him.

Today he was attempting to sound like a leader employing his most sincere tone to tell his minions how proud he was of his Hollywood squad and how he wanted to tag along on this search warrant to show his support of their efforts. He said this was their opportunity to ask about anything happening in the division and make their case for any tools or equipment they needed to do their jobs better.

Josie stopped listening. Once or twice a year Clark would come to Hollywood and make the same speech. She had given him the same list of equipment each time and hadn't seen a single item yet. Curtis coughed, and it sounded as if he'd said "bullshit." Clark, who obviously hadn't deciphered the insult, looked around the room and seemed puzzled by the ripple of snickering.

He finished quickly and told them Lieutenant Watts had a few words before they left. Watts stood and opened his mouth to speak but before he could say a word, the barely audible music came from somewhere in the back of the room.

"'It's Howdy Doody time. It's Howdy Doody time.' It's time for boys and girls . . ."

Watts's smile faded, and his freckles seemed darker, more sinister. The music stopped, and he stared directly at Art, who shrugged indifferently. Josie expected the lieutenant to get angry, say something and take charge, but he didn't. She could see he was struggling to control himself and she knew that was a mistake. He needed to deal with it, make a sarcastic joke, or tell Art he was an asshole. Ignoring the affront made him look weak. But then again, she thought, the guy is weak.

"I know Curtis wants to get this show on the road, so I'll let him do his briefing. Be careful out there," Watts mumbled and sat down.

"I'm inspired. How 'bout you?" Tomic asked just loud enough for her to hear.

"Sad," she whispered and sat back ready to enjoy Curtis's briefing which she knew from past experience would be entertaining.

Curtis was hands down the most knowledgeable detective in the division, and that was his curse. He knew too much. His briefings became rambling dissertations including every conceivable contingency and pitfall in serving warrants until it got so confusing, he'd eventually stop and say, "You know what I mean. Let's just serve the damn thing."

He handed out copies of his game plan and fifteen minutes later reached that point of information overload, so everyone got up, put on their nylon raid jackets with "Police" in large letters written across the back and LAPD badges stamped on the front, and got ready to serve his warrant.

Josie went to her locker to retrieve her ballistic nylon gun belt and holster with Velcro straps she could fasten around her leg. She used it for search warrants because the holster was covered by a secured flap. Search warrants generated frenetic activity with lots of cops and suspects yelling and running around. Not having her gun fall out or get grabbed in a tussle was one less thing to think about in her never-ending quest to recover the drugs at any cost.

She was ready to go and watched as the captain struggled to put on the protective vest Curtis had loaned him. Without thinking, she reached over and flipped it around, so the right panel was in front. He turned and started to thank whoever had helped him until he realized it was Josie. His nose and cheeks got a little redder under a road map of tiny blue veins before he walked away.

"Knucklehead," she said under her breath and noticed Tomic across the room staring at her before he made a jerking motion with his right hand. He picked up his utility bag and walked toward her.

"Come on, partner," he said, touching her shoulder. "Like I said, watch and learn."

The cars lined up in the parking lot behind Officer Fisher's black-and-white, and then they caravanned from the narcotics office for about a mile and parked a block away from the search warrant location on Fuller Avenue. Venice detectives had Dolores broadcast a message that their car had broken down a few minutes after they left the lot. Curtis decided not to wait for them. He knew in this gang-saturated neighborhood, it wouldn't take long for word to spread that the police had invaded their territory.

The house was boarded up and had security bars over most of the windows. Steel plating covered the front door, but Curtis had recently constructed a heavy-duty ram in his garage. He claimed it could generate enough force to knock down any door. Normally they would hit the lock with the ram, but the informant had advised Curtis there were bolts and bars on the interior of the door, so his plan was to hit it hard enough to rip the entire frame away from the wall.

Captain Clark stood on the sidewalk with the young female uniformed officer as Josie and the rest of the entry team ran up onto the front porch. Art and Too Tall had gone around to the back of the house.

"Police. We have a search warrant. Open the door!" Officer Fisher shouted, banging on the steel-plated door with his baton.

With Curtis holding the handle on one side and Donny on the other, they smashed the ram into the door, ripping it a few inches away from the frame. They brought it back again and swung harder this time, shattering the frame and spraying wood splinters, chunks of plaster, and drywall inside the house, onto the porch and entry team. The door fell flat on the floor as detectives ran over it into the house and quickly rounded up the occupants.

Josie chased a heavy-set woman into the bathroom where she was attempting to flush not only plastic baggies with what looked like rock cocaine but bundles of money down the toilet. When the woman realized the money had created a dam preventing anything from getting down into the sewer line, she stood on the tub and frantically tried to scramble out a tiny window. Josie pulled her off the tub and led her handcuffed into the living room where she sat on the floor with the four men who'd been found hiding in other parts of the house.

The men were dressed in stained tank-top underwear or were shirtless in dirty jeans. Most of them had matted hair and smelled of dried sweat and marijuana. Their dilated pupils and inability to stop fidgeting or talking told Josie they'd probably been hitting the base pipe with some regularity.

A chill went down her spine as she watched Tomic remove a double-barreled shotgun from a makeshift bracket above the front door. It was intended to prevent unwanted entry, but the door was forced open so quickly either no one inside had a chance to grab the weapon or they were so stoned they didn't care.

There were other guns stashed throughout the house, but from their tattoos and demeanor, Josie figured these dealers were "OGs" or original gangsters, the older parolees who knew how the game was played. They didn't get excited about being arrested. Most of them thrived in prison and had no fear of going back. It was the young gangbangers who did stupid things, got mouthy, and tried to shoot it out or fight with the police. There was a sort of understanding between the police and the "OGs." They knew when they got caught, jail was inevitable and resisting was stupid and painful. If they had an opportunity, they'd gladly kill cops but ambush in a dark alley was more their style.

Josie and Tomic searched the kitchen and found evidence of freebasing or reducing cocaine from powder to rock or pure cocaine for smoking as well as packaging materials to sell the product. A triple-beam balance scale and several recently used base pipes had been left on the counters which told her these guys were inhaling a lot of their profits.

Like most of these places, the house smelled like a sewer and was cluttered with filth, so no one put much effort into a thorough search. Cockroaches had taken possession of the kitchen cupboards and appliances, and Josie declared the rodent-infested bedroom a drug-free zone, meaning it didn't matter if there were drugs in there because she wasn't going to touch anything. Besides, Curtis had already confiscated more than enough rock cocaine to arrest everyone for sales.

Art and Too Tall stayed in the bathroom to dry and count the money pulled from the toilet and several piles of cash the woman hadn't had an opportunity to flush. As soon as Curtis was ready to leave with his arrestees, nearly a half kilo of cocaine, and a couple hundred baggies filled with rock cocaine, he got impatient and shouted from the living room for the two detectives to gather up the money and finish counting it at the office. They didn't answer so Tomic went down the hallway toward the bathroom and walked out alone a few seconds later looking upset.

“What’s up?” Josie asked as her partner pushed past her and out the front door.

Before she could go after him, Art and Too Tall came into the living room carrying two paper grocery bags stuffed with cash. They were laughing and talking . . . very unlike Tomic who had so quickly turned sullen and angry.

She found her partner sitting on the car hood and asked him to help board up the front door and broken windows of the rock house. He wasn’t interested in sharing his thoughts with her as they hammered nails into the plywood or on the drive back to the narcotics office. Josie had worked with him long enough to know it was pointless to try if he didn’t want to talk, so as soon as he parked, she removed her gear from the trunk and went inside.

The captain and Lieutenant Watts hadn’t stayed at the search warrant location more than a few minutes after detectives had made entry. Captain Clark had already returned downtown but Watts was in his office. Josie stood in the corner by the coffee machine and watched as Tomic and Behan had an animated conversation in the parking lot before going directly into Watts’s office. Immediately, the lieutenant’s door slammed closed, and Josie could hear the lock click on the other side. She sat at her desk and waited for over an hour before Behan came out into the squad room alone.

The rest of the squad had gone across the street to help Curtis book arrestees and contraband in Hollywood station, so she was alone with the squad leader. Josie adjusted her chair, so she could stretch her long legs and rest them on Tomic’s empty chair beside hers, folded her arms, and stared at Behan until he finally looked up at her.

“What do you want?” he asked.

“Where’s my partner?”

“Gone . . . he went out the front door.”

“What’s going on?”

Behan took a deep breath, got up, and sat directly across the table from her.

"Tomic said he's gonna talk to you in the morning but I'll tell you now because I know if I don't you'll break into the lieutenant's desk trying to find out."

Josie attempted to look wrongly accused but knew he was right because she'd done it on more than one occasion.

"Is Tomic in trouble?" she asked.

"Not the way you think. He says he saw Too Tall take money at the search warrant location and put it in his pocket."

She slid her legs off the chair, turned, and leaned closer to him.

"Why didn't he say something out there when he saw it, when the evidence was in his pocket? It's too late now." She was angry. Dirty cops were the worst kind of criminal.

"Because your partner's smarter than you, that's why," Behan said. "Too Tall hasn't got a clue Tomic saw him and we need to find out if he's the cop your snitch was talking about."

"We caught him stealing money; he might've talked to save his skin," she said, still not convinced.

"Why should he? He goes down for a few hundred dollars, but what if he isn't alone, or what if he killed Kent? If we do it your way, he loses his job, probably gets probation for a couple of years, but is he getting away with Kent's murder? And when he's gone, will we still have more dirty cops we can't identify?"

All of that was true, but she was irritated knowing Too Tall would be walking around carrying a badge and gun.

"Okay, what's Tomic's plan?" she asked.

"We'll get surveillance to watch him, bug his city car; that way we can find out if Art's in on it . . . but none of that's happening tonight. Go home and we'll talk to Tomic first thing in the morning."

"Why wait? Why not get started now?"

Behan got up and locked his desk. "Watts wants to run it by the captain and try to get SIS to do the surveillance. There's no way we can watch him."

Josie knew the Special Investigation Section or SIS was the department's premiere surveillance team, but she'd also heard those veteran detectives didn't like following other cops or working with Internal Affairs so nothing they were told by IA remained confidential.

"Has everyone gone? Are you leaving?" she asked, looking around the office and checking her watch. It was a little after six P.M. Josie couldn't remember the last time the Hollywood squad had shut down this early.

"Yes, so go. They're finished across the street. We're done until tomorrow," Behan said.

Before leaving, she helped Behan find a place to tack a copy of Curtis's search warrant schematic on the back wall of the office which was already covered with hundreds of similar diagrams for significant warrants the squad had served over the years. The date, number of arrestees, and amount of contraband seized had been scribbled across the bottom of each sheet. They couldn't find enough space, so he tore one of Too Tall's minor warrants off the wall, crumbled it up, and tossed it into the trash.

"If Tomic's right, that's just the beginning," Behan said, flipping off the light switch.

~ SEVEN ~

She thought about calling home to see if Jake was there but decided since it was such a rare opportunity to leave work early she'd surprise him. On the way, she drove past the "Freeway" bar and wasn't surprised to see Tomic's city car parked next to Sue Ann's yellow Toyota Corolla in the back lot. He would need her mindless chatter tonight, and the cheerleader wasn't about to let her favorite player get away early.

Traffic wasn't as bad as Josie had anticipated and she made it to Pasadena in less than an hour. She parked in front of her house and smiled at the neighbor sitting on his front porch across the street. He got up, gave her a dirty look, and went inside as she locked the driver's door. She thought he'd be in a better mood since she usually left the pile of junk parked in front of his house.

Jake's Porsche was in the driveway, but Nonna's Chevy Nova was nowhere in sight. Josie wouldn't allow herself to get too excited until she got inside the house and saw David in his pajamas and Jake sitting beside him at the dining room table working on a coloring book. She gave them both a hug and sat at the table.

"Where's Nonna?" Josie asked.

"Just left," Jake said.

"Really?" Josie asked, peeking under the table, pretending to look for the old woman and laughing when David did the same.

"Very scary if he's got your sense of humor," Jake said, getting up, giving her a kiss before going into the kitchen. As soon as he'd gone, David began describing his day at school and everything he'd done since the bus dropped him off that afternoon.

"Did you finish your homework?" Josie asked when the little boy stopped to take a breath. He nodded, and she added, "Did Nonna make you dinner?" He nodded again and started another story about how he crashed his bicycle and pulled up the right leg of his pajamas to show her a tiny bruise and Band-Aid on his knee.

"Better get Evel Knievel to bed," Jake called from the kitchen. "Or he won't get up in the morning."

David started to whine about not being tired, but Josie picked him up and carried him over her shoulder like a sack of potatoes into the kitchen, so he could kiss his father good night. She kept him up there and trotted around the living room, the den and finally climbed the stairs before dumping him onto his bed where he stopped giggling, crawled under the blankets, and told her how much he loved her. She pushed back his hair, kissed him on his forehead, and after a few minutes, he was asleep.

As soon as she got downstairs, the smell of baked salmon was thick in the air. Jake was finishing a sauce for the asparagus and asked her to set the table.

"Let's eat in here," Josie said, putting napkins and silverware on the breakfast table. She liked eating in the kitchen. Something about the formality of the dining room seemed to stifle their conversation.

A cold bottle of Chardonnay and two glasses were on the counter. She poured a little in both glasses and gave one to Jake. They touched glasses, but he put his on the table without drinking and hurried back to the oven to pull out the salmon stuffed with spinach. He filled the plates and put them on the table.

"Hope you're hungry," he said, pulling out a chair for her.

"No, I'm starving," she said, but waited until he was sitting across from her before tasting the fish. "This is incredible."

They ate in comfortable silence until she had finished everything on her plate and a second helping of salmon. She filled their wine glasses again and sat back.

"Tomic says he saw one of our guys stealing money this afternoon," she said while Jake was taking the last couple of bites. He stopped, lowered his fork, and looked up at her. She continued, "Behan thinks he might be the dirty cop our snitch was talking about before he got killed."

Jake had a puzzled expression and Josie knew why. She rarely talked about work, but she felt the need to share this with him tonight because he was not only a smart lawyer but had the ability to cut through bullshit and see the core of a problem. Something was bothering her about today's events but her usually reliable instincts weren't helping. She needed to engage his analytical mind, so she recounted every detail of the search warrant, the theft her partner claimed to have seen, and what they had decided to do about it.

"That's a serious allegation. Is Tomic certain that's what he saw?"

"He wouldn't say anything unless he was positive. I just don't like waiting for SIS. We should be watching them now."

"Them?" Jake asked.

"Too Tall and his partner, Art. We need to know if they're working together or with anybody else . . . other cops."

"Why didn't Tomic arrest Too Tall as soon as he saw him take the money?" Jake asked, reaching over to put the dirty dishes on the counter without getting up. "He probably would've told you everything for any kind of deal that kept him out of jail."

"That's what I said, but Behan doesn't agree. He thinks if Too Tall killed our snitch he'd gladly accept being fired because he won't lose his pension and he knows he'd most likely get probation for petty theft. We can't prove who killed Kent, so he might get away with murder, too, and even worse, we might never know if there are other dirty cops."

"You're not happy with that or with SIS handling this, are you?" he asked.

"No."

"But you can't do it yourselves and there's no one else, is there?"

She didn't have an answer and they didn't speak for several seconds as she stared at the table.

"I want Too Tall gone. I hate the idea of him going to the office every day, carrying that badge as if . . . you know," she said, her voice trailing off and finally she looked at him.

"Then I guess you and Tomic better find another way to get it done," Jake said. "You're smart. Figure it out." He got up and, leaning closer to her, said softly, "Next time, tell Tomic to arrest the guy because your favorite deputy DA promises he'd charge the worst possible felony and request enough prison time to scare the shit out of the toughest cop."

Josie pulled him closer and kissed him. "There's something irresistible about a bloodthirsty lawyer."

They never got to the bedroom, but Josie found lovemaking on the living room floor could be very satisfying. Two hours later, she was wrapped in an afghan on the lounger, drinking the last of the Chardonnay and watching Jake sleep soundly on the couch. She could never get enough sleep, but it was worse when something was on her mind. It wasn't easy to accept Tomic's explanation for not confronting Too Tall at the house. That's what was gnawing at her. Doing the smart calculating thing wasn't the way her partner operated. She would have expected him to be furious and drag Too Tall out of the bathroom in handcuffs. That was the Tomic way.

She finished the wine, put her glass on the floor, and pulled the afghan up to cover her arms. This is stupid, she thought. I'm overthinking again. Tomic's not perfect but I do trust him. She closed her eyes trying to clear her mind but couldn't purge that little speck of doubt taking root in her brain.

~ EIGHT ~

The telephone was on a small table across the room from her recliner. Josie heard the persistent annoying ring in her dream until it finally woke her. The room was cold, but someone had tucked a heavy blanket around her. She glanced at the couch; it was empty. She threw off the blanket, wrapped the afghan around her naked body, and stumbled to answer the phone.

"What?" she said, not happy with the irritating wake-up call.

"You planning on coming to work today, Corsino?" Behan asked in his most pleasant voice.

"Yes, sir," she said, trying to focus on the small Waterford clock on the fireplace mantel. It was ten A.M. "Shit, sorry, overslept."

"Just get your ass in here," he said and hung up.

She stood there for several seconds listening to the dial tone, trying to shake the Chardonnay cobwebs out of her brain. Finally, she stuck the phone back in the cradle, picked up the blanket, and hurried upstairs to take a shower. In less than fifteen minutes, she was dressed and in her car headed toward Hollywood. Nonna's car was in the driveway when Josie left but she hadn't seen her mother-in-law. David's school bus always picked him up before nine, so Jake's mother should've gone home over an hour ago, but she was probably doing laundry, cleaning the bathrooms. or performing any number of those domestic chores Josie hated and avoided. A cleaning lady came once a week, but the elder Mrs. Corsino was never satisfied with the quality of work and spent hours "touching up" after her. Even though the old woman's frequent presence in her home sometimes annoyed Josie, she appreciated her help and valued her love for David who in turn adored his grandmother. Josie guessed there wasn't much of anything else in the woman's life to occupy her time and energy. She'd come to the conclusion that David's happiness, spotless toilets, and an empty clothes hamper more than made up for a bit of aggravation.

Tomic and Behan were alone in the narcotics office when she arrived. She sat at the table next to her partner and waited for one of them to say something.

"Red told you what's going on, right?" Tomic said, looking at Behan.

"He told me," she said and paused before asking, "I still don't understand why you didn't bust him on the spot."

Behan started to answer for him but Tomic interrupted saying, "I almost did, but then I wasn't sure I saw what I thought I saw . . . I couldn't tell if Art was in on it, so I decided it might be better to wait . . ." He exhaled and sat back. "I don't know what the fuck I was thinking."

"Doesn't matter now, IA and SIS have it. They'll come up with something," she said, attempting to make him feel better even though she wasn't confident either of those divisions was capable of doing a thorough investigation.

"There's been a change of plans," Behan said. He hesitated, glanced at Tomic.

"The captain's not going to ask SIS to help and IA decided they're not going to, in their words, 'pursue' my complaint against Gilbert," Tomic said, finishing what Behan was reluctant to say.

"Why?" she asked, in a high-pitched voice she hardly recognized as her own.

"A few days ago, Gilbert made a personnel complaint against Tomic, and IA is saying Tomic's allegation smells like retaliation," Behan said.

"Gilbert made a complaint about what?" she asked, turning to Tomic.

He shook his head, and Behan said, "We don't know. The captain hasn't served him yet . . . probably this afternoon."

"So what you're telling me is Too Tall gets away with stealing money and keeps playing cop while the department screws with Tomic," Josie said.

"No, I'm telling you we're on our own. There's no IA complaint and no SIS surveillance. It sucks but that's how it is," Behan said. "Gilbert's dirty and we have to prove it ourselves. But you've got other things to worry about, Corsino. Butch bailed out last night."

"How?" she asked. "I booked all his money."

"Abby posted his bail," Tomic said and when Josie didn't react right away, he added, "Abby Morrison from The Carnival."

"I remember who she is but we can't worry about Butch now. We need to concentrate on nailing Too Tall," she said, getting up and glancing into the hallway. She thought she heard someone come in from the parking lot, but there was no one by the door. "He's got to be our priority," she said in a softer voice.

"I think it's all connected," Tomic said. "If Too Tall's our dirty cop, I'm guessing he's responsible for what happened to Kent and if I'm right, finding Kent's killer should lead us straight back to him."

"Who's here?" Dolores called out from her desk in the lobby. She walked through the lieutenant's office and stood in the doorway of the Hollywood squad room waving the sign-in board. "Why don't you people do this? It's a simple task, but you don't care because I'm the one who has to listen to the lieutenant," she whined, looking at each of them and back to Behan.

"Sorry, Dolores, it's Josie's fault," Behan said, smirking as Josie, standing behind the secretary, raised her middle finger in his direction.

"It's never anybody's fault, but Howdy Doody always yells at me. Curtis and Donny are in court. At least they called in," Dolores said, giving the clipboard to Behan. "If the lieutenant asks, I haven't got a clue where Art and Too Tall have gone, but then again that's actually your problem. Isn't it, Detective Behan?" she asked with a forced smile.

As soon as Dolores went back to her desk, Behan moved closer to Josie and said, "If all else fails we can always do a sting operation on Too Tall. He took money once, and odds are, like any other thief, he'd do it again."

"Okay," she said without much conviction. Josie wanted to do the sting now and fire him. On the other hand, she understood all that would do is prove he was a thief, so she was willing to be patient a few days if it meant finding enough evidence to tie him to Kent's murder.

"The two of you go back to The Carnival and talk to Abby. Find out why her sudden interest in Butch," Behan said. "Threaten her with extra enforcement in the club. Marge Bailey's back as a vice sergeant. She won't be intimidated by the Testa name."

"Marge wouldn't be intimidated by the Al Capone name," Josie said.

Before they left, Behan reminded Tomic of his meeting later that day with Captain Clark.

After he got served with his personnel complaint, they'd all know what Gilbert was alleging. Tomic didn't say anything, but Josie thought he seemed worried which told her he didn't have a clue what Too Tall's allegation would be. Her partner wasn't a saint, but he tried not to cross the line that could get him into serious trouble . . . a firing offense. Rules and regulations weren't a priority with him, but she couldn't remember anything he'd done that was worthy of a personnel complaint, at least nothing Too Tall would've known about or was smart enough to figure out.

"Have you got any idea what he might've told IA?" she asked, when they were alone in the car. Josie knew he'd prefer not to talk about it, but she had to be certain he wasn't keeping anything from her. If they got into a life or death situation—a daily occurrence in Hollywood—she had to know they were still working as a team.

He didn't respond right away, but as she was about to repeat the question, he said, "Corsino, there's nothing I haven't told you.

Let's drop it. In a couple of hours, we'll both know what asshole told IA."

His expression never changed, and she wasn't certain if he was telling the truth but decided to drop the subject. She'd trust him until she couldn't.

ABBY WAS in her apartment above The Carnival and let them in as soon as Tomic rang the bell. She was dressed in a long, black, silky caftan with a blue chiffon scarf and walked directly to Josie and gave her a quick unexpected hug. Josie got a whiff of expensive perfume nearly buried under the heavy odor of hair spray and perspiration.

"I didn't think you were coming back," Abby said, smiling at Josie. She was ignoring Tomic, but offered Josie a drink and pointed to the couch. "Make yourself comfortable. There's someone I'd like you to meet."

"Thanks," Tomic said, sitting next to Josie. "Nice to see you too."

"I'm pissed at you, Tomic," Abby said, dramatically dropping onto an ottoman. Josie thought she was attempting a girlish pout, but it emerged as an angry scowl.

"Really," Tomic said sarcastically. "I couldn't tell."

"Your detectives came to my home and threatened me."

"I don't have detectives. All I got is me and Corsino. Who the hell are you talking about, lady?"

"That tall long-haired creep with the dark glasses you work with and the quiet one that's always tagging after him, they come here this morning and say they'll close my club if I don't help them."

"Gilbert?" Josie asked.

"I don't remember his name, but I won't forget him," she said, her eyes narrowing to serpentine slits.

"What did he want from you?" Josie asked, sensing she had a better chance than Tomic of getting answers.

"Tells me I've got to give up Butch," Abby said. She took a deep breath trying to control her anger. "Threatens me . . . like I'd give that slimy insect the time of day."

"So, I take it you didn't give up Butch. While we're on the subject, why did you post bail for a guy you claim to hardly know?" Tomic asked.

Abby didn't respond but shot him a disgusted look, then almost as quickly her expression softened as she stared past them. Josie turned to see what was behind her as an older white-haired man had come into the living room. He was short and stocky, but dapper in a shirt, tie, and business suit. When he got closer, Josie could see a large pearl pin on his tie and a pair of pink pearl cuff links peeking out from his jacket sleeves.

There was no mistaking how much he resembled Abby. They had the same Roman nose, high brows, olive complexion, and that menacing demeanor of predators born to take advantage of the weak.

"Gaetano Testa," he said, introducing himself and shaking hands with Josie and Tomic. He was friendly and chatty, asking them about Hollywood station and asking personal questions—were they married; did they have children; how long had they been cops—he seemed genuinely curious, especially about Josie, and showed no animosity about the fact they were sworn to put men like him out of business and into prison. He moved like a caged lion and talked constantly until Abby brought him a glass of whiskey, and he sat on the chair closest to Josie.

Josie gave vague answers to most of his questions, but he didn't seem to mind and, like his daughter, ignored Tomic and professed to be fascinated by her and her choice of professions. She knew Gaetano was trying to be charming and congenial, but he couldn't conceal his true nature. His eyes studied her like his next meal, so his jokes and compliments didn't have the desired effect. She was Sicilian too, but they had nothing else in common and if he thought their shared heritage would make a difference in the way she dealt with him or his daughter then he had seriously misjudged and underestimated her.

"We need to talk to Butch," Josie said to Abby as soon as the old man got up to refill his glass.

"Like I told the hairy creep, he isn't here."

"Then where is he?" Josie persisted. She calculated it was time to test just how much Abby and her father would tolerate.

Tomic didn't say anything. He was smart enough to have figured out these two were more apt to cooperate if he stayed out of the way.

Guy wandered back from the bar and leaned over Abby's shoulder, mumbled something in Italian that Josie couldn't hear. When the old man sat again, he said to his daughter in English, "Tell her. What do you care about this *strano*?"

Josie guessed "strano" meant strange one in Italian, so maybe Butch was one thing she and the old man could agree on.

The father and daughter argued for several minutes in Italian. It had been years since Josie had spoken that language with her family and relatives, but to her surprise she understood most of what they were saying. Gaetano was upset that Abby was protecting the degenerate "freak with blue hair." Abby, in a somewhat respectful way, was telling her father to butt out of her business.

"*Basta*, enough, Papa," Abby groaned after several minutes, raising her hands in defeat. "I'll tell them." She stared at Josie for a few seconds before saying, "But just you two. If the tall creep finds out, we're done."

"We're done when I say we're done," Tomic said, staring at Abby.

Josie was watching Gaetano. The veins in the old man's neck were bulging and it was clear he wasn't pleased with the way Tomic spoke to his daughter, but he stared at his drink and didn't intervene. From everything she'd heard about the Testa family, especially the old man, Josie figured his willingness to let Tomic's remark go unchallenged was peculiar.

Abby's expression changed. Her mouth tightened, and she was obviously controlling her irritation with the insult but nevertheless gave them an address on Santa Monica Boulevard.

"There's nothing but post-production factories on that block," Tomic said. "What's he living in, a shipping crate?"

"The guy who owns the place lost his house and business. They can camp there until the bank throws them out."

"Another loser hits the gutter," Gaetano said with a smirk, flicking the tips of his fingers off his chin, a dismissive gesture Josie had seen older Italian men use.

Abby ignored him and escorted Josie and Tomic around the wall to the foyer. She held the door open until they were on the landing.

"He'll be there. I bought that building from the bank and I ain't throwin' nobody in the gutter," she said.

"You never told us why you posted bail for Butch," Josie said as Abby started to walk away.

"That's right," Abby said and kept walking as the door automatically closed and locked behind her.

The address she gave them was a few blocks from the club but there wasn't enough time for Tomic to find Butch and still get to his meeting with the captain.

Josie wasn't eager to go downtown but knew it would be easier and faster if Tomic didn't have to drop her off at the Hollywood narcotics office. Interacting with Captain Clark wasn't one of her favorite things, but she could stay out of the way until her partner was done. Besides, the captain rarely came out of his office unless he had to attend a cocktail lunch or a press conference.

She knew being a woman wasn't the only reason Clark disliked her. A few months ago, she had gone downtown to pick up secret service funds and found him asleep in his new car. She opened the driver's door to see if he needed help and was nearly knocked over by the strong odor of alcohol. She worried he might wake up and try to drive, so she went inside and got one of the administrative detectives to come out to the parking lot with her.

The detective pleaded with her not to get him involved saying the captain was a nasty drunk who'd eventually sober up and drive home. Although she believed Clark was a jackass, leaving his fate to chance seemed like a high risk, low probability solution. He was more likely to wake up drunk, drive away, and kill himself or worse, some innocent person. She opened the hood and ordered the lower-ranking detective to point to any removable part that would prevent the car from starting. He did, and she yanked it out.

The next day, Josie heard the captain had become more obnoxious than usual when he woke and couldn't start the car. He swore he would find a way to fire the person who'd disabled his ride. Since cops are notorious for not keeping secrets, Josie suspected everyone in the division, including Clark, knew that she was the culprit, but she wasn't worried he'd carry out his threat for two good reasons. First, she was a female civil service employee in the city of Los Angeles, and only Supreme Court justices had more job security. Second, the last thing Clark wanted was an inquiry into why he was passed out in his car.

She tried to stay out of his way, hoping he'd eventually realize she'd done him a favor, but losing the moral high ground to her apparently wasn't something he could accept or reconcile with his perception of female inferiority. Josie found it worrisome that Tomic's career was in the hands of such a man.

Most of the administrative staff, including their lieutenant, had gone to lunch, so Josie sat in the lieutenant's office and watched his television while Tomic went down the hall to meet with the captain. The lieutenant had a leather chair that reclined a little and a small refrigerator close enough to reach without getting up. No wonder these guys never leave their cushy inside jobs, she thought, resting her feet on the desk and retrieving a cold soda. She sat up to open it and noticed a folder sitting on top of his in-basket. It was labeled "West Bureau Narcotic Seizures—Reconciliation Stats."

"What the hell does that mean?" she said out loud, picked it up, and flipped open the cover. It was an audit of West Bureau's four geographic divisions including Hollywood. Every contraband seizure for the last year was listed and compared with a tally from Property division's records where they should've been booked.

Josie was trying to read as fast as she could and watch the doorway at the same time, afraid the lieutenant might walk in and catch her. After flipping through several pages, she went directly to the summary page and, after a cursory look, it was clear to her the report had concluded the Hollywood squad confiscated more narcotics than they booked into Property division.

"Shit," she said, tossing the folder back into the basket. Loud voices were coming from the hallway and she recognized the lieutenant's secretary's as one of them. She put the unopened soda back in the refrigerator and sat back with her feet on the desk and stared at the television.

"If you're not doing any work, get out of my office, Corsino," the lieutenant said, hanging his jacket on a coat tree. He didn't seem upset as he gently pushed her feet off his desk. She got out of his chair.

Josie didn't know him very well, but they had chatted briefly at the division's social gatherings and training days. He was near retirement and made no secret of the fact this admin job was the safe boring place to finish his career. She liked his easygoing manner but knew he had stopped doing any real police work a long time ago.

"Be happy to give you a job here if you're tired of playing in the streets," he said, sitting behind his desk.

"Thanks, Henry, but no thanks," she said, lingering a few feet from him. "I do have a question if you're not too busy."

"I'm overwhelmed. Can't you see," he said, indicating the uncluttered spotless desk top.

"I read your audit on West Bureau. Why did you do an audit on West Bureau? And exactly what did you find?" she asked.

He glanced at the folder in the basket and then back at her.

"Didn't anyone ever tell you it's bad manners to snoop?" Before she could respond, he said, "It's just a routine audit."

"What did you find?" she asked again.

"You read it; you tell me."

"Property division doesn't have a record of some dope my squad seized and supposedly booked there."

The lieutenant sighed, got up, and walked around to the front of his desk until he was too close to her and in a barely audible voice said, "I can't talk to you about this, Josie." She took a step back from the odor of stale tuna and onion, but he continued, "It's way above your job classification. My advice is forget what you read and let nature take its course. None of this concerns you."

"Then who does it concern?" she asked as he walked out of the office and waited by the doorway for her to follow.

"Can't tell you that," he said. When she reached the hallway, he added, "Trust me, you'll know soon enough."

Her first thought was the audit might've been the reason for Tomic's personnel complaint but that was crazy since she certainly would have noticed if he booked less narcotics than they seized. The next logical choice had to be Too Tall . . . steal money or steal dope. What's the difference?

She was so caught up in her thoughts, Josie almost bumped into Tomic in the hallway. He had finished with the captain and was looking for her. Josie searched his face for some indication of how the meeting had gone, but his stoic expression revealed nothing.

"What's the allegation?" she asked, when they were in the parking lot.

He didn't answer right away but as soon as they got into the car, he said, "Somebody supposedly saw me take a few balloons of heroin before I booked the rest."

"Where was I when this happened?"

"You weren't there. It's after I checked it out of property for court."

"And of course, there's heroin missing, right?" she asked, and he nodded.

"I remember the case . . . big seizure, about fifty balloons. I went to court, testified at the prelim, got the chemist report introduced into evidence . . . I don't think balloons were missing."

“How do they know somebody in Property division didn’t take them?” she asked. “As I recall, that case took a long time to get to a prelim.”

“They don’t, except they’ve got this witness saying he saw me take a handful of balloons out of the property envelope while I was in the men’s restroom at the courthouse after I testified. Of course it was Gilbert. He was there that day. That’s why they didn’t believe me about him stealing money. They think I knew he saw me and I made up the theft to discredit him,” Tomic said and tapped his forehead with his fist. “Why didn’t I arrest the asshole when I saw him put money in his pocket? I’m a fucking idiot.” He was quiet for a few seconds and then turned to look at her and said, “Clark is recommending a board of rights. He thinks I should be fired.”

“Clark’s a moron. He’s the least of your problems. How many balloons are gone?”

“Twenty . . .”

“Too Tall had to have taken them. How else would he know which case had the narcotics missing unless he took it or knows who did?”

Tomic sat up and looked at her. What was obvious to her had finally registered in his worried mind.

“You’re right, Corsino. I’m damn sure nobody, especially that shithead, ever saw me take anything.”

“We know it was all there when the lab tested it. You said when you testified the chemist’s report had listed fifty. Do you think there were still that many in the envelope when you were in court?”

Tomic sighed and said, “I think so but who knows. I didn’t count them again . . . I guess it could’ve been short.”

They agreed their next stop should be Property division in the basement of Parker Center. The police administration building was only a few blocks away on Los Angeles Street. All property officers were civilians, but their supervisor was a police sergeant who had worked with Tomic when he was in uniformed patrol. The man was disagreeable and curt with most cops, but he liked Tomic. Josie suspected their antisocial natures made them compatible.

The sergeant immediately agreed to let Tomic look through the logs that documented when property was checked out or returned from a court hearing or lab testing. It only took a few minutes to find the entry where Tomic booked the heroin after the search warrant; the date it was taken by Scientific Investigation Division or SID for testing, and the date it was brought back; the date Tomic checked it out for court and returned it; and another entry when it was checked out for a court hearing.

"I only checked it out once. The guy pled to a lesser charge after the prelim," Tomic said, pointing to the second court date. "This wasn't me."

"According to this sign-out sheet it was," the sergeant said, pointing to the entry with Tomic's scribbled signature and serial number. Wheezing a little as he spoke, he was overweight with bloodshot eyes and was smoking a cigar. Josie thought the cigar smelled like dirty socks and was certain this walking time bomb for a heart attack shouldn't be smoking in the building, but she kept quiet because he was helping them.

"Who's this property officer that signed for the release?" Josie asked.

"Eddie Small."

"Can we talk to him?" she asked.

"You could if he was here. Got fired . . . for stealing."

"Narcotics?" Tomic asked.

"Nah, just money and some cheap jewelry," the sergeant said.

"Do you know if IA interviewed him?" Josie asked, knowing they should have but probably didn't.

The sergeant shrugged and said, "They never mentioned nothing to me."

Tomic got the property officer's address from the sergeant and while they chatted a few minutes, Josie studied the log and compared Tomic's last signature to the others. It was difficult for her to see much difference, but a handwriting expert should know. Tomic would have to tell his union representative to get the comparison done before the disciplinary board of rights got started. In her mind, it didn't change anything as far as Too Tall was concerned. If he was IA's snitch, he knew the heroin was missing so either he signed Tomic's name and took the narcotics or had Small do it.

THE PROPERTY officer lived in LAPD's Rampart division just east of Hollywood. Tomic was eager to find and interview Butch, but Josie convinced him they should stop at Small's house first. She understood her partner was focused on finding Superman's killer, but she knew his priority had to be discrediting Too Tall's allegation and saving his job.

Crime was out of control in that central Los Angeles area the police department had labeled Rampart. Gangs consisting of El Salvadorans and other immigrants from Mexico and Central and South America ran amok among a dense population of illegal aliens and poor families, a few square miles where killings and assaults were the highest in the city.

There were no addresses or only partial numbers on the curb identifying most of the rundown houses and apartment buildings on Small's street, but Josie could narrow it down to what she figured had to be the right property.

Any doubt they might've had was immediately dispelled when Tomic spotted Too Tall's city car parked on the street in front of that location.

~ NINE ~

Fortunately, Tomic recognized the car before he drove past it and could quickly turn into a driveway about a half block north where there was tenant parking located behind the apartments. He made a U-turn in the lot and parked where his car couldn't be seen from the street.

Josie got out and stood near the corner of the building where she had a clear view of both Too Tall's car and Small's house. No one paid much attention to yard maintenance in this neighborhood, so overgrown bushes and weeds provided plenty of cover. She could make out Art sitting in the passenger seat. His head was down, and he seemed to be reading and probably hadn't noticed Tomic's abrupt departure off the street.

After twenty minutes, Art got out of the car and lit a cigarette. He paced over the dead grass and dirt on the parkway and then onto the sidewalk, frequently checking his wristwatch. She thought he appeared to get increasingly agitated until finally he flicked the cigarette butt into the street and marched up the sidewalk toward the house. Before he could reach the front door, Too Tall came out with a shorter, light-skinned black man. The man was barefoot and wore sweatpants with a faded gray T-shirt. He hopped a step or two on the cold cement and rubbed his arms for warmth. Josie guessed coming out of the house half-dressed wasn't his idea. She immediately recognized the design on the front of his shirt, the number six over palm trees. Six was Hollywood division's number identification within the department. The shirt had seen better days, but it was identical to those Hollywood officers sold to make money for their station fund.

She'd seen Small's personnel photo still attached to the employee board at Property division and knew it was him, unshaven and looking frozen and shitty, but him.

Too Tall was doing all the talking and occasionally poked the smaller man in the chest to make a point. Even from a distance, Josie could see the detective was upset. Art stood to the side and didn't get involved. His body language said he wanted to leave, but Too Tall was in charge, and he wasn't finished.

However, when Too Tall put both hands around the smaller man's throat, Art finally stepped in. He calmed down his partner, prying his fingers away from Small's neck, and managed to convince Too Tall to go back to their car. Small didn't move. He stood with his head bowed, arms hanging limp at his sides, as the city car started and pulled away from the curb. He waited like that for several seconds before looking up and staring at the empty street.

There was no doubt in Josie's mind they had to talk to Eddie Small as soon as possible. After Too Tall's visit, he'd either be pissed off and want to spill his guts or be too intimidated to open his mouth. The way he stood there shivering, with his fists clenched, made her believe it was the former. It might not be easy to convince him they could keep him safe and encourage him to talk, but she knew they had to take a chance. She waited until he went into his house, then jogged back to Tomic's car where her partner was sitting on a concrete block wall with the driver's door open listening to the police radio.

"Art just checked in with Dolores for messages . . . asshole told her they were clearing from a foot patrol on Hollywood Boulevard," he said when Josie got closer.

"We've got to question this guy now," she said after describing everything she'd seen. "I've got a feeling he's either gonna rabbit or

Too Tall's coming back to make him disappear forever. Neither way will be good for you."

Tomic didn't respond but slid behind the wheel and waited for her to get in the passenger side. He drove across the street and parked in front of the house next door to Small's. They got out and walked across the neighbor's lawn to the corner of Small's house where Tomic motioned for her to go to the rear as he stepped onto the porch. Josie knew every criminal's first instinct was to escape and the favorite route was by way of the back door. She hurried to the rear yard, ducking under the windows. She used a rusted, nearly gutted Chevy El Camino truck parked on concrete blocks and surrounded by dead weeds as cover. The back door was protected with wrought iron bars and had a dead bolt. There was one tiny window to the right of the door that looked like opaque bathroom glass.

She heard Tomic shout and what sounded like pounding or kicking on the front door. Seconds later, the security bars covering the back door flung open and a terrified, still shoeless Eddie Small jumped out and stumbled off the wooden steps onto the walkway. He lay there on his back rubbing his knee and groaning as Josie holstered her gun and stood over him.

"Going somewhere, Eddie?" she asked.

Tomic ran around the corner of the house but stopped as soon as he saw her standing over the man.

"I don't hafta talk to you," Eddie said, rolling up his sweatpants leg to examine his bruised knee.

"No, you don't," Josie said, leaning against the El Camino. "You can hide in your house until Gilbert comes back and takes care of you like the messy loose end we all know you are."

Eddie crawled onto his good knee and tried to stand but Tomic had to keep him from falling again.

"I don't need no help," Eddie said, pushing Tomic's hands away. "I don't need nothing from you."

He tried to walk but couldn't put any weight on his leg. Tomic wrapped his arm around the smaller man's waist, practically lifting him up the back steps and into the house. Eddie was mumbling and rambling on about police abuse but didn't resist. They went through the kitchen into the cluttered living room where Tomic dropped him onto a couch.

"Why you gotta be so rough," Eddie whined.

"Because you're a fuckin' asshole who doesn't know when somebody's trying to help you," Tomic said

Eddie snickered and said, "Yeah, trying to help me . . . like your lunatic buddy . . . I get canned . . . but nobody gives a fuck 'bout him . . . I need a doctor." He groaned trying to straighten his leg.

Josie could see his knee had swollen to twice its normal size. "I think you broke your knee cap, but you're probably not going to live long enough to get it fixed," she said.

"Ain't nobody gonna kill me."

"Not if we keep you safe."

"You're here so you must already know'd what he done; why've you gotta harass me?"

"You were there," Tomic said, sitting on the couch. "You saw him do it?"

"Can't believe you people. Don't you know that fool's a junkie? When he took all them balloons . . . I told him 'that's too much, fool. They gonna catch us,' but he tells me he's hurtin' bad, gotta have it."

"Did you tell anybody what he did?" Josie asked.

"I snitch on him; he snitches on me. Now I been fired, so fool's tweaking, thinking I'll spill my guts on account of how I ain't got nothing to lose."

"Will you?" Josie asked.

"Bet your fine ass I will," Eddie said. "Fucker's nuts . . . him and bat boy. You think I'm gonna give them a chance to do me in first."

"You saying his partner knew what Gilbert was doing?"

"What do you think . . . fool's got a righteous habit. He's usin' and down every day, stealin' everything in sight. That little man's with him all the time; he's gotta know or he's the damn stupidest creature on this earth," Eddie said and shook his head. "You expect me to believe all you narcs never figured that ten-foot hairy ape is on the needle . . . that's pretty fuckin' suspicious if you asked me."

No, just really fucking stupid, Josie thought. She was remembering all the times Gilbert had to lie on the bench in the holding room with the door closed because he said he had migraines and couldn't assist with warrants or arrests. Or, how he would suddenly doze off while sitting at his desk because "he never got enough sleep" or how he always wore those glasses, tinted just enough to mask the size of his pupils. She knew he was lazy and screwed up, but it never occurred to her he might be nodding off or scratching at his beard and arms more than normal or wearing dark glasses to hide something. She should've checked his eyes for pinned pupils because he was displaying a lot of symptoms associated with being under the influence of an opiate, but it never crossed her mind because cops shouldn't and don't use heroin . . . lesson learned.

Tomic called Behan at Hollywood homicide and told him what Eddie Small had said. The supervisor directed them to take the injured man for medical treatment at Central Receiving and then bring him to Hollywood station and wait there. He would go to the district attorney's office in Santa Monica and start the process to set up witness protection. While he was gone, Behan would have one of his detectives interview Small on tape and get a formal statement.

Josie took the phone and asked, "Is there any way to keep Lieutenant Watts and Captain Clark out of this, maybe coordinate with the IA captain instead."

"No, Corsino, there's no way. These guys are under Clark's command, but I don't have to notify him or Watts right away . . . until we're ready. I'll have everybody meet at Hollywood station in a couple of hours."

"Too bad," Josie said.

"I can keep them out of our hair for a while," Behan said. "But that's all."

"I can't believe Art would go along with any of this. He's no hard charger but . . ." Josie didn't finish her thought because Behan had hung up. She gave the phone back to Tomic.

"He's pissed."

"He's like you. Dirty cops make him crazy," Tomic said.

IT WAS early evening before Tomic and Josie finished getting medical treatment for Small's cracked knee, and his leg was in a full cast when he finally hobbled on crutches into the lobby of Hollywood station. They escorted him to the detective squad room, gave him coffee and a vending machine sandwich, and locked him in one of the interview rooms. A few minutes later, a veteran homicide detective went into the room and recorded Eddie's statement. Josie listened to the interview and was surprised how detailed Eddie was in repeating his story. It was a good accounting and left no doubt that he knew he was incriminating himself while implicating Too Tall. Eddie swore he saw the big detective take the balloons of heroin he had accused Tomic of stealing. He even elaborated on how Too Tall had practiced Tomic's signature several times before signing the log book and told the detective that Too Tall had taken narcotics on at least a half-dozen other occasions.

Josie knew enough about opiates to be certain Gilbert would have puncture wounds somewhere on his body and if they were lucky he'd still be under the influence. She was relieved for Tomic's sake but had a sick feeling in her stomach. Arresting another cop wasn't something she ever wanted to do. It was no secret she'd have to accept an assignment to Internal Affairs at some point in her career if she ever wanted to promote to a command position, but as much as she hated corrupt cops, investigating men and women who wore the same uniform she did wasn't something she relished.

When Behan returned from the district attorney's office, he called Watts and Clark and briefed them. Lieutenant Watts had Dolores broadcast a message ordering Too Tall and his partner to come to the narcotics office. Too Tall acknowledged her message and arrived by himself about ten minutes later.

The lieutenant escorted him across Wilcox Avenue to the Hollywood station and they waited in the detective lieutenant's office for Captain Clark to get there. Josie, Tomic, and Behan sat in the detectives' squad room. They didn't speak, and Gilbert didn't look at them as he walked past.

"He knows we know," she said, as soon as Gilbert was in the lieutenant's office and out of sight. "You think we've got Superman's dirty cop?" she asked Tomic.

"Maybe," Tomic said.

"We'll check his alibi for the night Clark was killed," Behan said.

Josie didn't say anything, but she was having doubts that Too Tall was their killer. He needed heroin, not rock cocaine, and she couldn't get the idea out of her head that Abby Morrison was somehow involved in Clark's death and drug dealing. Too Tall had no connection to The Carnival and Abby had made it clear she despised him. Josie had no proof, but her instincts were telling her Butch was their best lead in finding whoever murdered his ex-lover and finding Clark Kent's dirty cop. The thought made her uneasy because it meant there was another cop still out there masquerading as one of them.

It was nearly midnight when Internal Affairs finished interviewing Too Tall. He admitted injecting heroin he'd stolen from LAPD's Property division downtown and told investigators he'd had a habit for nearly a year. His excuse was back pain, but Josie figured like most hypes he just liked the way it made him feel.

Everyone including Too Tall knew his career as a cop was over, but the remaining question was whether or not he'd go to jail. He'd eventually be charged with theft of the drugs and for being under the influence, but the department was always reluctant to pursue locking one of its own behind bars, even the bad ones.

When the interview was over, an IA sergeant asked Behan to do the narcotics exam and schematic to attach to the arrest report. He agreed because he said he didn't want another cop to have to do it, but he also made the sergeant promise as a favor he could have a look at Eddie Small's confidential personnel package.

Josie watched the video feed of Behan's exam from another room. Tomic had refused to stay, saying Josie and Behan could find him at the "Freeway" when they were finished.

Too Tall stood when Behan came into the room. He seemed subdued, no rather resigned, to his fate, Josie thought. She moved closer to the screen as Behan told the other man to sit and he sat next to him.

"I know the fucking drill, man," Too Tall said, dropping onto the chair beside Behan.

"You going to tell me where you shoot up or do I need to do a strip search?"

Too Tall leaned over, removed his left boot and pulled off his sock. He raised his leg and put his foot closer to Behan. Behan grabbed his foot and rested it on his knee.

"That's it. Started in the groin but that's too painful. Between the toes is someplace no copper's ever gonna look," Too Tall said.

Behan didn't respond but he pulled a small magnified light out of his back pocket and examined Too Tall's foot. Josie could see he was counting puncture wounds, estimating the age of each hole and marking the schematic to show where it was located.

"If I look right now, am I going to find another place you've been sticking yourself?" Behan asked.

"I'll strip if you want but except for a couple marks here," he said, touching his groin, "there's nothing."

"Show me."

Too Tall unbuckled his belt and dropped his pants. He pulled back the edge of his briefs and Behan used the light to examine the groin area and then checked his bare legs, arms, hands, chest, right foot, his neck, back, and buttocks. Behan told him to get dressed again and lowered the lights in the interview room. He told Too Tall to close his eyes and then after a few seconds open them in the darkened room. Behan shined the low light from the magnifier slowly into one eye and then the other. Josie knew as light gets closer to the eyes, pupils respond by getting smaller, but that wasn't going to happen with Too Tall. The heroin would keep his eyes fixed and pin-pointed even in the dark.

"Don't you want to know why?" Too Tall asked when he was dressed.

"Doesn't matter," Behan said. "What do you know about Clark Kent?"

Too Tall took a cigarette out of a pack on the table and lit it. "I know he's dead, but that's got nothing to do with me."

"Why'd you want to find Butch?"

Too Tall studied Behan's face as if he were attempting to decipher just how much the other detective knew and then said, "I wanted to make a case on Abby Morrison to get her off my back. Rumor was Kent stole a major stash of coke from his dealer and Abby had paid for some of it and wanted it back. I find it; I got leverage."

"You mean Billie told you Kent stole it. Did you want the coke for yourself or to sell?" Behan asked.

His features twisted into an angry snarl before Too Tall said, "Fuck no, I'm no base head and I don't deal drugs. I'm on the needle for pain . . . that's it. Billie told me about rumors of a dirty cop and I figured I could finger Tomic and keep you from looking at me. I know he saw me take that money . . . get him before he gets me."

"Where's Art?"

"Like I told the sergeant, I drove him to Parker Center and haven't seen or heard from him since."

"You also told the IA sergeant Art knew what you were doing. Is he a junkie too?"

Too Tall laughed quietly and said, "Not that tight ass."

Behan asked a few more questions before Too Tall became sullen and nonresponsive. Behan left the interview room and Josie watched the IA sergeant handcuff Too Tall and leave with him. He would be booked at Parker Center and released on his own recognizance with a promise to appear. Josie figured jail time was unlikely for a cop with a drug problem. The department and the DA's office rarely sought more than probation, AA, or restitution in this type of case. The deputy DA had taken Eddie Small to his temporary new residence where he would stay a day or two. No one expected he would need the witness protection program any longer since Too Tall had confessed to everything and there was enough physical evidence without the property officer's testimony.

As they walked back to the narcotics office, Behan told Josie what he'd found in Eddie Small's personnel package. Eddie had worked in Hollywood division as a property officer several years ago. He stayed less than a year, but that's most likely where he first met Too Tall.

"That explains the old Hollywood T-shirt he was wearing," Josie said, standing near the driver's door of her car.

"Eddie left Hollywood under a cloud. There was property missing but they could never tie it to him, so in true bureaucratic fashion he got transferred to a bigger Property division downtown where there was more to steal. I need a drink. See you at the Freeway," Behan said, walking away before she could say anything.

He didn't ask because they both knew she was going. Like most cops there was no way she could go home and wind down enough to sleep unless she talked to her partners about what had happened that day. They'd critique, praise, and criticize each other's actions until they were certain it couldn't have been handled better. Nobody held back, but Josie believed it was good. Things that should be said were brought out and not allowed to fester. Everyone learned if he or she was willing to listen. Josie wondered why working cops couldn't or wouldn't talk that way with command staff or management and remembered Tomic's words. Watch and learn. If she got promoted, she'd make them trust her enough to discuss these things. They'd know she was more interested in getting the job done and getting to the truth than protecting her road to promotion.

Sue Ann was holding court at the Freeway when Josie arrived. In the dim light, the little bartender looked about sixteen years old. She bounced from one end of the long oak bar to the other serving beers and lots of whiskey or tequila shots. It was a cop refuge and they responded positively to her gritty humor, tobacco-damaged voice, and baby doll looks.

Curtis was the one who started calling her the cheerleader and the nickname stuck because she was always high energy and loud. Her laugh could be heard over any music on the deafening jukebox. A chain-smoker, Sue Ann only put down the unfiltered cigarette to drink her gin and tonic. She seemed to adore Josie's partner, who sat quietly at the end of the bar watching her like the best floor show he'd ever seen.

She'd stop in the middle of a story or joke to go to Tomic and give him a long sloppy kiss or a bear hug and then continue what she'd been doing, only to repeat the gesture twenty minutes later. Sometimes she'd sneak up behind him, put her arms around his waist as he sat on a barstool talking, and stay like that until she had to tend bar. She was a child/woman, playful and lacking that confining self-consciousness of adulthood. Tomic was gentle and patient with her, but Josie suspected if Sue Ann were to suddenly leave him, that would be okay too.

She sat beside Tomic while Sue Ann was busy at the other end of the bar and told him what had happened with Too Tall.

"Good," Tomic said when she finished. "Looks like I'm gonna stay employed, so we'll come in early tomorrow to look for Butch."

Josie lifted her glass of whiskey and nodded in agreement before downing it.

"Sweet Josie," Sue Ann shouted, leaning on the bar inches from Josie's face. Her breath was a sour combination of stale tobacco and alcohol. "Another?" she asked, snatching the empty glass from Josie's hand.

"Why not," Josie said, as Behan sat beside her. Tomic moved so Behan was between them and they huddled closer to discuss what had happened that day. Sue Ann put Josie's drink on the bar. Tomic ignored her so she stepped back and watched from a few feet away. Josie could see she was pouting and not pleased. She was a pleasant diversion for Tomic, but when he was with Behan, Josie, or anyone in the squad, Sue Ann was on the outside. She would never be privy to Tomic's work, that part of his life he kept from his wife, kids, and lover. Josie was included, and she knew from the expression on Sue Ann's face as well as a similar look she'd gotten from Tomic's wife and the spouses of most of her male partners, they didn't like her because of that inclusion. She was a woman like them but a warrior in blue, as well, tested and proven; they weren't and never would be.

Josie had to admit when she allowed herself to think about it that once or twice she'd seen the same expression on Jake's face. For just a few moments on those nights when she came home late, avoided talking openly and frankly about her work, she thought her husband looked and acted as if he might not like her.

~ TEN ~

Her son's room was warm and had the faint lingering odor of Jake's aftershave when Josie checked on the boy during the early morning hours. He was sleeping on top of the blankets again, hugging his ugly toy puppy. The black poodle had been David's favorite stuffed animal for years. He named it Max after a drug-sniffing dog he'd met at a Narcotics division picnic. Much to Nonna's displeasure, toy Max was a broccoli-sniffing canine that saved David from the dangerous vegetable until Jake insisted dogs, even stuffed ones, didn't belong in the dining room and declared broccoli safe to consume again.

Josie showered and slipped into bed, snuggling close to Jake. Her feet were cold, but he didn't react when she rubbed them against his. She wanted him to wake up and hold her, so she could get warm and fall asleep, but he didn't move, his back a silent wall between them. Josie turned onto her other side and curled up hugging her pillow. Disappointed but too tired to worry about her lover's snub, she started to drift off when he rolled over and tucked his arm around her waist, pulling her closer to him, pressing his naked body against hers. The last thing she remembered was the warmth of his breath on her neck as she fell into a deep wonderful sleep.

They made love a few hours later at dawn leaving Josie rested and ready to begin her day, but instead of getting up, she stayed in bed another hour, talking and sharing with him in a way they hadn't for a long time. She wasn't eager to lose the intimacy of that moment, but Jake had a hearing in a few hours. While she dressed, he made breakfast for her and David and by the time Nonna arrived, the boy was ready for school and Josie was putting dirty breakfast plates in the dishwasher.

It was a good . . . no, a necessary morning, she thought, driving back to Hollywood. The persistent fear that her family was inching away had been silenced for yet another day.

Tomic was already in the office when she arrived. He was wearing the same shirt he'd worn the day before which told her Mrs. Tomic hadn't slept with her husband last night and the cheerleader probably had. His bloodshot eyes and unshaven face were a good indication the evening hadn't gone well.

A year ago, in a moment of alcoholic weakness, Tomic had revealed that Sue Ann was bipolar with borderline personality disorder, and she could instantly morph from sweetness to maniac without much provocation or warning. He insisted that if she took her meds, the cheerleader was fun and stable; however, when she didn't, he very often became the most convenient target of her rage.

Josie's Catholic upbringing made her wonder if the woman's personality disorder was God's way of punishing Tomic for cheating on his wife and kids, but she knew better. Sue Ann was what her partner needed and wanted even if his being with her was akin to playing a lovers' version of Russian roulette.

Tomic had planned on going out early that morning to locate the building on Santa Monica Boulevard where Abby said Butch was staying, but Curtis and Donny insisted on hearing all the details about Too Tall's arrest. Art was still MIA, but he hadn't been named in any of the reports so there was no urgency in finding him. Dolores was the only one who seemed to be worried about the missing man. She was afraid he might harm himself rather than face the shame and possibility of losing his job and reputation.

"Don't worry about Art," Behan said, maneuvering around the secretary with his morning mug of coffee and bloodshot eyes.

Donny jumped up from Behan's desk chair as soon as he saw the supervisor. "You're wasting your time, Donny. I never leave anything about you on my desk where you'd find it."

"Art's not hard like the rest of you guys," Dolores whined. "I am worried."

"I guarantee he's got a rep, and his union lawyer has already filed for that big, fat, stress pension," Curtis said, giving Dolores a quick hug. "It's those quiet ones you gotta watch out for, sweet thing."

Dolores shrugged, smiled at him, and slowly went back through the lieutenant's office to the front lobby. She was near tears, but Curtis always treated her like his little sister and his reassurance seemed to calm her a little.

"Hollywood squad is shrinking . . . you're leaving, boss, and now Too Tall and Art are gone. The four of us can't work the whole division," Donny said.

"Not the way you work," Tomic said.

"Fuck you, Tomic. I put as many bodies in jail as you do."

"No, that's your partner. You're along for the ride."

"Knock it off," Behan ordered, as Donny moved toward Tomic. Donny's face was flushed, and he looked angry, but Josie and probably all of them, including Donny, knew he wouldn't fight her partner.

She'd never seen Tomic lose a fight, but not because he was always the biggest, strongest, or best fighter. He told her losing on the streets meant dying, and he wouldn't allow anyone to beat him, ever.

"Do the best you can with what you got," Behan said. "And I'll try to find some loaners to help out until the captain brings in new detectives."

"Get Vern Fisher," Tomic said.

"He's that uniform P-III across the street," Curtis added, and, grinning at his partner, said, "He makes more dope cases than you do, Donny."

"Asshole," Donny said. "All of you are fucking assholes . . . including you, Corsino." He left the squad room, kicking at the nearest chair on his way out.

"Me? I didn't say anything," Josie protested.

"He knows what you were thinking, hard not to notice he never leaves that table except to piss or help Curtis," Behan said and added as an afterthought, "Probably have to take Vern's probationer too, but it might be good having another woman in the squad," Behan said. "Maybe this one will listen to me."

"But you belong to Hollywood homicide," Josie said, smirking at the obvious dig.

"I'm still splitting my valuable time, Corsino. I'll try to have Vern and his partner here tomorrow."

Tomic was done talking and motioned for her to meet him out back. He locked the shotgun in the trunk of his car, pulled up to the gas pumps, and by the time he'd filled the tank, Josie had finished her second donut and was ready to go.

The production building on Santa Monica was two stories with a brick facade. From the outside, it looked well-maintained as if it might still be functional. Josie rang the buzzer and waited before knocking on the front glass door. No one answered. It was difficult to see through the tinted windows but there didn't seem to be anyone inside. Tomic went around to the rear and after a few minutes he shouted for her to join him.

He was standing in front of an open loading dock of what looked to be a vacant warehouse, on the alley side of the building. The heavy metal door had been rolled up. A man who appeared to be in his thirties or early forties, dressed in Levi's, cowboy boots, and a long-sleeved dress shirt, was sitting on a folding chair behind a card table, drinking Corona from a bottle. There were two empty beer bottles on the table and a guitar on his lap.

"What can I do for you?" the man asked with a hint of a Texas drawl.

Tomic made the introductions and the man invited them to join him, pointing to narrow stairs at the end of the dock.

"We're looking for Butch . . . Brian Thomas," Josie said. "Abby Morrison told us he was staying here."

"Gone," the man said, looking at a stack of chairs against the wall. "Grab a seat, take a load off, and we'll talk." He slid the guitar off his lap onto the floor, resting it against his leg.

He said his name was Lance McCray from San Antonio, Texas. He was tall, thin, and sickly pale with long stringy blond hair tied back with a rubber band into a ponytail.

"Do you know where he went?" Josie asked.

"Nope," Lance said, finishing his beer. "Woke up this morning . . . him and all his smelly belongings were cleaned out. Can't say I'm sorry."

"Is this your building?" Tomic asked.

"Was, till I smoked it away. Now it's the property of the Testa family."

"What do you mean smoked it away . . . crack cocaine?"

"I figure Butch is lucky. Heroin's his drug of choice. He steals to feed his habit because the needle keeps him from getting sick."

"How's that lucky?" Tomic asked, setting his chair near the table.

"My crack pipe was my lover and best friend . . . kept going back for more, wanting her to make me feel like the first time we did it . . . she never did. By the time I realized what was happening, I was broke, sick, and didn't have a friend I hadn't borrowed or stolen from . . . house gone . . . life's work gone," Lance said as if he were reciting the lines from a sad song. "I'm flat broke an' lonesome, like when I drifted into this godforsaken town five years ago."

"What kind of work did you do?" Josie asked.

"Music producer . . . before I sold or pawned all my equipment and furniture, this was a recording studio and stage . . . made millions, but I smoked or snorted it away. I loved this business . . ." He stopped and shook his head as if it was too painful to talk about.

"You seem pretty clean now," Tomic said.

Lance laughed and said, "Can't afford it anymore. I already scraped off every speck of the white lady from inside my base pipe, licked clean every straw or mirror I ever cut lines on. I'm mostly sober now and sadly I do understand how much I lost." He stopped, looked up at Tomic, and with a wry smile added, "Truth is, friend, if you put a loaded crack pipe on this table right now, I'd start smoking again without a second thought or regret."

No one spoke for a few seconds. Despite her strong negative feelings about drug users, Josie felt sorry for him. His life was ruined, and he knew that but was helpless to turn it around. She also knew Lance was right about heroin. It was addicting but nowhere near as debilitating as smoking crack.

"Butch didn't give you any idea where he might've gone?" she asked, as he reached into a Styrofoam cooler under the table for another beer.

"He's a street boy. I'm guessing he's out there hustling to make enough money to get as far as he can from ol' Lady Macbeth."

"You mean Abby," Josie said, and he nodded. "She bailed him out of jail. Why would he want to get away from Abby?" Josie asked.

"The boy isn't book educated but he's got plenty of street smarts. He figures the only reason she bailed him out was to keep him close to her because she thinks he's hiding that dead guy's stash."

"Is he?" Tomic asked.

"He says no."

"Did you buy from Kent?" Josie asked.

"Sometimes."

"Did he give you a code name?"

"Nightingale," Lance said, touching the neck of his guitar. "I had a pretty nice sound once."

"Got any idea who killed him?" Tomic asked.

"No, but I know he had plenty of enemies . . . made no secret about being a snitch. He bragged he could get anybody arrested . . .

made it sound like he had more than one dirty cop in his pocket," Lance said, picking up the guitar and fingering a few chords.

Josie noticed Tomic's right fist tighten. He was pissed because he knew what Lance was saying about Kent was probably true. Like all informants, Superman lied and tried to look more important than he was. Tomic had been good to him but wouldn't want anyone believing he did Clark Kent's bidding.

After a few minutes of playing bits and pieces from different songs Josie didn't recognize, Lance stopped and let the guitar slide to the floor again. He got up and walked into the warehouse. She was sorry he stopped. It was obvious the man had talent, and she enjoyed listening to him. Music was always a big part of her life. Her Sicilian dad had bookcases full of records and would sing along with Italian operas. She was happy when her son showed an interest in playing the piano.

"Gotta piss. Let yourselves out," Lance shouted over his shoulder and disappeared behind a row of shelves.

Tomic wasn't willing to rely on the man's word that Butch wasn't there. He and Josie walked through all the first-floor rooms and the living quarters upstairs, but nothing of value was found—no Butch and no contraband.

All the faucets from sinks and other hardware had been removed and probably sold. A few cheap rugs and old curtains remained but the master bedroom was bare except for one open sleeping bag in the middle of the room and an old-fashioned lantern sitting on a suitcase. The only sign that Butch had ever been there was a used syringe she found in the corner of the room.

They finished their search and left without seeing Lance again. The table, beer cooler, and his guitar were still there when they climbed down off the loading dock. Tomic drove directly to the chicken shack where Josie and Marge Bailey had located Butch a few days ago, but he wasn't there or anywhere they looked on Santa Monica Boulevard. No one had seen him at the halfway house on Western where most of the Santa Monica young men hung out when they weren't hustling.

After nearly two hours of searching, Tomic went back to the chicken shack and they picked up a late lunch to bring back to the narcotics office where they could eat and think about their next move.

Josie knew Too Tall was a hype, but she couldn't think of any logical reason he'd have to kill Superman. She doubted he was the same dirty cop Kent had mentioned since IA had searched Too Tall's locker, home, and car and found no indication he ever used, sold, or attempted to sell cocaine. Kent had made it clear that his dirty cop was selling crack. She was certain it had to be somebody else.

The office was empty, even Dolores had gone to lunch. Josie put the bag of greasy chicken on her desk and looked at Art and Gilbert's empty chairs. She went around to the other side of the table and tried to open their personal desk drawers. Gilbert's was unlocked, and it was obvious the Internal Affairs sergeants had dumped out the contents, searched, and just thrown everything back in. She sat in his chair and began going through the paperwork.

"What are you doing, Corsino?" Tomic asked when he returned with two cups of freshly brewed coffee.

"I know IA already searched but odds are they didn't know what they were looking for."

"Let's eat and I'll help you. Is Art's drawer open?"

"No, but I can pick these locks."

"I've taught you well."

"Taught her what?" Behan asked from the hallway. "Never mind, stupid question. Did you find Butch?"

Josie described the meeting with the music producer Lance McCray and their efforts to locate the street hustler.

"Want a piece?" she asked, holding up a chicken breast covered in a thick greasy layer of fried batter. "I've almost reached my maximum Valvoline tolerance."

Behan took the offering and covered it with a generous amount of hot sauce to mask the oily taste. "So, what's next?" he asked, using several paper towels to clean his hands and face when he finished.

Josie wiped her hands and pulled out the desk drawer again. "I'm going to search Too Tall's and Art's desks because Abby Morrison told us they'd been looking for Butch . . . after that, don't have a clue."

"Kinda strange nobody's heard from Art yet," Tomic said.

"He seems to have disappeared. IA tried his apartment a couple of times to interview him and he's not answering his phone," Behan said. "Too Tall wasn't really his friend . . . I don't know if he had any real friends. I'm carrying him AWOL on the books."

"Odd duck," Tomic said, sitting beside Josie and quickly unlocking Art's desk drawer with a paper clip.

She removed and examined every piece of paper in Gilbert's messy drawer. There were copies of old search warrants, department orders and directives, pictures from surveillances, court subpoenas, and a stack of notes with clues he'd jotted down and kept for future reference. Most of the notes were months old and the information wasn't relevant any longer, but she found a couple that were written within the last week. One was from the day Too Tall and Art had captured Billie and made her work for them. *"AM lost kilos—find street competition"* was all the note said with the date scribbled in the corner.

"Mean anything to you?" Josie asked, showing the note to Tomic.

He took the piece of paper from her and after staring at it for a minute said, "AM is probably Abby Morrison. Don't know who the street competition would be."

"Doesn't help much. You find anything?" she asked, glancing into Art's organized desk drawer.

"I've confiscated the Howdy Doody tape to create embarrassing moments in the future, but there's a dry-cleaning bill from a place in Venice with a contact address that's nowhere near the apartment address he's got on file. We can check it out tomorrow.

I've got something to do tonight," Tomic said, not looking at her as he closed the desk drawer.

Josie knew "something to do" was most likely meeting with the cheerleader, but she didn't care. It would be nice to get home early again. The thought had barely flickered in her mind when Marge Bailey walked into the office and sat on the corner of Behan's desk.

"I'm about to harass the Godfather's spawn at The Carnival, Red. Thought you guys might like to participate."

"Take Corsino. I've gotta do my other job. Homicide team picked up a suspicious death off Melrose this morning," Behan said.

"Better yet," Marge said, grinning at Josie.

"Try not to do anything that causes me paperwork or headaches," Behan said.

"Don't worry, boss. The Testas don't make complaints," Josie said.

"I'd rather not fish your bodies out of Hansen Dam either," he said. "Why don't you go with them, Larry. You're the only one who can handle that Morrison woman."

"Not anymore. Her affections belong to Corsino . . . can't keep her eyes or pudgy hands off Josie," Tomic said.

"She hates my fuckin' guts," Marge said with a grin and asked Josie, "Can you leave now? I've got some stuff to go over with you before we start."

Josie figured there was no good reason to stay. She'd finished searching Too Tall's desk; Tomic was done for the day; Behan was leaving, and she had no idea what Curtis and Donny were doing.

"What do you need to show me?" Josie asked as she was crossing the street with Marge walking in the general direction of the Vice office at Hollywood station.

"Nora's bar, I'm starving," Marge said, making a slight turn through the division's parking lot in the direction of the restaurant.

"I just downed a pint of grease from the chicken place."

"Good, then you can drink and watch me eat."

It was still a little early, so the bar and restaurant weren't crowded. They found a table in the bar and Marge ordered their biggest hamburger, fries, and two glasses of Cabernet. Josie knew she and Marge had the same metabolism and could eat or drink practically anything without gaining weight. That's what she told herself when she got a large order of garlic fries.

"Thought you just ate," Marge said, sipping the wine.

"Need to have something to mix with the alcohol. What are we doing at The Carnival?"

"Selective enforcement . . . with a touch of harassment. My guys have been collecting violations in that place all week, but we have time to catch up first."

"You married?" Josie asked.

"Not anymore. I know you are. How old's your kid now?"

"Seven."

"Is Behan married?"

"So much for catching up. No, but he's looking for wife number four if you're game."

They finished the wine and food but stayed and talked. Josie unloaded everything she knew about Behan because that's what interested Marge, but they had stories to tell too. They could laugh now about some male cops who'd decided women didn't belong on the street, and about their feeble attempts designed to make women quit, the subtle slights, and outright threats, but they also talked about those stronger men who helped and gave them a chance.

"Remember that asshole on morning watch at Rampart that put live rats in my locker trying to scare me?" Marge asked, when they were getting ready to pay the bill.

Josie laughed and said, "I remember the next day you put a five-foot gopher snake in the back seat of his car, and the moron wet his pants. Best part was the note you taped to the steering wheel."

"Meet the female reptile that ate your dickless rodents, shithead," Marge said, as if she were reading from an imaginary note, then sighed and added, "Those were fucking Hallmark moments."

When they got to the Vice office, Marge's detectives and undercover officers had already gathered for roll call. She briefed them on the objective for the night, making it clear Abby Morrison's Carnival would be their only target. The plan was to allow the UCs an hour inside the club before Marge would enter with Josie and her detectives to cite Abby for dozens of violations and make arrests. They'd been scouting the club for several days, documenting code violations, offers of sex, and drug use. Even before tonight, Gaetano's daughter had accumulated civil and criminal violations that would cost her thousands of dollars in fines and bail money for several of her employees.

Josie read the case file while she and Marge sat in the car waiting for the UCs to complete their work for the night.

"The Queen of Hearts is not going to be pleased with your excellent work," Josie said, closing the file and giving it to Marge. "Is there any law or municipal code section the woman doesn't ignore?"

"Fuckers don't park in the handicap spaces . . . otherwise no," Marge said, glancing at her watch. "Showtime, Corsino."

She keyed her radio and told her detectives to enter The Carnival and block the exits. They would keep patrons contained inside the building until all the suspects had been rounded up. The noise, lights, and strong odor of marijuana, tobacco, and sweaty bodies enveloped Josie as she walked through the main entrance of the club. Most patrons were oblivious to the police presence and kept dancing and drinking. The floor manager passed them in the lobby and immediately used the wall phone to call Abby Morrison.

Josie watched as the vice officers escorted a dozen handcuffed arrestees out the front door. Marge cornered the manager, and ten minutes later, Abby appeared from somewhere inside the club. Her office was on the second floor, adjacent to the apartment. It had a large window that looked down onto the club's main dance floor and stairs that gave her access to the kitchen and rear door. Josie remembered the layout from an arrest she'd made before Abby owned the club.

"Sergeant Bailey, what are we up to this evening?" Abby asked with a frozen smile that was anything but sincere.

"We're assisting with your criminal infestation," Marge said. "Pest control, a free LAPD service."

"I had no idea. Whatever have they done?" Abby was suppressing a yawn.

Marge detailed the employees' criminal charges, handed Abby a stack of citations for the club's code violations, and said, "And these are yours, Mrs. Morrison, with dates for compliance and appearances before the state and city licensing boards . . . any questions?"

"Yes," she answered, her eyes narrowing. "But this is obvious harassment. My lawyers will have a lot more to say in the morning to people who matter." She turned away from Marge and seemed to notice Josie for the first time. "Detective Corsino, I didn't realize you worked with the vice department."

"I don't," Josie said. "I was hoping to find Butch here since you were kind enough to buy his way out of jail."

"Apparently, my generosity wasn't appreciated. He's vanished without a word," Abby said with a smirk.

"Do you know where he might've gone?" Josie asked.

"Not yet," Abby answered, stuffing the citations into the pockets of her black caftan. "Is there anything else, Sergeant?" she asked, turning toward Marge again.

"The Carnival is closed for tonight and will stay closed until you appear at the citation hearings. As soon as you get everybody out of here, we'll leave, and you can start contacting all those people that matter," Marge said.

Abby didn't respond. She gave Josie a sideways glance and left.

"I'd say that woman really hates you a lot," Josie said, watching Abby waddle across the nearly empty dance floor toward the stairs to her office.

"What a shame. I'm fucking crazy about her. She just improved my arrest stats a couple hundred percent tonight."

"Don't open any suspicious packages. I have a feeling Miss Abby holds a grudge," Josie said. She was joking, but if Tomic was right, the Testa progeny didn't have a sense of humor when it came to her business interests.

"As do I," Marge said with a slightly raised right eyebrow, then added, "But on a weirder note, Tomic was right. That woman has got a thing for you."

"What are you talking about?"

"She can't take her fucking eyes off you, Corsino. You didn't notice?" Marge asked as they got into her car.

"I know she and Gaetano act like we ought to be *paisanos* as if we all belong to some Sicilian brotherhood."

Marge made a U-turn and drove back toward Hollywood station.

"Nah, this is personal. She's got a thing for you."

Josie didn't respond. She knew Abby was treating her differently than other cops, but figured it was their shared Italian heritage. If being Sicilian gave her leverage with the Testas, that was fine. She'd use it to her advantage. Abby and her father might believe they'd get special treatment from her, but they'd be seriously mistaken.

She was hoping Jake would be awake when she got home, and he was. He and his mother were in the kitchen drinking coffee and talking. Nonna looked embarrassed when Josie opened the side door as if she'd been caught stealing the silverware. She got up slowly, groaning, nodded at Josie and put her cup in the sink.

"I'm going to bed. You two talk," Mrs. Corsino ordered, exiting the kitchen.

"What's wrong with your mother?" Josie asked when they were alone.

"She's worried about David."

"Is he sick?"

"No, nothing like that," Jake said, getting up and giving her a quick hug and peck on the cheek. "Want some brandy?" he asked, getting two glasses and filling them a little more than usual. He gave one to her and they touched the rims before she took a sip. Jake waited a few seconds before sitting at the table again and gesturing for her to take the seat his mother had just vacated.

"Let me put my stuff in the den and take off my gun first," she said, putting her glass on the table. She left her purse, jacket, and gun belt on the chair in the next room and out of habit put the semiauto on the fireplace mantel where David couldn't reach it.

Jake handed her the glass when she sat next to him.

"What's up?" she asked, thinking something was about to happen she wasn't going to like.

"The school wants to put David in a special class."

"Good 'special' or something we should worry about 'special'?"

"The class would emphasize the arts and he'd be with kids who had musical or artistic talent. I think it's a bad idea. Mom thinks I'm right, but she's worried you won't agree."

"Your mom's right this time. I don't agree. That's good 'special.' "

"He's already shy and awkward around other kids. He needs to be in with the herd."

"I'd agree if he were a palomino but he's a very talented kid who needs to be encouraged. He'd be with other kids like himself, make friends, and not have to compete with the stallions," she said, thinking it was a stupid analogy but kept things simple.

Jake sighed and asked, "Don't you want him to be a normal boy, play baseball and basketball . . . date girls?"

"He's better than normal, Jake. He can do those other things, but his talent should be encouraged," she said.

"He's seven, plenty of time to develop his talent. Now he should be a kid."

Josie finished her brandy and said, "Do we have to decide tonight? I'm really tired."

"This isn't something you can put off, Josie. He's your son too. Mom shouldn't have to be concerned."

"I agree. This has nothing to do with your mother. I've given you my opinion. I think we should put him in the class . . . I'll sign the permission slip now if you like. Give it to me," she said, holding out her hand. Jake stared at her empty palm for several seconds but didn't say anything. She suppressed a laugh and added, "Right, that's what I figured." She gathered her belongings from the den and went upstairs to their bedroom.

Why bother to discuss something if you've already made up your mind, she mumbled to herself as she reached the third-floor landing. Josie guessed Jake had most likely told the school he didn't want their son in a special class. They'd been married long enough for her to know when he wasn't asking for her input but actually trying to get her to agree to something he'd decided on his own.

She knew David was talented, and he'd do well with or without that class. Winning this argument wasn't worth days of pouting and hurt expressions by Jake and his mother. She wouldn't bring the subject up again and knew her husband and his mother would silently celebrate their victory thinking she was preoccupied with work and had forgotten about it or had once again relented.

Her willingness to relinquish authority in matters concerning her son was becoming a sore spot for Josie. She knew David needed her involvement in those decisions that might affect the rest of his life, but not asserting her motherly rights occasionally made it easier to keep her family together. It was a fact, if she allowed Jake and his mother to have their way, there was less scrutiny and criticism from them about all those hours she wasn't at home being a loving mother to her boy.

A nagging guilt was always the result of not fighting for her maternal principles, but she knew her addiction to police work was consuming and would prevail. What really bothered her was that her preference for chasing bad guys over spending more time with her son didn't concern her enough to do something about it.

~ ELEVEN ~

Behan kept his promise, and the next morning Vern Fisher and his probationary partner, Madison Worthen, or Maddy, as Vern called her, were in the office waiting when Josie arrived. The captain at Hollywood division had agreed to loan them to narcotics for a single deployment period or approximately four weeks. From the expressions on the two officers' faces, Josie guessed neither of them was thrilled with the arrangement.

They sat in the places formerly occupied by Too Tall and Art and were looking through handbooks Curtis had assembled for newly promoted detectives coming into the division. Josie guessed the patrol training officer could probably write his own primer on narcotics enforcement, but he was dutifully turning the pages and answering Maddy's questions.

"Thanks for helping out," Josie said, sitting at the table next to Tomic.

Vern looked up and gave her a half smile which said what he would never say out loud, i.e., do you think I had a choice?

"She needs patrol time, but I guess this is good experience," he finally admitted, closing the handbook. "Just tell me what needs to be done."

He was dressed in grungy clothes and looked comfortable, ready to mix in with the community of drug users and dealers that roamed the boulevards he usually patrolled like a neon light in uniform in a black-and-white. Josie thought his partner could walk onto any high school campus and fit right in. She was small and looked about fourteen in tight jeans, tennis shoes, and a hoodie.

"Maddy, do you have any questions?" Josie asked in an attempt to get the young woman to talk.

"No," she answered, not looking up from the handbook.

"I think you should ride with me for a couple of days," Josie said, returning Vern's stare. "Tomic can work with you," she added, nodding at the training officer. "That will ease both of you into the squad's routine . . . or what's left of the squad's routine."

It was smart to split them up, give each the benefit of a detective partner who knew how things were done, but that wasn't the only reason Josie suggested it. There was something peculiar about the girl's behavior. Most probationary officers were stiff and afraid to exhibit any personality for fear of being accused of acting too "salty," but this was different. Maddy was subdued to the point of disappearing. Josie thought she was too tentative and figured a few days away from Vern's stern demeanor might allow the woman to breathe, improve her self-esteem and confidence.

Josie had always felt comfortable doing police work. Behan told her after she'd been in the squad a few weeks that, "You're not always right, Corsino, but at least I know you're not afraid to make a decision." She hoped some of her self-assurance would rub off on the probationer. Good cops need both expertise and confidence in themselves. The department was promoting women at a rapid pace, but Tomic was right. There were too many indecisive, clueless ones moving up.

Maddy looked at her partner and then at Josie before saying, "Yes, ma'am, if it's okay with Officer Fisher."

"It will be good for you. Josie knows a lot about dope. Just remember, even in soft clothes, you're still on probation," Vern said without hesitation.

"And don't call me 'ma'am,' use first names until you put that uniform on again," Josie said. "Street people can smell cops . . . ma'am and sir are dead giveaways."

Maddy nodded and blushed, making her look even younger. There wasn't any argument from Tomic about splitting up their team for a few days. He liked Vern and was always more than willing to work with him. The two men were similar in a lot of ways—introverted, grumpy loners who did things their way and didn't much care what other people thought or said. Josie was certain her need for conversation annoyed Tomic, so he'd be pleased to have someone as moody as he was in his car all day.

It was almost another hour before Josie finished giving Maddy basic instructions on how they would work as a plainclothes team in an unmarked car. Most of the street people knew Josie was a cop, and didn't challenge her, but she tried to emphasize how important it would be to stay alert. Complacency was a problem when cops worked out of uniform. The casual clothes seemed to lull them into a state of situational sloppiness that often proved fatal.

Behan was the only one remaining in the office when Josie and Maddy finally got into Josie's new car. It was a Ford Mustang she'd appropriated the morning after Too Tall resigned and had no further claim on it. His car was much nicer than the dilapidated pile of junk she had been driving. Josie instructed her new partner on how to use the narcotics frequency and remove the shotgun from the rack in the car trunk. She loaned Maddy her spare two-inch revolver and a holster that could be concealed under her hoodie, showed her how to keep the handcuffs in her back pocket where they could be reached with her left hand, leaving her gun hand free, and moved the badge over on her belt, so it couldn't be seen until it was necessary. Josie intended to let Maddy walk ahead of her on Hollywood Boulevard knowing with her teenage appearance it wouldn't take more than a few minutes before she'd get approached to buy drugs. The first time Josie saw the young woman smile was when she explained what Maddy should do if someone offered them to her. She seemed pleased with the opportunity to be a decoy.

The car was idling in the driveway as Josie was about to turn onto Wilcox Avenue when she noticed Stella standing on the corner near the front door of the narcotics office waving at her. Stella took several steps back into the shadows along the side of the building as soon as Josie acknowledged she had seen her.

"Come with me, Maddy, but don't say anything," Josie ordered, parking the car on the wrong side of the street and getting out.

Stella walked past the car and kept going until she was half a block away and into a driveway with a cinder block wall and plenty of overgrown bushes for concealment.

"Who's that?" Stella asked, pointing at Maddy. She was sweating a little, nervous and edgy. Josie recognized the early symptoms of withdrawal.

"My new partner. What's up?"

Stella gave Maddy a long look, coughed, and said in a raspy voice, "She's like fucking thirteen . . ."

"What do you want, Stella?" Josie asked again. She knew it wasn't easy for Billie's lover to talk to the police, so something had to be very wrong.

"The baby . . . she's sick. Billie won't do nothing . . . strung out. I gotta help myself; you gotta go get it."

"Let's get something straight. I don't gotta do anything. Where's Ashley?"

"My place . . . I think she's dying. Billie's shitfaced, won't let me do nothing. I'm fucking sick, gotta go," Stella said, groaning and grabbing her stomach in pain. After a few seconds, she looked at Josie, shook her head, and slipped between a shed and the wall, disappearing in the alley that ran parallel to Wilcox.

"What's she talking about?" Maddy asked. She'd stayed a few feet away down the driveway but obviously had been close enough to hear. Josie had almost forgotten she was there.

"Let's go. I'll explain on the way," she said.

As they drove to Stella's apartment on the corner of Hollywood and Western, Josie gave her new partner a little background information on the two hypes. Some crucial details she kept to herself. Billie was hers and Tomic's snitch. They were the only ones who needed to know the whole story. In their business, a good informant was invaluable, and when this loan was over, she didn't want Vern appropriating Billie or Stella.

The Midtown motel was on Western just north of Hollywood Boulevard behind a gas station. There were a dozen rooms, all on the ground floor. Most of the windows faced east or west and were covered with aluminum foil or heavy curtains. Every narco team in Hollywood had served at least one warrant at this location. She and Tomic had recovered heroin in two of the rooms from local dealers.

The door frame on Stella's room had been replaced recently and there was damage around the dead bolt lock indicating that on at least one occasion a ram had been used to make entry. Most of the doors at The Midtown had similar damage.

Josie told Maddy to watch the front window for any movement inside while she knocked on the door. The curtain was pulled back a little. A few seconds later, she heard the dead bolt click and the door opened a crack; the odor of marijuana and the stench of rotting garbage polluted the morning air. Josie pushed the door open with her foot, drew her Beretta from the holster, and held up her hand like a traffic cop to keep Maddy from charging into the room. She knew an addict's loyalty went to the highest bidder and something didn't feel right about Stella's frantic performance. Maybe the baby was sick or maybe this was a ploy to get a couple of cops to walk willingly into a trap.

"Motherfucking cops . . ." Billie shouted with her back to them inside the room. She was saying something else, but her words were slurred. She nearly toppled over picking up a soda can off the floor and when she regained her balance, threw it across the room hitting the window then squatted on the couch after kicking the piece of furniture several times.

"Follow me," Josie whispered and pointed her weapon at the ground until she was through the door, did a quick tactical sweep of the front room around Billie, told Maddy to check the bathroom and kitchen as she cleared the bedroom.

Josie found no one in the apartment except Billie. She always anticipated sifting through some level of grime when dealing with hypes, but this place wasn't that bad, a little messy and odiferous but Stella kept it from becoming the standard filthy crash pad.

Billie was in a short, dark blue, terry cloth bathrobe and barefoot, sprawled on the couch, nodding off every few seconds when Josie returned to the room. Her hair was a new shade of bright orange, tied back with what looked like a piece of string.

"Where's Ashley?" Josie asked.

Josie had seen an empty crib in the corner of the bedroom and baby clothes piled on the dresser.

"Stella . . . she's got the kid," Billie mumbled, fighting the opioid stupor. Seconds later, Josie heard her name shouted by Maddy.

She hurried to the bathroom and found her partner standing outside the open door, the color drained from her face, arms hanging limp at her sides, a pink towel held tightly in her right hand. Josie pushed past her into the small room and saw Ashley's tiny motionless body lying on another pink bath towel in the tub, her skin pale, bluish.

"Did you check if she was still breathing?" she asked, and Maddy, looking dazed and staring at Josie, slowly nodded her head.

"I think she's . . . dead," Maddy whispered.

"Get the paramedics," Josie shouted. It seemed to startle Maddy and she turned quickly, hurried outside to the car radio.

Josie sat on the edge of the tub and lifted the baby onto her lap. The body was emaciated and cold, but two fingers on the left hand appeared to move slightly; there might have been a faint pulse. It was difficult to tell if she was still alive, so Josie took the towel from the tub and partially wrapped Ashley to keep her warm, cradled the bundle in her arms, and performed CPR waiting for the paramedics.

The wail of sirens began in seconds and when the paramedics arrived, they took over. Ashley was alive, barely. Half an hour later, no one spoke as one of the young firemen wheeled a gurney carrying the baby and all the medical paraphernalia that kept IVs and oxygen pumping precious life into less than six pounds of fading humanity.

Billie never moved from the couch during those frantic moments as cops and firefighters fought desperately to save her baby. She was oblivious to the activity around her. It took a few minutes to get her attention after the commotion stopped and everyone had gone, but Josie explained that her baby was at the hospital emergency room. Eventually she seemed to understand and became more coherent. Her eyes filled with tears as Josie explained what had happened and bluntly told her what the paramedics had said. Her daughter had a seizure, probably linked to her inherited heroin addiction, and, short of a miracle, would not survive the night.

"We'll drive you to the hospital if you want to be with her," Josie offered, sitting on the couch beside Billie.

"I want Stella to go," Billie said. She wiped her eyes with the sleeve of her bathrobe and for the first time seemed to realize she needed to pull the robe tighter to cover herself. "Sorry, guess I oughta get dressed."

"Stella's not here," Josie said. "What happened? Why did she leave you and the baby alone?"

Billie used the bathrobe sleeve again to blow her nose and stared up at the ceiling, not answering. Josie waited.

"Nothin' fuckin' happened," Billie finally said and quickly snapped, "And you, Miss high school homecoming bitch, what're you starin' at," she shouted, glaring at Maddy who was quietly leaning against the wall with her arms crossed.

"Leave her alone, Billie. She's worried about your baby which is more than I can say for you," Josie said, knowing those words would hurt the woman but hoping they might get her angry enough to tell the truth.

"I fuckin' worried plenty. Stella's the one, she promised . . . soon as stuff turns to shit, she splits. What am I supposed to do with the fuckin' kid?"

"Act like a decent mother and take care of your baby. That would be a great place to start," Maddy said, moving away from the wall and taking a few steps toward the couch.

Josie was surprised by the reserved young woman's sudden verbal attack, not expecting her to assert herself, especially with someone like Billie.

The words seemed to surprise Billie too. She didn't react immediately, but after a few seconds started to get up. Josie stood quickly and pushed her back onto the couch.

"Don't even think about it," Josie said. "She's just out of the academy and will kick your ass all over this room."

Billie sat back, gave Maddy a hard look, but didn't attempt to get up again.

"Stop fucking with us and tell me what happened, or I'll arrest you for child endangering and you can detox in jail," Josie said. She took the handcuffs out of her back pocket and held them in front of Billie's nose for emphasis.

"Where's Tomic? Gotta talk to Officer Tomic first."

"Get up," Josie demanded and motioned for Maddy to assist her. "You're under arrest . . ."

Before she could finish, Billie waved her hands over her head and said, "Okay, okay, don't get all mutherfuckin' gestapo on me."

Maddy stood beside Josie and they stared at the informant as if her next words would be the trigger for imminent incarceration.

"This ain't right, you know, me grieving and all . . ."

"Stop stalling," Josie demanded.

"Stella and Butch, they don't tell me nothing but her and that spikey-blue-haired, ass fucker's been sneakin' around, whisperin' behind my back, bitches always got tar and Mexican brown. You know what tar is, Baby Dick?" she said, looking up at Maddy.

"Stella and Butch? That's an odd couple," Josie said.

"Yeah, ain't they though."

"You're still not telling me what happened."

"Damned if I know. Stella's freakin' this morning . . . tapped out, no product, wants me to give her some a my shit . . . no fuckin' way. Bitch panicked . . . coming down big time, screams, swears at me, says the baby needs help . . ."

"You just said she always had plenty of stuff," Josie said.

"Did up 'til this morning, and now I'm out too."

"Has Butch been here since Abby bailed him out?" Josie asked.

"Couple a times, I give the creepy ass-wipe a hard time so he don't come round when I'm home."

"Where's he staying?" Josie asked.

Billie hesitated, wouldn't look at Josie, and shifted her weight on the couch. "Don't know for sure," she said, still not making eye contact.

"Guess or spend the night in Hollywood jail."

She sighed and said, "What the fuck, he ain't nothin' to me . . . mighta went back to that dump on Santa Monica."

"Lance McCray's warehouse?"

"Yeah, the base head . . . easy mark . . . kill his own mother for a fuckin' rock."

"Would Stella go there?"

"Unless Butch sold some more rocks, he ain't holdin' what my wetback bitch needs . . ."

"What's that?" Josie asked, interrupting her.

"Cash to get Mexican crap. All that crack he's got stashed won't do nothing for her gut pain," she said, starting to wiggle on the couch. "I told you what I know. Let me get up; I gotta piss, real bad."

"We're done with you. Call me when Stella comes back or if you change your mind about going to the hospital."

"Ain't going to no fuckin' hospital. Tell Stella," Billie mumbled, dry-eyed with a hard expression that said loud and clear—find somebody who cares.

~ TWELVE ~

It was an unusually chilly fall in Los Angeles, no rain of course but the winds made the air feel colder than Josie liked. She had spent most of her life in Southern California and changing weather was an unwelcome anomaly. Maddy had worn a jacket and Josie took hers out of the trunk before driving to the building on Santa Monica Boulevard. She was unfamiliar with this car, so it took a few seconds to find the heater and she left it on full blast while attempting to reach Tomic over the radio. He finally responded, explained he'd just left Vern who had to testify in Superior Court downtown, and agreed to meet them at Lance McCray's abandoned warehouse in twenty minutes.

The warehouse parking lot was empty when Josie arrived. She knew it might be better . . . smarter to wait for Tomic but figured Maddy should be enough backup until he got there.

This time, the heavy steel door to the loading dock had been pulled down and there was no sign of Lance or his guitar. Josie climbed up onto the platform and tried the side entrance. It was locked too. Not a problem, she thought, and sent Maddy back to the car to retrieve her picks from the glove compartment.

In less than a minute, Josie had the simple lock opened and they were inside. There was dim light from the dirty windows on the first floor, but without heat, it was colder inside the building than outside. She pulled her semiauto from the holster and saw

Maddy do the same. The young woman kept the muzzle of her weapon pointed at the floor, had a small flashlight cradled in her other hand, and watched Josie as if to see what her next move should be.

"Be quiet and keep your light and gun muzzle off me," Josie whispered.

Maddy nodded and seemed a little excited but not the least bit worried or scared. Her body language said she was confident and ready for whatever was about to happen. Josie walked cautiously through the empty, cavernous warehouse, checked the bathroom and front office area, and continued searching until she was certain no one was on the first floor.

A staircase with about two dozen steep metal steps was located to the right of the lobby door. She climbed slowly until she reached the second-floor landing, took a long look around her, and then motioned for Maddy to follow. This was the living space—bedroom, private bathroom, kitchen, and dining area. They were about to go into the kitchen when Josie heard a muffled noise that sounded like someone dragging furniture in the bedroom down the hallway. It was the same room where she'd seen the single sleeping bag but nothing else.

She motioned for Maddy to follow her back into the hallway but stopped and took cover behind the kitchen door when she heard a creaking noise coming from the stairwell. The area was dark, and it took a while for her to realize Tomic was the intruder. She stepped out where he could see her and put her finger over her lips to keep him from speaking.

Josie pointed down the hall toward the bedroom and whispered, "I heard something. Might be Lance or Butch."

He stepped back and motioned for her and Maddy to take the lead. Josie moved quickly but cautiously past the empty bathroom, stopping just outside the bedroom where the door was ajar. She pointed her gun at the opening as she moved to the other side where she could see through the crack. There was no need to discuss with Tomic how they would make their tactical entry. They'd done it hundreds of times. She indicated to Maddy that she was to follow Tomic. He kicked open the door, hitting the wall, and Josie entered in a crouched position to the left. Her eyes swept the room, peering over the front sight of the 9mm semiauto.

A small bong still filled with grayish smoke was on top of a card table close to Lance McCray, who was sitting on the only chair, slumped over with both hands clutching the glass base pipe. Otherwise the bedroom was empty. The window leading to the fire escape was open and made the room slightly colder than a refrigerator.

For a moment, Josie thought Lance might've passed out in his freebasing euphoria, but a closer inspection revealed a thin strand of wire embedded in his bloody neck. He wouldn't let go of his damn crack pipe even as his killer was practically decapitating him, she thought, and said out loud, "Evil drug."

"Don't see many garroting homicides," Tomic said, carefully lifting the dead man's long blond hair, revealing an almost foot-long piece of doweling, an inch in diameter, that had been used to twist the wire.

"I'm no expert, but it looks sort of professional to me," Josie said. "Not your typical hype burglar . . . more like somebody Abby or Guy might know."

"Maybe," Tomic said, taking a police radio out of his inside jacket pocket. He talked to Dolores at the narcotics office and gave her the address and a few details on the dead man for the paramedics, Behan, and his homicide detectives. He told her they would remain at the warehouse until Behan arrived.

A gust of cold air caused Josie to zip the front of her jacket and glance at the open window where Maddy was standing close to the ledge, staring out at the street. She seemed unphased by the weather, but her cheeks and nose were turning a shade of pink and Josie saw her body shiver before she stepped away.

"You okay?" Josie asked, putting on gloves and slamming the window shut. The younger woman nodded and looked serious when Josie added, "Not exactly the sane life you had in a black-and-white, is it?"

"Do you think I can come back here after I make probation?" Maddy asked and stared hard at her as if there was only one acceptable answer.

"Eventually, sure. Get some experience and when you're ready, I'd help you get in the division."

"Wish I didn't have to wait."

"I'm sure juvenile narcotics or the buy-team program would put you undercover now because you look so young, but my advice is don't do that. Stay in the field a couple of years. You'll be a better cop."

A big smile now, a shy thumbs-up, and Maddy turned back to the window.

Josie didn't smile. She understood what it meant, the cost of loving a job with an exciting challenging lifestyle that inevitably pushed every other important thing or person into the shadows of your life. She liked Maddy but knew any attempt to discourage or warn her about the pitfalls of narcotics enforcement was pointless. The signs were all there. Madison Worthen had been given a taste of this crazy world of drugs and the woman was hooked.

Behan and a team of homicide detectives arrived within twenty minutes, shortly after the paramedics declared their victim dead. Josie watched the big redhead scrutinize the area around the body and as he examined the neck wound, he asked, "Who found him?"

"We kind of all did," Tomic answered and then explained how they made entry into the bedroom looking for Butch.

"Busy first day, huh," Behan said to Maddy who was intently watching him work. "Murdered base head, dead heroin baby . . ."

"The baby died?" Maddy asked, interrupting him and taking a step back.

"Sorry, thought you knew," he said, groaning and turning to Josie. "Corsino, I'm an idiot. I just figured you already heard." He had to know how many times and in so many ways she had tried to protect that baby, having the Department of Children and Family

Services take it away from Billie, only to have a sympathetic court remove the baby from competent foster care and give her back.

"It's okay, Red. I knew she was really sick. It's just . . ." She shook her head and swallowed the next words like the bitter taste of bile. Ashley wasn't hers; the odds of survival were always against the damaged infant; nevertheless, Josie felt as if someone had just kicked her in the gut and was grateful there wasn't much food in her stomach or she would've vomited all over Behan's crime scene.

Josie believed Billie might be a little despondent for a while over the death of her baby, but Stella would be devastated, and it wouldn't be a surprise if the tough little Mexican woman took her anger and revenge out on her lover.

"Stop thinking about it, Corsino," Tomic said, gently rubbing the back of her neck. "You and I both know that poor kid never had much of a chance."

Josie nodded but knew she'd never forgive herself for not doing more and guessed neither would Stella.

~ THIRTEEN ~

Nothing, in her personal life had changed, but there was zero possibility Josie would work late that night. A baby had died and for some inexplicable reason her kid had become so much more vulnerable. It was stupid because Ashley's death didn't affect David or her family. Her fear was irrational, but the job had made her that way. She'd seen too many dead babies, too many evil human beings willing to hurt and kill for no reason. Random malevolence was scary stuff, so she'd come home earlier tonight to be with her son. By tomorrow the apprehension would pass and she'd be able to work again.

Jake had a late meeting in the district attorney's office and when he called to tell his mother she'd probably have to sleep over again, he was surprised but sounded happy to hear Josie's voice.

"Have you looked in the spare bedroom yet?" he asked after she told him David had been fed, bathed, and put to bed by his mother. Mrs. Corsino had stayed a few minutes trying to be pleasant and making an effort to communicate with her daughter-in-law, but Josie wasn't in the mood for conversation, so the older woman reluctantly said good night and went home.

"No, why would I," she answered, suspiciously. Josie wondered what he and Nonna had conspired to do that would piss her off this time.

"Go upstairs and tell me what you think. I'll wait."

She did and opened the door next to David's. It had been their junk room, an extra bedroom that had never had any real purpose. Most of the old furniture and all the boxes were gone. In the middle of the room was a shiny black baby grand piano, a small couch that had been in the downstairs den against the wall, and two empty bookcases.

"Holy shit," she said too loud, and put her hand over her mouth thinking David might have heard her, but no sound came from his room. She turned off the light, closed the door, and went to the master bedroom where she picked up the receiver near her side of the bed.

"Where did that come from? Can we afford something that expensive?"

He laughed and said, "I had it delivered this morning, after mom and I cleaned the room and no we can't afford it, but I bought it on time, a hundred and fifty bucks a month for the rest of our lives. Do you like it?"

"I love it, but I can't play. What does David think? Has he tried it yet?"

"He did, great sound. He loves it too. Mom and I were hoping you'd be home after he went to bed; otherwise, he'd spoil our surprise."

Josie couldn't remember the last time she felt this good about her mother-in-law. Nonna and even Jake had never supported David's piano lessons, complained he was too young and needed to be outdoors more. Buying a piano was something Josie alone had been determined to do.

"What made you and your mom have this change of heart about lessons?" She had to ask.

"Guess I felt guilty about not putting him in those special classes without discussing it with you first."

She didn't pursue his explanation for this sudden turnaround, but when Josie hung up, her suspicious nature kicked in and she wondered what the real cost of this Steinway was eventually going to be.

Sleep didn't come easy that night. She got up twice to check on her son for no particular reason. The second time, she found Jake still dressed in his business suit standing near the bunk bed watching the boy.

"When did you get home?" she asked, after he gave her a long, I've-really-missed-you kiss.

"About an hour ago, had some work to finish downstairs. Are you really okay with the piano?"

"Yes," she whispered.

David wiggled onto his other side. She turned to leave and motioned for Jake to follow.

They went to their bedroom, made love, and Josie was finally able to shut down her thoughts and fall asleep.

The next morning, Nonna didn't come, so Josie could spend time alone with her son helping him get ready for school, making breakfast and waving as the bus pulled away from the corner. She would be late for work but didn't care. Life would get back to normal by tonight . . . anyway her idea of normal. The anxiety had eased, and she was once again thinking about Superman's killer and the irritating possibility of another dirty cop.

TOMIC WAS waiting in the Hollywood narcotics office when Josie arrived. Vern had been subpoenaed back to court and would probably be there for the rest of the week. He took Maddy, so she could observe and learn the proper way to testify. She had two cases in court at the end of the week where she'd found rock cocaine in suspects' pockets while working patrol and she would have to testify too. Josie and Tomic would team up again until they returned.

Before she could sit at her desk, Lieutenant Watts, who couldn't see into the squad room but must have heard her voice, shouted for her to come into his office. She shrugged at Tomic who made a fist with his right hand, pretending it was a puppet and whispered, "It's Howdy Doody time."

"Yes, sir?" she asked, and at the lieutenant's request closed the door behind her.

He pointed at the chair in front of his desk. He was sitting behind the desk and still hadn't looked up at her.

She sat and waited until he finished writing before repeating, "Yes, sir?"

Curtis and Donny and some of the Venice squad must have arrived. The activity and volume of noise outside the lieutenant's door had increased. Watts stared at the door. She knew he'd never admit the raucous cop banter annoyed him because he wanted to be accepted as one of them, but they had already decided, in a lot of significant ways, he wasn't and never would be.

"I'm worried about the Hollywood squad," he said, sighing and leaning back in his chair. "There's just too much smoke."

"Sorry, what?" Josie asked, genuinely confused.

"Gilbert or whatever you call him . . . Too Tall, he's an addict and a thief; Art has disappeared; Tomic is accused of stealing heroin, not to mention his informant . . . what's his name, Kent, is killed right after the two of you meet with him. There's more but . . . a lot of smoke."

"So what are you trying to say? You think Larry Tomic and I are dirty because Too Tall was an addict and tried to frame my partner." She was angry, but her voice was calm and strong. "You should know informants get killed all the time. Kent knew it. He even joked about us taking out a life insurance policy on him."

"Look, Corsino, I'm not accusing you or Tomic of anything. I just want you to know people are talking about how much corruption has touched your Hollywood squad. You have a potentially promising career and we don't want you to get caught up in the mire of what may or may not be going on in there," he said, pointing at the closed door.

"We?"

"Captain Clark and I were discussing the possibility of promoting you to Detective III to fill a position in the administrative unit. You'd have to take the oral exam, of course, but you're the best candidate in the division. This promotion would be a stepping-stone, make you eligible in a year to take the lieutenant's test. Just think about it," he said, before she could respond.

Josie wanted to tell him what unnatural thing to do with his admin position but instinctively kept that thought to herself. She had dreamed of becoming a Detective III in the Hollywood squad and filling Behan's job. She would have jumped at that offer, but also recognized ambition was her Achilles heel. She was savvy enough in department politics to realize turning down this offer would be stupid and deadly for her future in Narcotics division.

The most disappointing aspect of the admin job was leaving the field. The position was attractive because it meant regular hours to be home with her family and maybe even eliminate the need for Nonna's presence and influence in their daily lives. The bigger picture was she loved narcotics street enforcement but wanted to be a lieutenant too . . . eventually, come back here, take Watts's job and do it the right way.

"Okay, thank you, I'll think about it," she said, getting up. "Is that all, sir?"

Now he looked directly at her and said, "Yes, but keep your eyes open and don't wait too long to make your decision, Corsino. Any taint of dishonesty or unsavory behavior will ruin your chances for what could be an exceptional opportunity."

Threat received and understood, she thought, returning to the squad room where conversation stopped, and all eyes were on her.

She shook her head and mouthed the word, "later."

"Oh, come on," Curtis whined, and whispered, "Outside?"

They gathered their utility bags and other gear as if they were leaving to work the streets. In the parking lot, as they loaded up their cars, Josie told them everything that had been discussed in the lieutenant's office including the offer of a promotion.

Donny congratulated her, but Tomic and Curtis stood silent.

"You think it's a bad move?" Josie asked Tomic.

"No, I think it's a great opportunity but for all the wrong reasons. They want you out of here. That's for sure."

"You'll go crazy in an office," Curtis said. "But on the other hand, as soon as a three spot opens up in the field, you can go for it, transfer back to an enforcement squad . . . maybe here. You got scary tactics, lady, but you'd be a great boss and I'd work for you anytime," he said, grinning.

"Thanks, Curtis . . . I think. Why would they want me out of here, Tomic?"

"Damned if I know, but I recognize shit when I smell it. Captain Clark hates your guts because you made him look like the fool he is, and our lieutenant isn't exactly the mentoring type. The only person he ever thinks of promoting is himself, so why are they making you an offer you can't refuse?"

"I can do admin stuff but I'm not that good. There are a dozen detectives at my rank who would be better," she said and gently punched Donny's arm. "You would be better."

"Probably," Donny said matter-of-factly.

Josie smirked and said, "We have time to figure this out before I have to give him my answer. Until then, don't taint me with your unsavory behavior."

They looked at each other and then at her with quizzical expressions at first that seemed to ask, "was that a joke?" followed by "did-you-just-insult-us?" scowls. She smiled but didn't bother to explain. Thin skins didn't survive in this squad, so she figured her comments would be cast off as some sort of indiscernible girl humor.

Curtis and Donny got into their car to begin the daily prowl, searching the streets for Hollywood's abundant drug dealers. Tomic told Josie he wanted to break their similar routine and find Art first. Josie agreed because she guessed the missing detective might have information about Butch and her instincts told her Superman's skinny blue-haired ex-lover was the key to who had killed their informant. She also hoped Butch might give them a clue to Raven's identity, the alpha bird and likely contact for all that missing cocaine Kent was supposed to have delivered to his bevy of feathered friends. If it was another dirty cop, the Hollywood squad needed to find and arrest that person to prove all those corruption red flags were wrong.

Before his arrest and termination, Too Tall was looking for the missing cocaine and Butch. He might have discovered something that would help them find Butch who was hiding not only from the police but from his benefactor Abby Morrison. Art had always been Too Tall's shadow and like a human sponge, unobtrusively absorbed everything he saw or heard. If his partner knew something, Art did too, but Josie was certain that unlike Too Tall, he was timid and could be bullied.

She believed it would have been understandable if Too Tall had refused to talk to them but strange that Art had disappeared and wouldn't contact anyone in the department. He hadn't been accused of anything, but his job was in jeopardy not only because he knew and ignored Too Tall's addiction but because of his unexplained lengthy absence. Most likely he would get fired, but he'd earned a pension, a small one; nevertheless, it was there to claim. Josie wondered why he didn't just resign or retire, take his monthly check and go away. The whole disappearing act didn't make sense to her.

The client address on the dry-cleaning bill Tomic found in Art's desk was in Venice on a street close to the canals. That area had been populated by beat generation diehards, hippies, college professors, and left-wing radicals who couldn't quite let go of the minimalist lifestyle demanded by the anti-war and other revolutionary movements.

Real estate developers were steadily and quietly buying up the dilapidated buildings along the canals and researching ways to clean the stagnant smelly water. There was talk about reviving the neighborhood with expensive, trendy homes or condominiums. Garage apartments and rent-controlled housing would soon be things of the past.

Josie had lived near this place during a lengthy undercover assignment earlier in her career. It was the hub of counterculture activism. She always figured that proximity to the ocean and the prospect of clean canals would inevitably destroy the funky Venice she knew and loved. It would eventually evolve taking with it the last remnants of life from the fifties, sixties, and seventies, those tumultuous, outrageous decades of change unlike any others. To her surprise, it made her a little sad.

"That's the one," Tomic said, pointing at a duplex set back from the street as he parked his car about a half block away. "The right side is his place. Piece of crap car in front is registered to him."

She saw a silver Toyota in the driveway and all the curtains were closed in that unit.

"So how do you want to do this?" Josie asked.

"The usual, I'll knock, and you grab him when he runs out the back."

"No reason to change a perfect plan."

The yard wasn't fenced so Josie could easily work her way behind the property next door and wait by the back door where she could intercept Art's escape. The canal ran directly behind the duplex and the rancid smell cautioned it had become the watery grave of human waste and other nasty garbage. As she looked around, Josie thought the neglected broken sidewalks, piles of debris in every yard, and out of control shrubs and weeds completed the picture of a place where someone had a vested interest in making it uninhabitable for current residents.

After a few minutes, she began to worry. She hadn't heard the usual banging on the front door, no shouting or panicky dash out the back. What was Tomic doing, she wondered, and was about to move around to the front of the house when the screen door opened slowly. Art was holding it for her to enter.

"Hi, Josie, come in," he said as if the last week had never happened.

Tomic was standing behind him beside an older blonde woman who had her long thick hair loosely braided and hanging down her back. Art stepped aside, allowing Josie to enter and she followed him into the living room. The woman's name was Kit. She owned the house and the four big dogs that ignored everyone but their mistress. They sat around her like a security force, daring anyone to reach in and attempt to touch her. Art hovered behind her chair almost as if she were a shield. He was wearing a faded blue T-shirt and sweatpants, socks but no shoes, and his normally neatly trimmed hair was shaggy and seemed a lot grayer than the last time Josie had seen it. She thought he looked weary and older.

There was ample seating in the small but uncluttered room. The place reminded Josie of those houses where she'd hung out during her undercover days. There were always plenty of chairs for comrades or fellow activists to sit and endlessly debate "the marvelous foursome": Marx, Engels, Lenin, and Mao. She always viewed those discussions as political masturbation—made them feel great for a while but otherwise a pointless and self-indulgent exercise that could never lead to what they wanted, the equivalent of sex or better yet, love, which in their case translated to the violent overthrow of the United States government.

Kit offered drinks and went into the kitchen, followed by the dogs and Josie. There was no chance Josie would leave this woman or Art alone in a room before she or Tomic had a chance to look for weapons. She relaxed a little because the couple appeared to be very much at ease. Kit even joked about finally getting Art to leave the house now that he had been found.

"Why was he afraid to leave?" Josie asked, helping her take glasses out of the cupboard. The dogs, two German shepherds, a rottweiler, and some breed of white shaggy terrier, must have decided she wasn't a threat and rubbed gently against Josie's legs as she moved around the kitchen.

"He really won't talk about it, but anybody can see he's scared shitless about something," Kit said.

Josie had a gut feeling Kit, who came across as uncomplicated, maybe a touch simple, wasn't telling the truth. She guessed the woman was in her late forties or fifties. She was heavyset and wore baggy lounging pants and a man's dress shirt. She had very pale skin, didn't wear makeup, had a nonchalant almost careless manner, and seemed to Josie more like a mother or confidante than a lover to Art.

"How do you know him?"

Kit snorted a quick laugh and said, "He came here in uniform one night years ago after I called the police. I thought I heard a prowler. There wasn't one, but we hit it off and we've been friends ever since." She poured lemonade in four glasses and handed two of them to Josie, adding, "My place has become his refuge."

"Refuge from what?"

"This time? Who knows, but whatever it is, he's scared. I can tell you that much," Kit said, picking up the other two glasses and leading the way back into the living room.

The two men were sitting side by side on the couch now. Their conversation seemed intense, not loud but angry. They looked up at the same time and stopped talking.

"What?" she asked the two expressionless faces staring at her and gave Tomic one of the glasses.

He put the drink on the coffee table and stood. "Let's get out of here, Corsino," he said.

"No way, sit down and tell me what's going on."

His lips tightened and then came the Tomic sneer, his go-to reaction when he knew she wasn't allowing him to boss her around. "We're wasting our time with this asshole," he mumbled and sat on the edge of the couch with his arms crossed, glaring at her.

"What did you tell him, Art?" she asked.

Art glanced at Kit who was sitting on a card-table chair she'd moved closer to him. Her expression was frozen in a fake smile, so he turned to Josie.

"I didn't do anything," he whined, avoiding eye contact with her. "I told him Too Tall might've been taking money from the Testas."

"Might've been taking money?" Josie asked incredulously. "Stop bullshitting. You know he took money . . . to do what?"

"Give Abby a heads-up on vice raids . . . drug busts, that kind of stuff," he answered timidly.

"What'd you say to Tomic just now that pissed him off?" she asked, looking at her partner.

Art took a deep breath and said, "His warrant last month at Cozy's on Melrose, that's a Testa place. They knew we were coming."

Josie remembered serving that search warrant. They had buys inside the club. It was almost a guarantee they'd find cocaine but came up dry, not a speck of rock or white powder, not even a dirty razor blade or rolled-up dollar bill.

"How much did they move before we got there?"

"About . . . twenty kilos," Art said hesitantly.

"No wonder you're pissed," Josie said, turning to Tomic who was visibly on low boil. They all knew that would have been the largest cocaine seizure a narcotics field enforcement unit had ever made, probably more than any of the major violator squads had come up with this year.

"Maybe you didn't rat us out, asshole, but you knew what your partner was doing and didn't say or do anything to stop him," Tomic said.

Josie could tell it was tormenting him not to swoop down on Art and beat twenty-kilos worth of satisfaction out of the frightened little man.

"They woulda killed me. Look what she did to your snitch," Art blurted out.

"You know for a fact the Testas killed Superman?" Josie asked.

"That's what Gilbert told me . . . Abby had Kent taken out."

"Too Tall told you he knew Abby killed my snitch?" Tomic repeated with more than a hint of skepticism.

Art nodded and said, "If they find me, I'm a dead man too."

"Why? What else are they afraid you'll blab?" Tomic asked.

"I know they got a contract on that blue-haired little creep," Art said, his voice growing stronger.

"Butch?"

"Don't remember his name. Whatever reason Too Tall gave you for finding him was a lie. He was helping the Testas. They wanted their coke and a pound of flesh."

"Was Too Tall dealing for the Testas . . . is he Raven?" Josie asked.

Art had a puzzled expression and finally shook his head and said, "Nah, he got paid for information, that's all. He's a hype, needs money to buy heroin . . . anything he can't steal."

"Is there another cop working for the family?" she asked.

"How should I know. They got judges and city councilmen. I'm guessing buying another cop's no big deal."

Suddenly Josie had an urge to hit him. It was a big deal. Art and his partner had tarnished all of them. In the public's mind . . . hell, in the department brass's mind, it was never just one or two bad cops. The rest of us had to know or should've known, she thought, and any compassion she might've felt for this pathetic soon-to-be ex-cop was gone. She would do her best to see him and his partner behind bars.

Josie put the handcuffs on Art because she knew Tomic hated doing it. He was squeamish about arresting other police officers, even this one who had cost him his moment of glory. She wasn't. In her opinion, dirty cops were like any other criminal, only worse. Respect and preferential treatment belonged to the warriors, not the imposters.

Art seemed almost relieved when he realized he was being arrested. He was willing to give up everything he knew about his ex-partner's criminal activities and was smart enough to figure out he'd probably get immunity for providing the district attorney with "bigger fish." He led them to a floor safe in Kit's bedroom, removed a notebook, and gave it to Josie. True to his fastidious nature, he'd kept a detailed accounting of everything Too Tall had done for Abby. Josie thumbed through pages filled with dates, times, payments, and copious notes, his insurance policy, he claimed, in the event Too Tall or the Testas threatened him.

The notebook documented Art's accusations and it was enough with his signed statement to temporarily put him behind bars as an accessory. However, Josie was fairly certain the DA wouldn't file charges on anybody including Too Tall or Abby based solely on what Art had given her. It was a start, but she knew they'd have to find independent corroborating evidence. Until then, Art would be safely tucked away in a Central Jail cell isolated from other prisoners so the Testas couldn't get to him.

~ FOURTEEN ~

Behan met them at Central Jail to give booking approval for Art, who assured everyone he had no intention of attempting to post bail. He understood his best chance of surviving the Testa clan was incarceration and isolation with witness protection before and after he testified. Josie promised him she'd set up a meeting with the DA the next morning to begin the process of providing him with a new identity and safe location, but for today, tracking down Too Tall—hopefully, before Abby and her father realized he was of no further use to them—had become her priority.

She contacted Curtis, and, over Donny's protests, he agreed they would help her and Tomic with the search. The loanees from patrol were still in court so Josie walked over to the Vice office in Hollywood station to recruit Sergeant Bailey and her crew.

The office was empty as usual, except for Marge who didn't allow her officers to linger inside the building unless they were writing reports or booking arrestees.

"Let the fucking Testas have Gilbert and Art too . . . good riddance," Marge said, after Josie asked for her assistance.

"Gladly, if we didn't need him," Josie said. "If what Art says is true, Too Tall could be the key to finding Superman's killer."

"Why should we believe anything that loser Art swears to?"

"Because it all kinda makes sense and I'm really hoping they're the only dirty cops we find."

"And if they're not?"

Josie was tired of explaining. She stared at her friend and said, "Then we get the rest of the damn assholes and clean house."

"Wow," Marge said laughing. "I just heard Josie Corsino almost swear. That's a first. How come you never swear?"

"I don't know, no reason," Josie said, but she knew why. Words always worked better for her than anger. Swearing meant she was so angry she couldn't say what she meant and, as far as she was concerned, losing control was a sign of weakness, a fatal character flaw in this man's world of policing.

"Just don't fucking do it anymore, sounds weird coming from you," Marge said, taking a last big gulp of coffee.

Josie leaned closer and calmly whispered in her ear, "Fuck off," causing her surprised friend to cough and spit a mouthful of café mocha across her desk.

"Not fucking funny, Corsino," Marge shouted, holding up a soggy piece of paper as Josie disappeared into the hallway, laughing.

Too Tall's home address on file with the department was no longer accurate, according to Art, and probably hadn't been for years. The big man refused to reveal where he was living, but Art had deduced from piecing together bits of information that his ex-partner was staying somewhere close to Hollywood, maybe even in the division.

Staff at the methadone clinic where the court had ordered Too Tall to go as part of his plea-bargained detox and rehab program had never seen him. He had signed up, but was a no-show, same story for his Narconon sessions.

"Not really into the whole fresh start thing, is he?" Tomic asked as he and Josie got back into his car.

They were leaving the rehab center on Sunset and headed toward Hollywood Boulevard where a few of the more prolific heroin dealers occasionally set up shop. Too Tall, like all hypes, needed a fix about every six hours, more or less, and he wasn't going to get it at the local pharmacy. He might have a dealer who'd deliver, but if he lived in Hollywood that would be rare.

The pricier areas such as Brentwood or Malibu might rate that kind of service, but not the streets of Tinseltown. Heroin dealers were rare in this division. Josie and Tomic had so many informants that as soon as someone set up shop and started selling, his fate was sealed . . . he went to jail but not before most of his customers had been picked off and arrested.

Cocaine addicts had it much easier. Rock houses were everywhere. If one got busted and shut down, another would pop up within hours. Every base head was more than willing to make deliveries for a taste of the product. What Superman had been doing wasn't unusual. The difference was most delivery boys killed themselves with drugs and didn't get beaten to death with a baseball bat.

The plan had been to sit on the roof of the arcade across the street from the Saint Francis Hotel and if they were lucky, see Too Tall do a transaction with one of the local dealers. Josie had just made a clean spot so she could sit on one of the air ducts when a code-three radio call "Officer needs help, shots fired" came over Tomic's handheld radio on the Hollywood frequency. Josie instantly recognized Marge's strong, steady voice, not a trace of panic or fear in her broadcast.

There was no need for Josie and Tomic to discuss their response. In seconds, they were off the roof and back into his car speeding south toward Santa Monica Boulevard where Marge had directed responding cars.

Hordes of black-and-white cruisers, detectives' plain vehicles, squads of uniformed motor officers, and the beat-up-looking utility cars belonging to Hollywood's Vice and the narcotics squads already filled the four-lane boulevard when they arrived.

Marge's tan Chevy sat in the intersection of Highland and Santa Monica with a sea of empty space surrounding it except directly in front of her car where a newer model black Buick sedan was attached, front bumper to front bumper—like two steel bulls with locked horns, eerily quiet now, but there had been a ferocious battle.

Supervisors were making a futile attempt to clear some of the police vehicles off the street. A fire truck and ambulance were parked on Highland north of the boulevard, but two firemen and paramedics were in the intersection hovering over someone lying near the open driver's door of Marge's car. Josie pushed her way through the crowd of blue uniforms, ignoring the Hollywood watch commander who tried to send her back the way she'd come. She could hear him shouting at her as she stood over her friend.

Bandages covered the side of Marge's head and neck. Her torn blouse was covered in blood. Josie had to remind herself to stop panting and breathe normally. Seeing another cop hurt, especially this one, made her angry and queasy.

"What happened?" she asked the vice lieutenant standing behind the paramedics. He was an older, experienced cop who by all accounts was infatuated with his newly acquired, irreverent, foul-mouthed sergeant, not in a sexual way but like a father.

"Check out the other car," he mumbled, not looking up from where they were working on Marge.

Josie could make out two men sprawled on the front seat of the black Buick. Like in Marge's car, the windshield had been shattered by what appeared to be gunfire, and they had been hit. From the lack of activity around them, Josie guessed they were dead.

"She did that?" Josie asked, glancing down at Marge who was leaning on her right elbow now attempting to sit up.

"Some of it," the lieutenant said. "Hollywood patrol unit coming back from court finished the job."

"Has she been shot?" Josie asked as she turned to see that he was pointing at Maddy and Vern, both in uniform standing beside their patrol car talking to Tomic and two men in suits. Before the lieutenant could answer, Marge had struggled to her feet, cursing at the paramedic who was attempting to cajole her onto a stretcher.

"I don't fucking need your fucking stretcher," Marge said, but the trauma must have taken its toll because mid-sentence she started to lose her balance. The young paramedic helped her sit and eventually lie on the stretcher. Her eyes closed when he covered her torso with a thin blanket, and she was quiet again.

"No, I don't think so," the vice lieutenant said, helping lift the stretcher into the ambulance. "But she did hit her head pretty good . . . glass cuts too." He climbed inside beside Marge and told Josie not to worry; he'd stay with Marge until she was either discharged or admitted into Cedars-Sinai hospital and call the narcotics office with an update.

The ambulance slowly drove around the cars and when it reached open road the siren blasted and it picked up speed. Josie watched it for a few seconds then walked over to where Tomic was standing. The two uniformed officers and the men in suits had gone.

"Where's Vern and Maddy?" she asked.

"Shooting team took them downtown for their interviews. No problem. They probably saved Bailey's life," Tomic said. He moved closer to the Buick but stayed behind the yellow tape. "Did you see this?" he asked, motioning for her to join him.

"Do you know how it went down?"

"According to Vern, the Buick rammed Bailey's car and the two assholes inside started shooting at her. She got out behind the driver's door and fired back. She might've hit one of them and Vern or Maddy got the other. Shooting team's gotta figure that one out."

"Does anybody know who they are?" Josie asked. The bloody faces weren't familiar, but it was difficult to make out features behind the broken glass.

"Not yet. Robbery-Homicide's got this one . . . Behan's pissed. He says his guys should handle it."

"Who'd want to take out Marge . . . this bad?" she asked, but had a feeling she already knew. This smelled like the Testas' handiwork.

"We'll know more when these assholes are ID'd. Come on, let's get outta here. There's nothing more we can do here, and Curtis just radioed he might have a lead on Too Tall."

Josie took a last long look at the dead men. That detective voice inside her head told her to stay, take prints, search the dead men's pockets and every inch of that car, run the license plate and not stop digging until she proved who tried to kill her friend. The only thing she really wanted to do now was drag Abby in handcuffs out of The Carnival and throw her in the back seat of a black-and-white. But she turned and followed Tomic to his car. We'll do it by the book . . . for now, she'd decided.

There was a logical way to investigate this crime and there was the LAPD way. Police officers were involved so RHD or one of the downtown divisions had to handle it. Hollywood's detectives were some of the best in the city. They knew the territory and local suspects, so of course they wouldn't be allowed to take the lead. She had grown up in this organization and had learned it was pointless to resist the lunacy. The case would get solved because one of their own had been attacked, but the LAPD bureaucracy always found the most convoluted way to get it done.

The shooting scene wasn't far from a pocket park on Gower Street where Curtis and his partner wanted to meet. The south end of Gower below Melrose was mostly a low-rent residential area for immigrants from Mexico and South America, and this two-block patch of green had been intended to be a playground for the dozens of kids who lived nearby. Maintenance wasn't a priority in the impoverished areas of Los Angeles so over the years the grass had become mostly dirt and weeds, the swings were unsafe, and children avoided the sandbox after too many used syringes were found buried in what had become mostly a pile of dirt. The park was now a hangout for gangs and drug dealers. No decent parent would allow a child anywhere near the place.

Curtis and Donny were sitting on one of the picnic tables near the parking lot when Josie and Tomic arrived. They were almost back to back, eating McDonald's hamburgers, and watching the terrain. In this location, diligence was much more important than conversation. She knew Curtis had the nerves and constitution of a Navy Seal and could snack during a gun battle, but he wasn't careless and getting caught off guard wasn't going to happen. On the other hand, it wasn't in Donny's nature to be comfortable having lunch in the middle of a gang-infested park, but he usually went along with his partner, never backing away from any of Curtis's crazy ideas or quirks.

"Want some nuggets?" Curtis asked, handing a small container with two pieces of breaded chicken to Josie as soon as she and Tomic got out of the car.

She took them and asked, "Where is he?"

"About three blocks south on the east side of the street," Curtis said.

Tomic sat on the end of the bench and asked, "How'd you find him?"

"Snitch," Donny said. "They have the same dealer."

"Still on the needle," Josie said. She was disappointed and had hoped when Too Tall lost his job he would get clean.

"No, marijuana. Snitch swears he's off smack," Donny said. He slid off the table, collected all the lunch debris and dumped it into the nearest trash can.

"That's a first for this place," Tomic said, watching him wade through garbage and litter to reach the container.

"You gonna door knock? Want us to hang around?" Curtis asked.

"No," Tomic answered quickly. "Josie and me can handle this one. Thanks for your help."

Josie started to disagree but changed her mind. Maybe her partner was right. Too Tall had been one of them, not some unpredictable street thug. They should be able to talk to him without backup.

The house was exactly as Curtis had described it, a tidy white bungalow on the east side of Gower. The front lawn was a weed garden, but it had been freshly mowed. Most of the homes on this block were old but kept up. It seemed the occupants had tried to create a pleasant, livable neighborhood.

There wasn't an answer to either the doorbell or their knocking, so they walked around the corner of the house and down a cement driveway to the garage. The front barn-style doors were closed and secured with chains, but Tomic opened an unlocked side door and they located Too Tall inside surrounded by three Harley motorcycles in various stages of disassembly. He was wearing protective goggles and headphones and welding a front extension onto a motorcycle frame.

He looked up and saw them but didn't seem surprised, more disappointed. He turned off the torch, put it on the workbench, removed his headphones, and stared down at the floor for a few seconds. Josie thought he seemed different, not just his appearance but his demeanor was calmer . . . more peaceful. His hair was tied back with a rubber band and he had the beginnings of a decent beard and mustache. His hands were covered with grease that he wiped off with what looked like an old T-shirt before approaching them.

"Let's go in the house," he said and led the way across a small concrete slab with a cheap metal firepit, and through a kitchen door into the bungalow. "Sit down," he said, pointing at four chairs around a Formica-top table that appeared to be a cheap throwback to the fifties. He pulled his chair away from the table and sat, crossed his arms, and asked, "What do you want?"

"The truth, everything you know about Abby Morrison, and Clark Kent's murder," Tomic said.

"What makes you think I know anything," he said, smoothing his mustache with his left hand.

"Art kept a diary. He gave it to us," Josie said.

Too Tall almost smiled, leaned forward with his head bent, staring at the floor again for several seconds before sitting back and slowly shaking his head.

"Not a major surprise. Little man, short on intestinal fortitude, with an active imagination."

"You're really not in a good position, Too Tall, to be judging people," Tomic said, interrupting him.

"Tony or Mr. Gilbert will do . . . these days only my friends call me Too Tall."

"All right Tony, what the fuck do you know about Clark Kent's murder? We can talk nicely here, or we can drag your ass to the station and book you on all those illegal things Art says you did," Tomic said calmly.

"It's his word against mine. He's a liar, and you can't arrest me without proof."

"Wrong. Maybe we can't get it filed, but we can definitely throw your sorry ass behind bars and pretty much make your life hell," Tomic said.

Too Tall was quiet for a moment and turned to Josie. She stared back at him. They both knew Tomic was right and even temporarily, jail was not a good place for cops, but at the moment, he seemed more amused than worried about the prospect of incarceration.

"I need a beer, want one?" he asked, getting up and opening the refrigerator. From where he stood in the kitchen, most of the appliances were within his long arm's reach. Josie could see the living room and the door to the bedroom from where she sat, and as far as she could tell, Too Tall wasn't living badly or in squalor. Everything in his home was well-used, but clean and orderly. She realized he wasn't escaping or coping; he belonged here.

They declined the beer, and he came back to the table with a bottle of Budweiser. Josie and Tomic glanced at each other for a second but didn't say anything. It was obvious the man wasn't intimidated or struggling with a decision. She had learned after years of interviewing suspects that there was a point in any interrogation when the intelligent, bolder individual might decide to talk or not. Any pressure at that point was usually counterproductive.

"Do you believe that crap in Art's diary?" Too Tall asked Josie.

"I'm keeping an open mind," she said.

"All right, first thing you should know is Art's a lying piece of shit. I don't know what he wrote or told you, but he was Abby's primary contact, not me. Second, I'm off the hard stuff, little weed most days but no heroin . . . cold turkey, no methadone, nothing, so there's no way you can put a dope case on me."

"Tough guy," Tomic said.

"No, I just don't need it anymore. Soon as I stopped working in a shithole I hated, the pain was gone."

"Right," Tomic said sarcastically.

"Don't care if you believe me or not. I'm not living a lie anymore . . . doing what I love," he said, pointing in the general direction of the garage full of motorcycles. "All that other crap is outta my life, so I'll tell you what I know because it doesn't matter."

"Might not matter to you, but if you broke the law it matters," Josie said.

"I should of told you Art was warning Abby, but nobody, especially no cop, ever got hurt. The squad lost some dope. That's all. I did what I had to do to take care of myself, to survive."

"Bullshit," Tomic said.

"Yeah, maybe, but it's done, and I can't change the past," Too Tall said and finished the beer.

"What about Clark Kent?" Josie asked. She believed him. It made sense that Art might've had a way to shift blame to his partner if he ever got caught. Art was a sneaky little bastard, and he wasn't stupid.

Too Tall shifted his position uncomfortably, crossing and uncrossing his long legs.

"Clark was a simple guy . . . you know that, Larry," Too Tall said and then waited for confirmation from Tomic that never came, so he continued. "He worshipped you. Abby knew that. She used him to get to you. There was no other dirty cop . . . except Art and me."

"So why did he tell us there was. Was he going to give you up?"

"No. Abby had asked Art a bunch of questions about how we handle informants. After Clark got killed, I figured she killed him."

"She knew we'd document our meeting with him and everything he told us the night he got killed," Josie said. She was beginning to understand.

"Did Abby tell you to make that IA complaint against me?" Tomic asked.

He nodded and said, "I think she told Art to make it look like you were a dirty cop who killed his snitch to shut him up. I went along with him because I hate your guts. You're a selfish, pompous ass and the bonus was I got to keep the heroin. Her plan was a bust because she trusted a rat like Art and that idiot Eddie Small to make it work."

"So, who'd she get to kill Clark Kent?" Tomic asked.

"Don't know. Her old man takes care of that stuff. But that's the part that doesn't fit because she always protected Clark."

"How do you know what her old man does?" Josie asked.

"Art told me."

"Did the Testas order a hit on Marge Bailey?" she asked.

"What happened to Bailey?" Too Tall asked and seemed genuinely surprised.

"Couple of assholes tried to gun her down on the street," Tomic said.

"Is she . . . ?"

"No, but what do you think your chances are if Abby or her father's thugs find you?" Josie asked.

"I'm not hiding. They've got no reason to kill me. If they try, I got a few nasty friends of my own," he said, touching the faded Harley-Davidson emblem on his shirt.

"Were you privy to any of her business dealings?"

"Would you trust a hype with anything important? Art was useful, but probably expendable . . . same as Clark, I guess. Killing him had to be a way to get to you." Too Tall shook his head and added, "It's crazy. Abby really liked the big guy. If she had him beat to death after the way she mothered him, that's some cold-hearted bitch. Maybe she killed him, but it doesn't make any sense to me and I don't see any way you tie her to his murder."

"Maybe, but if the time comes that we do find even a tiny bit of proof, your testimony as a firsthand witness to her drug dealing might help put the lid on her coffin," Tomic said. "You actually believe she hasn't thought about that possibility?"

Too Tall was quiet. The deep furrows in his forehead told Josie he was thinking hard, and she could almost visualize the sparks flying as the wiring in his marijuana-soaked brain short-circuited. He pulled the rubber band off and back on his ponytail, smoothed his hair, and after several minutes, straightened up and seemed to come to a decision.

"I was a cop a long time. I know you're not here to arrest me. What is it you're trying to get me to do?"

"Get close to Abby," Josie said. "A dirty ex-cop can be a valuable asset to her. Offer to work for her."

"Doing what?" Too Tall asked incredulously.

"Whatever she wants . . . short of killing," Tomic said.

"You want me to be a snitch."

"More like an undercover cop without benefit of backup," Tomic said. "Except for Josie and me."

Too Tall slowly shook his head but didn't speak. The internal struggle had begun again. Fear, survival instinct, anger, self-pity among other emotions were most likely flooding his mind. He had discovered a lifestyle that gave him peace and purpose. Josie figured she and Tomic were yanking the happiness rug out from under his feet.

"If she has even a hint I'm working with you, I'm a dead man."

"Then don't screw it up. My guess is you're already on the old man's hit list. If you help us, we can try to protect you until we put her away," Tomic said and added, "We'll arrange adjoining rooms for you and Art in witness protection."

Too Tall closed his eyes tight and leaned his head back as if he were in pain. "Just shoot me now," he mumbled. "Hell couldn't be worse than having Art in my life again."

"Sorry, bad joke," Tomic said, not sounding the least bit sorry.

"You can forget about witness protection. I'm not hiding from that fat bitch or her asshole father. Like I said. I got friends too. I'll help you put her away because it helps me, but when we're done, both of you, Art, or anything to do with the fucking LAPD are out of my life forever. That's the deal."

Too Tall made a phone call to Abby Morrison while Josie and Tomic waited. She agreed to meet the ex-cop at her club after closing that night. He was reluctant to wear a wire until Josie convinced him Narcotics division's Major Violators section had transmitters for their UCs that were virtually impossible to detect—pens, tie clips, etc.

He agreed to meet them at the division's electronic unit downtown an hour before his meeting with Abby. At that time, they would brief him on what was expected and how the Hollywood squad would protect him inside and outside the club. Too Tall's right to carry a concealed weapon had been revoked after his drug arrest but Tomic insisted he carry a sidearm for protection.

The Testas were as cold and vicious as any street gang when it came to killing anyone who interfered with their business . . . as Marge found out. Tomic had told Josie that Abby's husband wasn't the only person close to her who had disappeared without a trace or was murdered without a clue or link back to the club owner. As much as Tomic disliked Too Tall, he refused to send the man into a "den of maniacs" without a way to defend himself.

They had a few hours before their meeting downtown. Josie wanted to visit Marge Bailey at the hospital but Tomic had to brief Behan on the deal with Too Tall and get his permission to use electronic surveillance. It might be difficult to persuade the cautious supervisor to allow not only the use of an ex-cop junkie as a UC, but placing him in a situation where he could be killed. Even Behan might balk at that scenario, but she was confident he would let them try because there was that chance it might work.

She decided to let Tomic argue their case and she would drive to Cedars-Sinai then meet him later at the electronic unit. Marge had been on her mind all afternoon and Josie knew the only way to stop thinking about her friend was to see her.

The security guard at the visitors' desk had reluctantly directed her to the room in the North Tower on the third floor. It was well after visiting hours, but he was resigned to the inevitability of concerned cops reaching their wounded comrade regardless of hospital rules. As soon as Josie got to the end of the sterile, freshly polished hallway, she knew why the hospital staff had given Marge that room. Other injured police officers had stayed in the facility and the nurses most likely knew what to expect. Cops were a family. They understood how suddenly and easily one of them could be badly injured or killed. Survival was a cause for celebration and they did just that with noisy gusto.

Two vice officers and a sergeant were leaving when Josie arrived, and a tiny Filipino nurse was shooing two more detectives out of the room. She gave Josie a stern look and warned her that visiting hours were over, and she'd better keep the noise down or face the same fate as the other offenders.

The room was actually semi-private, but the other bed was empty for obvious reasons. Marge was propped up in bed. Her blonde hair was disheveled and matted. Bandages partially covered her head, neck, and shoulder. The visible half of her face was bruised and had several small scratches. Her left hand and arm were bandaged but she was eating from a take-out food container with the other hand. A white Styrofoam box was on the narrow table that had been adjusted to fit over her legs. The smell of fried chicken and fresh rolls caused Josie's stomach to growl.

"Corsino, sit here and help me finish this," she said, patting the bed.

"Are you gonna live or what?" Josie asked and took a chicken leg out of the box.

"What do you think? Dumb fuckers barely touched me."

"You look like shit."

"Doc says broken collarbone, bullet went through my neck but missed all the important stuff, another one grazed me right here above my ear," Marge said, touching her bandage with a piece of bread before stuffing it in her mouth. "My arm caught a round and the fucking car crash did the rest of the damage."

"When will they let you out? You can stay with me. We've got room and my mother-in-law is dying to cook and clean for anybody."

"Thanks, but I've got it covered. I'll be here at least three or four more days. All I need is real food and my guys are making deliveries."

There was a hairbrush in the bathroom, so Josie carefully worked on combing Marge's hair. Twenty minutes later, most of it was unmatted and looked nearly normal. Josie found extra pillows in the closet that she put on the bed and stretched out next to Marge. They were lying side by side talking when Maddy knocked on the door and pulled the curtain back to enter the room.

"Oh, sorry to interrupt . . ." Maddy said, blushing and backing away.

"Anybody that saved my life can fucking interrupt me any damn time they want. Get the fuck in here."

Maddy smiled and gave Marge a gentle hug.

"You look so much better," she said.

"I look like hammered dog shit but thanks anyway. Want something to eat?" she asked, holding up the nearly empty box. Maddy shook her head and sat on a chair near the bed. "Wait, I've got a better idea. Corsino, can you reach the top drawer of that small cabinet?"

Josie could and retrieved an unopened bottle of Pinot Noir. She held it up, asked, "Whose bright idea was this?"

"Who else," Marge said, and Josie immediately knew it was Behan. His remedy for health and happiness was usually alcohol.

It took nearly half an hour, but the three women finished the wine. The aftereffects took a few minutes longer which for Josie and Marge meant a pleasant buzz, but for Maddy it was truth serum. Clearly not an alcohol drinker, she got silly and finally began acting like a young woman again and not the robotic soldier that Vern's probationary training had tried to create.

She laughed and joked and had a stinging sense of humor, imitating her training partner's constant admonitions about, "how this job has to be done for all those people who depend on you to get it right, Officer Worthen." Her expressions and movements were dead-on for Vern's.

"In this business, you only get one chance or you're dead," Maddy warned as she paced in front of the bed matching his slightly hunched walk and stern frown. "Watch. Don't talk unless it's to say, 'yes sir.' You got that, boot? When I tell you to search a suspect, he will have dope . . ."

She stopped suddenly and sat on the bed. The color drained from her face and Josie thought she was going to be sick.

"Let's get you in the bathroom," Josie said, trying to help her stand. "Don't want barf all over Marge's antiseptic sheets."

"I'm not sick," Maddy said, pushing Josie's hand away.

"What's the matter?"

"Don't worry. We're not gonna tell fuckhead you made him look like an asswipe," Marge said.

"That's not it." Maddy took a deep breath but wouldn't look at Josie.

"Something's bothering you. What is it?" Josie asked.

Several minutes later after relentless coaxing from the other two women, Maddy told them. She insisted Vern was in most respects the best training officer in Hollywood. He hated drug dealers more than any other sort of criminal except child molesters. Every day he vowed to put at least one dealer in jail fitting it in between patrol's regular calls for service, and he did. Lately she'd begun to feel uneasy about those arrests.

He'd only detain known drug dealers and would always do a pat-down search first and usually found something, but if he didn't, he'd go back and look in one or two pockets and then tell her to do another search. In every case, she'd find a single rock of cocaine or a balloon of heroin in one of those pockets. She had begun to believe Vern was planting the drugs before she searched.

"Did you confront him?" Josie asked.

"Sort of," she said, but hesitated before adding, "He got really mad when I mentioned it and said sometimes he'd left contraband he found, so I could find it again and be the one to testify . . . as part of my training. He told me I should know what I'm talking about before I start accusing another officer of misconduct."

"His method's odd, but I guess it's one way to train," Marge said. "Does smell a little bit though."

"A lot," Josie said. "I've got to get downtown but let me talk it over with Behan. I'm afraid there's only one way to be certain, a sting, and if he's planting dope, even on bad guys, he's toast."

Maddy fell back on the bed over Marge's legs, put her hands over her face, and said, "What if I'm wrong. He's such a great guy. I'll have to quit if I'm wrong. Even if I'm right, nobody will ever work with me again."

"Pull yourself together, woman," Marge said. "If the fucker's dirty, good riddance. If he's not, nobody will know it was you who told IA."

"Internal Affairs!" Maddy shouted, sitting up as if she'd been stuck with a pin. "Why Internal Affairs?"

"Because what you might've seen is a fucking felony."

Maddy moaned and whispered, "I really shouldn't drink."

~ FIFTEEN ~

It took a while, but Josie calmed down Maddy and she stayed until the younger woman curled up and fell asleep on the room's wide window bench. Josie didn't want to believe a veteran officer like Vern Fisher would do what his partner suspected, but she'd been in the department long enough to know sometimes smart cops do stupid things in the name of justice. As much as Vern hated drug dealers, she hated dirty cops, but he wasn't corrupt, just wrong. Her head told her the right thing to do was give the information to Internal Affairs, but some part of her was leaning toward confronting him instead and getting his word he would never do it again.

Coming up with a way to let him get away with past sins without losing his job dominated her thoughts as she sat in her car in the hospital parking lot. It was crazy. She'd jeopardize her own career if she tried to salvage what was left of his.

"You're an idiot. His stupidity is not your problem," she said out loud and started the car, but somewhere in the back of her mind there was this nagging flicker of hope . . . there might be a way.

When Josie arrived, Tomic and Too Tall were already at Central division in downtown LA at the corner of Central Avenue and Wall Street. Narcotics division occupied the entire third floor and had one room in the Major Violators section dedicated to radios and electronic equipment. That cramped space was the sole domain of Officer Carl Stern. He hoarded batteries and transmitters and new surveillance toys, doling out each item as if he'd paid for it out of his own pocket. Josie had been told he was a genius with electronics. She'd learned from personal experience, he was difficult to work with, had no common sense, and knew nothing about police work. His expertise in keeping their complicated equipment working was the only reason he hadn't been forced to retire years ago.

Too Tall seemed more relaxed than he'd been earlier that day as he listened intently to Carl explain how the tiny transmitter in his ballpoint pen worked. He decided to carry his 9mm Beretta on his belt instead of a two-inch revolver in an ankle holster. He wore a leather jacket that covered the gun, shabby faded Levi's with one end of a chain attached to the belt and the other end to his wallet in his back pants' pocket, heavy black biker boots, and the signature tinted glasses. His long hair was pulled back and beard trimmed, but Josie thought the overall effect on his tall frame was impressive and intimidating.

"Keep it here," Carl said, putting the pen as deep as he could into Too Tall's shirt pocket. "Don't zip your jacket when you're inside, don't touch or move it, and above all, do not lose my pen. Okay?"

"Okay for the hundredth time," Tomic answered. "Let's get the fuck outta here."

"Did you sign for the monitor?" Carl asked. "Are you sure you know how to use it?"

Tomic didn't respond but gave the nervous man a look that clearly said, "We're done or I'm killing you."

"Thanks for your help, Carl," Too Tall said and gave the older man a friendly pat on the back. His demeanor, Josie thought, was more appropriate for a man going to a social outing than an undercover cop about to walk into a deadly snake pit. He seemed confident and displayed none of the nerves she and most UCs would demonstrate in similar situations.

"Are you doing okay?" she asked him when they were walking out toward the parking lot.

"Do I look okay?"

She didn't answer, but Tomic said, "You look like a bullshitter who's sure he's the smartest dude in the room. I'm warning you—don't underestimate the Testas, especially Abby. She'd gut you for the fun of it."

A massive Harley was parked just outside the walkway leading to the lot. The extended front end and handle bars made it look bigger than any bike Josie had ever seen. Too Tall straddled the seat with his long legs, kick-started the engine, and the deafening roar grew louder reverberating off the walls of the large parking structure. He left her and Tomic standing side by side, covering their ears, watching him maneuver down the ramp toward the exit.

"Asshole," Tomic mumbled when it was quiet again.

Curtis and Donny had already set up surveillance at The Carnival and reported via radio that the club was starting to close down for the night and the crowd was thinning.

Josie decided to take her car and leave Tomic's on the roof of Central division's parking structure, a popular dumping ground for all sorts of vehicles. Nobody asked, or towed them, or cared why they were there. If he didn't have to drive, he could concentrate on the monitor.

The last few Carnival patrons were trickling out the front door and getting into cars by the time Josie found a spot to watch the location and be close enough to pick up any conversation from Too Tall's transmitter. Tomic fiddled with knobs and switches and swore at the apparatus Carl had given him until he got a clear signal and voice test from Too Tall's pen. He had parked his motorcycle near the stairs that led to Abby's apartment. There was a light burning on the second-floor landing, but it didn't illuminate much below that.

Josie had hidden her car across the street behind a U-Haul truck but close enough for her to barely see the motorcycle and Abby's apartment door with help from the streetlight near the alley. Curtis and his partner were on foot and could get inside the building quickly if necessary. After Too Tall gave his test message and before he climbed up the stairs, Curtis walked past the alley and gave him a thumbs-up to let him know he'd been heard.

The only noise on the receiver for several seconds was the sound of biker boots on metal stairs and the low crackling rustle of leather as it occasionally rubbed against the transmitter, then pounding on the security screen and voices.

"Well, well look what the garbage man left," Abby said.

"Fuck you."

"Don't piss on me, *cugino*. I didn't fire you."

"What'd she call him?" Tomic asked.

"Cousin," Josie answered quickly, but wondered if she'd understood what she'd heard.

"What?"

"How should I know. Be quiet and listen," Josie said, straining to pick up the broken conversation half in English, half Italian, and it became harder to hear clearly as soon as the door closed.

"Where's Uncle Guy?" Too Tall asked.

"What the fuck," Tomic whispered.

Josie was trying to convince herself not to get out of the car and drag Too Tall by his stringy ponytail down the stairs and back to the station.

Instead she said, "Probably something he should've mentioned upfront," and returned Tomic's cold stare.

"Daddy's back in Vegas cleaning up a few loose ends. Want a drink?"

"You got beer?"

Abby snorted a laugh and asked, "What do you think?"

"Give me a shot of Guy's good whiskey."

"Why the change of heart? I thought you wanted no part of the family business."

"I don't have a job, remember. I need cash."

His tone was nasty, not a plea for help, a demand.

It was quiet for several seconds and Josie could hear sounds, movement, but couldn't figure out what was happening. There was music in the background and Abby must have moved away from Too Tall. Her voice echoed as if she were in another room and then suddenly she was back.

"What good are you now. On the inside, we could of used you."

"I'm family. You can use me."

"Too bad it took you so long to figure that out. You know I gotta run it by Daddy first. You still got your gun and badge?"

"Yeah, my gun, but I'm not killing anybody for you. I'm not that bad off . . . yet. They took my badge and ID."

"We'll see. You got a place to stay?"

Too Tall laughed and said, "You know I do. I saw your hired half-wits sneaking around my house spying on me."

She forced a laugh and said, "Smart guy, you've always been a smart guy, Tony."

It was quiet for a few seconds except the rustling of the leather against the mic and Too Tall said, "What're you doing?" He sounded surprised but not in a nice way.

"You wouldn't be wearing a wire, would you Tony? Snitching for your old buddies in that Hollywood shithole."

"Get your hands off me, bitch. Snitching for what? I'm a free man. I owe those assholes nothing. If I wanted to get at you, I'd do it myself and you know it. Here, you wanna search me, look!" he shouted, his voice growing louder, angrier.

Abby swore in Italian. "All right, all right put your clothes back on. I'm not drunk enough to be looking at your fucking dick," she said, her words barely audible between bursts of uncontrollable laughter.

They calmed down, drank some more, and talked about family members for almost another hour. Josie guessed from the conversation that Tony's mother was Guy Testa's sister. His father was a chiropractor who'd kept his family as far as he could from the crime boss which would explain how Too Tall got through the police department's background check. The cousins didn't grow up together but apparently had kept in touch through other relatives.

Josie knew Italian families were close and even though the tiniest slight might result in years of not communicating, they always kept tabs on each other. She could relate to many of their stories from knowing her father's side of the family. Her mother was an Irish alcoholic; that was a completely different story.

It was nearly four A.M. by the time Too Tall left The Carnival to meet with them behind the Bank of America on Wilshire Boulevard. He had chosen the location for the debriefing because he claimed it was a place he could ride to on his motorcycle without being followed. The building was next door to a twenty-four-hour Winchell's donut shop so Josie and Tomic agreed. Curtis and his partner left, deciding sleep was a better idea than caffeine.

He had barely dismounted his motorcycle when Tomic approached and started his tirade about trust and "fucking, sneaky liars."

"If I told you she was my cousin, you wouldn't have let me go," he said, calmly leaning the bike on its stand.

"Damn straight," Tomic said louder, his face getting red as his temper flared. "That was our decision to make, not yours."

"How do we know anything you tell us is the truth? It makes more sense now that you were her source and not Art," Josie said.

"Were you listening? Did it sound like we've been working together?"

"No," Josie admitted after a few seconds. He was right. They were not two people who had talked to each other recently let alone shared much information before tonight.

"My dad's last name was Gilberti before his father changed it. He grew up in New York's Little Italy next door to the Testas. He loved my mom, hated her brother, and got us as far as he could from that family as soon as they were married."

"Not that far," Tomic said.

"Abby made contact when I joined the department. She's been trying to recruit me since I put on a uniform. I never worked for her or her father, but I made a huge mistake, got hooked on pain killers. I introduced her to Art this year, so he could snitch, and I could get my heroin."

"Should've told us," Tomic said, still upset.

Too Tall shrugged but didn't argue. He did tell them he wanted to have several more meetings with his cousin before asking her too many questions about Kent's murder.

"She probably doesn't trust me, and Gaetano's a fox. He'll want me to do something to prove myself."

"Like what?" Josie asked.

"Something illegal . . . rob, maim, how do I know. I already told her I won't kill. Here," he said, taking the pen out of his pocket and tossing it to Josie. "I won't be needing this."

"Far as I can tell, you never needed it, asshole. Pack doesn't eat its young," Tomic said.

"You don't know the Testas . . . anyway, they won't come after me as long as my mom's alive. She's the oldest and Guy's afraid of her."

"Get what you can as soon as you can and find out why they want Butch so bad. I've got a feeling that blue-haired hustler knows a lot more than he's telling us. I think they killed Lance McCray trying to find him." Josie was having a difficult time keeping her thoughts straight. There was more, but confusion came on the heels of exhaustion. "I'm really tired. Let's get out of here, Tomic," she said, getting into her car. Tomic was quick to follow.

She needed to go home, somewhere quiet to clear her head. This wasn't happening the way she'd anticipated. The questions were swirling in her head faster than she could answer them. 'Who was this guy really working with? How would they verify anything he told them without the wire? Was he playing them for fools or genuinely trying to help? How can you trust a reformed hype who lied as easily as he rode that monster bike?'

They'd gone a few blocks before Tomic asked, "We're not really working with that turd, are we?"

"Not sure, but maybe we should let him think we are," she said.

"This stinks. You know he's one of them and looking for a way to get back at us."

She sighed and said, "Maybe. I'm too tired to think straight. Why not let it play out and see what he does. We don't have to act on anything he gives us. Right?" she asked.

Tomic didn't answer and they were silent until she pulled onto the roof of the Central division parking structure. He said, "Good night," got into his car, and drove away in the direction of the freeway. The bar and Sue Ann weren't an option this morning. He rarely went directly to the cheerleader's apartment, so Mrs. Tomic and the kids might see Daddy when they woke.

SHE BACKED into her driveway beside Jake's Porsche minutes before Nonna should've been parking at the curb in front of the house, but the older woman wasn't there. The neighbor was picking up his paper and ignored her friendly wave. Josie had canceled her subscription to the *LA Times* the previous year, but Jake quickly renewed it. He said he wasn't going to be ignorant and uninformed about world events because she hated the paper's anti-police editorials. She picked up the thick newspaper tied with a string and realized it was Saturday.

Of course, David was already awake and playing in the backyard. On a school day he'd be hiding under the sheets pleading with Nonna for another ten minutes in bed. An empty cereal bowl was on the kitchen table, and Jake, in his pajama bottoms and an old T-shirt, was drinking his coffee on the enclosed back porch watching their son.

Josie poured herself a mug of coffee and gave her husband a quick kiss before sitting on the other uncomfortable wrought iron chair near the impractical little bistro table. He liked to escape here in the mornings and stare at the backyard while he drank his coffee. She preferred the cushioned kitchen chairs but needed to talk with him.

"Have you been at the hospital all night? I heard about Marge," he said, still watching David. "Is she going to be okay?"

"Pretty banged up, but she'll live. We did a surveillance after I left her at the hospital," she said and explained what had happened with Too Tall.

"How'd he pass the background check?" Jake asked when she finished.

"He never mentioned the connection and his family had no contact with the Testas for decades." She hesitated and asked, "What's our liability sending him into the viper's nest without backup or protection?"

"Are you paying him?"

"No, we haven't offered him a thing."

"Do you have to document the contact?"

"Yes . . . probably."

"Don't. He's a free agent. If he comes back with information, document at that time. Until then he's on his own. You're not directing or supervising him."

"Might've been a bit of directing," Josie admitted.

"Don't. Just take what he gives you. He already knows what you want, right?"

"Pretty much."

"You look awful. Why don't you sleep for a few hours and I'll make an early dinner?"

"Thanks, loving legal counsel," she said and got up but quickly sat again. "One more thing." She told him what Maddy had said about her training officer. "Vern is a great cop who got overzealous. I should make a personnel complaint, but it seems so . . . unjust, senseless."

"He broke the law. He's not so great."

"It's not that black and white."

"Yes, it is, Josie, and you know it. He made a choice like every other criminal. Wearing a blue uniform doesn't exempt you from the consequences of making bad decisions."

She didn't respond but got up and gently touched his unshaven face before going back into the house. Her head was pounding from lack of sleep, but she knew between dueling thoughts of Too Tall and Vern Fisher she had little chance of getting any real rest.

~ SIXTEEN ~

There was a principle of gravity Josie discovered the hard way: A seven-year-old doesn't weigh much until he decides to do a belly flop on your stomach while you're sleeping. She had managed to get a good six hours of oblivion before David decided it was time to get some attention.

Jake came running into the room, grabbed the little boy off the bed, and apologized as he carried him out under his arm like a giggling sack of potatoes, but the mission had been accomplished. She was awake. The shower finished the job and by the time Josie came into the kitchen she was rested, ready, and eager to play mommy for the rest of the weekend.

Unless Josie got called into the station, Nonna rarely came on Saturdays, so Josie and David ate in the living room while watching television, and left toys and games all over the house without constant annoying reprimands from the little Sicilian woman who followed the boy around picking up and cleaning.

Josie's son had inherited her aversion to tidiness. Jake tried his best to keep the house neat when his mother wasn't there, but he'd eventually give up and let the housekeeper pick up on Monday morning while his mother stood over the poor woman's shoulder and supervised.

The Hollywood vice lieutenant called just before dinner was ready, to tell Josie that Marge had left the hospital and gone back to her apartment.

"She signed herself out against her doctor's better judgment," the lieutenant said. His frustration and worry were clear. "Will you be seeing her?" he asked.

"I'm not sure," Josie said. She knew she wouldn't but didn't want to disappoint him.

"She said she couldn't rest in that place. So I'm hoping she'll just stay home and sleep," he said. "The captain's got a detail of Metro guys watching her and the apartment until we find whoever went after her. I'd just feel better if someone was there."

Then get off your whiny ass and go sit with her, Josie thought, but said, "As long as she's got a protection detail, we shouldn't bother her. Maybe have a couple of your vice guys drop off food or snacks later," Josie said. If Marge had nourishment and was being guarded, Josie saw no good reason to abandon her family on the weekend.

The lieutenant didn't sound pleased when he hung up, but Josie really didn't care. He seemed to expect her to drop everything, go to Marge's apartment, and babysit. She had other plans. This was the first opportunity she'd had in several weeks to spend significant time with her son and husband and she wasn't going to give it up unless there was a real emergency.

She convinced Jake to load up the dinner trays and carry food and drinks into the living room to watch a Disney special while they ate. David fell asleep before it finished and twenty minutes later was washed and in bed for the night without a fuss.

Josie cleaned the kitchen while Jake straightened up the rest of the house, then they turned down the lights and finished a very expensive cognac in the den. The phone hadn't rung since the lieutenant's call and Josie wondered for a moment if it was out of order. She could have checked but didn't. Jake stuffed newspaper under logs in the den's fireplace, lit them, and a few minutes later they were naked on the carpet making love in the warmth of a decent fire.

When David woke them the next morning, they were still on the den floor covered with a wool blanket and the fire had gone out. As the little boy crawled between them, Josie tried to focus on the Waterford clock on the mantel. It was before nine. David was hungry and complained he couldn't reach the cereal box in the cupboard or manage the full gallon of milk in the door of the refrigerator. Josie sent him back to the kitchen to wait while she gathered her clothes and underwear.

When she finally got dressed and knelt to give Jake a good-morning kiss, he pulled her back onto the floor and they probably would have repeated last night's experience if David hadn't come into the room again. He was impatient and tugged at Josie's shirt until she scrambled to her feet. Jake groaned and rolled over before promising to get up in a few minutes and make them a big breakfast.

Most of Josie's morning was taken up with napping, eating, or playing with her son. She'd nearly put Hollywood, Tomic, and Superman out of her mind when her partner called in the late afternoon.

"Major Crimes has identified the two dead bozos in the Buick," Tomic said. She could hear music, recognized his favorite song on the jukebox at the Freeway bar, and heard the cheerleader's husky laugh in the background.

"Anybody we know?" she asked before he felt the need to explain why he was at the bar. She didn't want to hear the same stupid lie he'd told his wife, so he could spend his day off with Sue Ann.

"Las Vegas residents, Organized Crime thinks they might be able to connect them to Gaetano. Don't know why the Testas would go after Marge."

"I do. She's been like a crazed flea in Abby's over-sprayed hair. Every chance she gets, Marge shuts down The Carnival. I'll bet it's cost Abby thousands of dollars in just the last week."

"Stupid . . ." Tomic mumbled.

"Why?"

"It's not the way to get her or her father."

"Must've been working or they wouldn't have tried to kill her."

"Annoy Abby for a few thousand dollars in fines and get killed. I don't see how that's such a great strategy."

"You got a better one?" she asked, irritated by his criticism.

"Put somebody on the inside."

Josie couldn't argue. Having Too Tall snitch on his cousin might turn out to be a huge advantage. She wasn't confident that even he could dig up enough to convict the Testas, but she'd been reasonably optimistic about their chances until Tomic got to the substance of his call. Too Tall had phoned him earlier.

"Asshole says he spent last night drinking with Cousin Abby . . . according to her, the coke Butch stole from Superman wasn't hers . . . told him she's been trying to get it because she paid for some of it and owes the supplier a favor. Know what I think?" Tomic asked but didn't wait for an answer. "I think asshole and his cousin are lying sacks of shit because I know it was hers and I know she killed Kent."

"Maybe, but I don't see her lying to him about owning the drugs, and if only some of the coke was hers, she really didn't have a reason to kill Kent."

"Fucker's trying to convince me Abby loved Kent like a brother . . . bullshit . . . she's saying the supplier, whoever the fuck that is, killed him . . . and Butch is either dead or gonna die when they catch up with him," Tomic mumbled. Josie could tell he'd done some serious drinking. His speech was slow and most of the words were slurring together. He became belligerent when he drank too much but she had a few thoughts she wanted to run by him anyway.

"I've got serious doubts Butch stole from Kent," she said. "I'm guessing those two geniuses took that cocaine to go into business for themselves. Kent wasn't very smart but even he had to know he could make a lot of money if the haul was big enough," Josie said.

"So then Butch rats out Kent to save his worthless skin . . . somebody kills Kent and McCray searching for the coke . . ." Tomic said, finishing her scenario, but stopping several times to organize his thoughts. "Abby's the one that bailed out Butch. She had him last."

"What If Butch confessed to her that Kent had it. She puts him in the warehouse for safekeeping, but McCray lets him escape. Butch finds someplace to hide himself and the stash, minus a few rocks he probably gave McCray to get him high," Josie said

"Who the hell is the supplier if it's not Abby?" Tomic asked, almost shouting after a long pause. "If he actually exists and sells to the Testas, he's gotta be a major dealer."

They were bouncing ideas off each other, throwing out possible scenarios the way they always did when an investigation got complicated, but this time it didn't seem to help, even made it worse.

Josie told him that first thing in the morning she would talk to detectives in Narcotics division's Major Violators section and ask if they were working on or knew of any active distributors in the Hollywood or Las Vegas area who could handle a Testa-size volume of business. Josie figured Kent might've been only one of this supplier's delivery boys, and just his ledger alone had a lengthy distribution list. She understood this was a big, messy investigation that should be handled by Majors, but it was tied to Kent's murder, too, so she was pretty certain Tomic, drunk or sober, wouldn't give it up without a fight.

~ SEVENTEEN ~

For two days at home, Josie had managed to avoid talking about a subject she knew would make her husband a very happy man. All weekend, the promotion Lieutenant Watts had offered her hovered like an ominous pigeon about to poop on her happy time. She understood it meant a raise, regular hours, and spending more time with her often-neglected family. It should have been a good thing, but she couldn't make herself tell Jake. Every time she thought about bringing up the subject, the words stuck in her throat like dry bread.

She finally admitted the truth to herself while driving into Hollywood on Monday morning. There was no way she could sit in the narcotics administrative office eight hours a day and watch other detectives make cases while she did paperwork. More money and better hours weren't enough incentive to lure her away from the street.

If she'd brought it up, Jake would've tried to talk her into taking the position, made her feel guilty, and when she told him it wasn't going to happen, his disappointment would have ruined their weekend. Two wonderful days of familial bliss and great sex were worth the deception. She could live with never telling him the offer had been made and rejected. The bigger lie, she knew, was believing she would find the time to make it up to David.

The office was empty when she arrived. Dolores wasn't at her desk; lieutenant wasn't there; Venice squad was gone, and the skeleton crew in Hollywood had abandoned its area. Josie picked up the check-in sheet near the radio's base station. Curtis and Donny were in court. Behan had been there earlier and left the Hollywood homicide number where he could be reached.

Tomic hadn't signed the sheet yet but that didn't mean he wasn't working. She wondered where Vern and Maddy would be today. Lieutenant Watts should have reassigned them back to patrol if Behan reported what Josie had revealed to him last night.

She'd decided not dealing with the information Maddy had disclosed about her partner would be wrong . . . wrong for everybody. It sent a terrible message to the probationer and gave her training officer a pass on serious misconduct. The decision was clear and easy when Josie wasn't dead tired. Vern had been a good cop but what he did, planting drugs on a suspect, wasn't an error in judgment. It was criminal.

"Morning, Josie," Maddy said. She was in uniform standing in the doorway.

"Hey, partner," Josie said and gave her a quick hug. "Back in the blues again."

"For a while . . . IA talked to me this morning. They're going to do the sting later today."

"I told you . . ." Josie didn't finish. She could sense the young woman wasn't in the mood to hear how she had done the right thing. "Do what you've got to do and move on. This isn't about you."

"Yeah, I know. I just came to tell you the buy team offered me a spot after probation. I remembered what you said but I'm going to take it, get out of sight for a while. I think it's best . . . you know . . . let people forget."

"You're going to be a good cop no matter where you go. I'd work with you anytime, anyplace."

Big smile. "Thank you, ma'am," she said, with a lot more confidence than Josie had seen a few days ago.

"As soon as you make probation, Marge and I will take you to Nora's and teach you how to drink."

Thumbs up. "Deal," she said, did an about-face, and was gone.

It was quiet in the Hollywood squad room. Josie sat at her desk and pulled a sheet of paper out of the drawer. She wrote Clark Kent's name at the top and drew lines to everyone connected to the dead informant. The one line above him was the word "supplier," aka Raven, with a question mark and her name and Tomic's were to the right side. She could have eliminated hers but leaving it made it easier to keep Tomic's name in the mix. More lines extended to Abby, Butch, Billie, Stella . . . Billie . . . Billie seemed to be hiding something, not a big surprise, but a woman had called 911 the night Kent was killed. Could that have been Billie, she wondered. Did she see the murder happen, find the body . . . maybe kill him?

Josie decided to go to communications, pull the tape for that night, and listen to the call. If it was any one of those women connected to Kent, Josie was certain she'd recognize the voice. But first she wanted to go across the street to Hollywood's homicide table. Ask Behan if the communications tape would be available without a warrant.

"Why not," Behan answered after Josie had explained what she wanted to do. "Talk to the captain at communications. He'll have them pull it for you."

"I doubt Billie's going to be all that helpful, but I've had a feeling all along she knows much more about Kent's murder than she's admitted. With the tape, I can put some pressure on her."

"Can't be all that pleasant having to deal with the woman after what she did."

"She's used up all her favors with me. If she's down, I'll book her. Truth is, Red, I can't stand the sight of her . . . or Stella."

"They're hypes, Corsino, what'd you expect, mother of the year? Speaking of which, I got a call from the coroner. Nobody's claimed the baby's body."

"What will happen to her?"

"If nobody claims her and they can't find a relative, eventually she'll be cremated, put in a paper bag about the size of my wallet and stored inside a metal box until she's buried in a mass grave at the county cemetery in Boyle Heights."

"Right," Josie said. She couldn't say any more. Anger had paralyzed her thoughts. She shook her head and left.

The ride downtown to Communications division, next door to LAPD's Parker Center administration building, was just long enough for Josie to compose herself. The senselessness of Ashley's life and death bothered her probably more than it should have, but the final insult of that sweet baby's burial was too much for Josie to stomach. Billie would step up and claim her baby or never get another minute's peace as long as Josie worked in Hollywood.

She parked at the erector-like parking structure across the street from Parker Center and walked to communications. The captain arranged to have one of the police officers who worked a division populated mostly by civilians help her find the right recording for that night. The call had come in on the 911 emergency line and turns out it was one of two calls regarding the incident. Almost five minutes before the woman had called to report Kent's body lying in the alley, an elderly man who lived in the apartment building had dialed 911 to say he'd heard someone screaming in pain but was too frightened to go outside. "Please send someone to help," was his final plea. He gave his name and apartment number at the Paradise. The dispatcher put out the call as a code-two emergency, "screaming man, possible ADW in progress," and assigned it to that area's patrol car.

There was no doubt in Josie's mind that the female voice reporting the discovery of Kent's mangled body in the alley a few minutes later was Stella's. She knew after several replays, it had to be the little Mexican woman exaggerating her accent, an unsuccessful attempt to hide her identity.

A senior civilian supervisor had joined the uniformed officer and Josie and assisted with the search. She was the one who knew how to retrieve the tapes for that night, and she played them for

Josie, but it was just a quirk that Supervisor Phillips had also been on duty when Kent was killed.

"I remember that call so clearly," Phillips said when Josie finished listening to the recording.

"You took the call?" Josie asked.

"No, but the emergency operator was in training, so I listened in to see how she handled it."

"What did you think?"

"She did okay. I told her later she should have tried to keep the witness on the line until the patrol car got there, but the caller sounded very scared."

Josie thought for a moment and asked, "I counted two cars and a sergeant responding to the call. Is that right?"

"Correct," the uniformed officer answered. He had written down the unit numbers for the patrol cars and the supervisor and handed the sheet of paper to Josie.

"Almost done with your tour here?" she asked the young, clean-cut and obvious probationary officer.

"Yes, ma'am," he said with a grin. "Can't wait to get on the other side of that radio call."

"Enjoy this break. You'll be in the meat grinder soon enough," she said and hoped that maybe by then he'd look older than a high school senior.

Josie wanted to go back to Hollywood and pull up the reports, field interview cards, and logs from that night. She was hoping there would be something, anything that the detectives missed that might help lead to the killer, but first she had to make a stop.

She checked the motel in Hollywood where Billie and Stella had stayed but their room was empty. The manager told her Billie couldn't pay the rent and had been kicked out that morning. He hadn't seen Stella and had no idea where she might've gone. Josie searched Sunset Boulevard from West Hollywood to Normandie Avenue and found Billie hustling on the east end close to the Rampart border. This area was mostly the low-rent district. None of the younger, prettier prostitutes worked here and it was strictly a last resort for the most desperate Johns.

It was clear Billie was on her own and wasn't doing well. She wore torn shorts, a halter top, and white plastic boots that reached to her knees. There were steps near the front of a closed auto repair shop where she was sitting, slumped forward, her legs spread as if she were asleep. Josie knew better. It was most likely an opiate stupor.

When Josie got closer, she could see and smell that Billie needed a shower and shampoo. A duffel bag was wedged in the corner of the stairwell. It probably contained the few things she owned or had stolen from Stella before leaving the apartment.

"Billie," Josie said, gently kicking one of the white boots a couple of times until the woman groaned and stirred.

"Fuck off," Billie mumbled and rubbed her eyes, trying to focus.

"Wake up, I need to talk to you."

"Josie? Hey, where the fuck you been?"

"Where's Stella? I need to find her."

"Dead and rotting in a gutter, I hope," she said, using the rail to help herself stand. She was unsteady but mostly coherent now.

"Listen to me, Billie. Did Stella tell you anything about what she saw the night Kent got killed?"

"Bitch never tells me nothing . . . her and that blue-haired bastard. Hope they're both dead."

"Have you seen either of them since Ashley died?"

Billie hesitated, and her eyes narrowed as if she were attempting to recall before saying, "Ashley . . . I think they took my baby."

"Your baby's dead. You know that."

"Leave me alone. I'm sick," Billie whined and grabbed the duffel bag. "Gotta get my medicine."

She dragged the bag across Sunset to the other side of the street. Josie knew where she was going. The methadone clinic was two blocks away on the boulevard, a government-sponsored way to supplement her heroin diet. Josie knew her vow to arrest Billie at every opportunity was stupid. The woman wasn't worth the effort and her own weaknesses would eventually deliver a much more effective vengeance for Ashley's death.

The encounter was a predictable failure. Billie either didn't know where Stella was, or she was too far gone to remember. Trying to get credible information from her was pointless and believing she would care or be capable of handling her baby's funeral arrangements was naive. It was depressing, too, because Josie knew nobody would step forward to claim the baby and she couldn't afford to pay for a decent burial without putting a serious dent in her family's savings. She was willing to do it, but knew she'd have to discuss it with Jake first. That's a conversation I'd rank right up there with a root canal, she thought, getting back into her car.

There were several places she checked looking for Stella, all the usual hype hangouts in Hollywood. Stella should need a fix every four to six hours, so it would depend on when she last scored if she'd be back on the street anytime soon scrounging for another hit.

After a couple of hours, Josie had exhausted her list of probable locations and decided to go back to the office. There hadn't been any message from Tomic and she worried his Sunday romp with the cheerleader might've had some dire consequences. She drove by the bar but neither car was there and only relaxed when she parked in the space next to his car in the narcotics lot.

"Where have you been," Tomic asked as she sat beside him at the table.

He looked rested but still had a day-old beard and seemed to be grumpier than usual. She recounted her trip to communications and how she had identified Stella as the 911 caller, but was unable to locate her.

"I'll put the word out. One of my snitches will know where she's hiding," he said. "Did you hear about Vern?"

"I know they were doing the sting. What happened?"

"Nothing. He didn't take the bait. Played it by the book."

"Maybe Maddy was mistaken about what she saw," Josie said. "What do you think?"

"I think she's too smart to make that kind of mistake."

"Me too," Tomic said. "IA is going to try again, but not tell Maddy when it's going to happen. They think she might've been nervous and her body language tipped him off somehow."

"That girl is solid as a rock. If anyone blew the sting, it was IA."

"Tough allegation to prove if he doesn't take the bait. Every drug dealer that gets arrested swears he didn't have anything on him," Tomic said and added, "But their investigators are going through security videos from the businesses nearby on days Vern made arrests, so who knows what they'll find."

"We've got our own problems," Josie said and told him about her plan to look at all the logs and reports from the night Kent died and then interview the uniformed officers who were on scene. Tomic agreed to interview the officers if she'd handle the paperwork.

She wanted to interview the old man at the Paradise who made the original call to 911, but Tomic insisted that would be a waste of time.

"The old fart's gotta be ninety. Homicide guys gave up trying to make any sense out of what he was saying. He kept getting confused or going catatonic," Tomic said.

Josie wasn't willing to ignore even the slightest possibility of any clue in a murder investigation that seemed to be going nowhere, not to mention that witnesses like Butch and Stella kept disappearing, so as soon as Tomic went across the street to do the interviews, she was in her car and headed toward the Paradise Apartments.

Christopher King was only eighty-four years old but did exhibit some symptoms of dementia. He lived at the Paradise Apartments on a government voucher with food stamps and a small social security check, and managed to survive among the drug dealers, prostitutes, and other street dwellers who occupied the building.

It had taken Josie almost fifteen minutes to convince the elderly man to open his door. He was convinced she was his daughter who had come to drag him away to a mental institution. When he finally agreed to let her in, though, King was completely lucid. He studied her ID and badge before offering milk and potato chips, his favorite meal.

They sat at a small table in his surprisingly clean kitchen set in the corner of a sparsely furnished apartment. She let him ramble on about his family, his work as a carpenter, how difficult it was to live in the neighborhood. When he seemed to run out of stories, she asked if he remembered the night he had called 911 for the police.

"Certainly," he answered. "I was frightened."

"Could you tell where the screams were coming from?"

"The roof . . . I think."

Josie got up and looked out the living room window. She realized King's apartment was not only on the fourth floor but one unit away from the fire escape.

"So, almost right above you."

"Yes," he whispered, and then said a little louder, "it was so quiet that night I could hear the police radio too."

"When did you hear that?" she asked.

"Just before the poor man screamed."

"You mean after you called the police."

"No before . . . I waited for the police to help him. I could hear them shouting up there, but the man kept screaming so I called 911 . . . Isn't that right?" he asked and suddenly looked puzzled. He got quiet and folded his hands on the table. "Did I tell you about my daughter?" he asked with a faint smile.

Josie stayed with him a few more minutes but it was clear he had lost touch with current events. Now he conversed in nonsensical disjointed sentences about different times in his life. She left him at the table after he'd gone silent, staring out the window, but still she found it was difficult to discount what he'd said before the confusion kicked in. He'd been articulate up to that point and was convinced he'd heard a police radio before Kent started screaming.

The probability wasn't good that anyone would believe the old man. On the trip back to the station, Josie was still debating with herself about whether or not his recollection was reliable. Every instinct told her what he said was what he heard, the way it happened. It made sense. If there was a corrupt cop, he could've had a police radio. He'd know exactly if or when a patrol car was assigned a call at the Paradise and have ample time to escape before they arrived. The killer didn't have to come down the fire escape. He could have used the stairs or the elevator and walked out either the front or back door of the apartment building.

She had to locate Stella and find out what the little Mexican hype had seen. Street people like Stella didn't wander far from familiar territory. She'd feel safe surrounded by places she knew and among her kind. That didn't mean one of her kind wouldn't give her up for the right amount of cash and Josie had snitches who would turn in their mothers for twenty dollars.

THE RECORD clerks at Hollywood station helped Josie find most of the paperwork related to the night Kent was killed. The murder book would be with the homicide detectives, but she had already asked Behan to review it, and he couldn't find anything in there they didn't already know.

She carefully checked patrol logs to determine when each officer arrived at the hotel and how long they remained at the crime scene, and she read every FI, or field interview card, uniformed officers had made around the time of the killing. No one had gone up to the roof of the apartments until detectives arrived, but they did check the alley and around the outside of the building. Every officer working that night could be accounted for before Kent was beaten to death.

The reports also stated there wasn't a night manager at the apartments; at least he wasn't awake and at the desk until sunrise and hadn't heard anything.

She wanted to take a look at the Hollywood station kit room where the radios, other equipment, and shotguns were stored. There wasn't anyone working, but Josie located the checkout sheet for the morning of Kent's murder. Every basic car and the report car had been issued two radios. No radios had been reported missing until the next night. Bingo, she thought. A radio hadn't been checked out, but it was gone and couldn't be accounted for by the kit room officer.

She found Jack Robertson, the kit-room officer, in the break room upstairs near the men's locker room. He was end of watch but had stayed to gossip, finish a snack and cigarette before heading home.

"Some asshole swiped it . . . maybe detectives or vice or one of yours," Robertson said when Josie asked him. He was older, had thinning gray hair, and an unhealthy pallor that said these days he spent more time in the kit room than in a black-and-white. He had rolled up the sleeves of his white T-shirt and carried a pack of Camel cigarettes in one sleeve. The shirt was tucked into a high-riding pair of new jeans. It was an odd picture with his skinny old-man arms.

"Could it have been someone on the watch?" Josie asked.

"No, I'm the only one that touches those radios. They know better than to help themselves," he said, grinding the half-smoked butt into an ashtray on the table.

"Anybody could've taken one when you weren't there," Josie said.

"Door's locked when I leave until the next watch comes on."

"I got in. It was easy."

"Like I said, narco, vice, or detectives. Blue suiters know better," he said and began coughing before reaching for another cigarette.

Josie didn't respond but thought, sure they do. The same way you know those things are killing you but you keep smoking them. She left before he could light up again.

She was on her way back to the narcotics office but glanced at Nora's across the street. The grumbling in her stomach was telling her it was time for a hamburger. Josie felt disappointed because she couldn't call Marge to share dinner and a glass of wine. Until last week, they hadn't seen each other or talked for years, but their friendship had remained as solid as it had been during probation.

Well, screw it, she thought. I'm starving, and she isn't here. As soon as she crossed the street, Josie saw the motorcycle parked near the restaurant. There couldn't be two bikes as big and unique as that one.

It took a few minutes for her eyes to adjust to the dim lights inside Nora's, but someone as large as Too Tall was easy to spot. He was sitting at the end of the bar drinking a beer. She slid into an empty booth in the corner and the bartender called out, "hamburger, fries, and Cabernet . . . for two?"

"Just me," Josie shouted back.

"Miss America's not coming?" he asked.

"Not today," Josie said. She knew he had a crush on Marge and suspected that half the time he never charged her pretty blonde friend for meals or drinks.

Before Josie's food arrived, Too Tall left the bar and carried his mug of beer to her table. He was dressed in full biker gear, black leather jacket, shabby Levi's, and boots. She wondered how he could see in this place with those tinted glasses.

"I was hoping you'd come here. We need to talk," he said, sitting across from her.

"Tomic told me you called."

"Look, I know Tomic doesn't believe me, but I'm not lying. Abby is family, but I'm very aware she's evil scum and there's plenty of shit she's done that should put her in prison, but I honestly don't think she killed your snitch."

"How can you know that?" Josie asked. "She could've hired anyone to do it."

"No, she wouldn't kill Kent . . . I'm certain . . . and definitely not McCray. She was trying to help him," he said and finished the last swallow of beer. He pointed at the glass when the waitress brought Josie's food and she returned with another full mug.

Josie listened but she wasn't convinced that Abby hadn't ordered both the killings. Too Tall thought he knew his cousin, but Josie understood how the criminal mind worked. Affection had nothing to do with whether someone like Abby or her father killed.

"I found a note in your desk after you left," she said, changing the subject because she remembered something she'd forgotten to ask him. "It looked like a clue where you wrote about having to find the street competition and had Abby's initials. What was that all about?" she asked.

He wrinkled his forehead and looked confused for a moment before saying, "Abby told Art that her street dealers were getting hit hard. She thought somebody was targeting them and wanted to know who the competition was."

"She thought one of our informants was snitching on her dealers to eliminate the competition?"

"It was bullshit. Art went through all the informant packages and nobody was getting paid for info on street dealers. Her dealers were just stupid. Patrol caught some of them. Tomic and Curtis got the rest."

"What are you going to do now?" Josie asked. "If you're so sure Abby's not involved in the murders, are you done working with her?"

"No, I think I might be able to get you a connection to the hitmen on Sergeant Bailey. I'll stay in the fold a while longer," he said, stood, and finished his beer. "I'll be in touch," he added and put the empty mug on the bar before leaving. He disappeared from her sight, but she could hear his boots on the lobby's tile floor and the rattle of the wallet chain in his back pocket with each step. She wasn't sure if Tony Gilbert had chosen a side, the police or the Testas'. Maybe he had and was playing her for a fool, but her instincts were telling her to stick with him a while longer.

She finished her meal and the wine. It was late, and she was curious to hear what Tomic had learned from his interviews. She paid the bill. The bartender always called her "Sweet thing" but never offered her a free meal. He seemed to know it was pointless.

Her partner was at his desk when she got back to the office. Everyone had returned. Dolores was with the lieutenant. Curtis and

Donny were writing reports, and since the Venice squad detectives were in their office, the noise level was back to deafening decibels.

She told Tomic about Christopher King at the Paradise Apartments and what she had learned at Hollywood station, but didn't mention the meeting with Too Tall. He had made up his mind about the ex-cop and she wasn't in the mood to argue with him.

Tomic had talked with all the officers who'd worked the morning Kent died. None of them had gone up to the roof of the apartments until detectives arrived and none of them had seen anyone near or inside the building. Two officers and a detective had talked to King that morning and all of them diagnosed him as "feebleminded."

"I believe Christopher King heard a police radio before Kent started screaming," Josie said. And she added before Tomic could argue, "He can be clearheaded for brief periods and there's a radio missing from the Hollywood kit room which kind of supports his story."

"It wasn't a Hollywood copper King heard on that roof; every one of them and both supervisors on morning watch are accounted for right up to his 911 call," Tomic said. "If he heard a police broadcast, it was another division or somebody with your missing radio."

"A cop killed Superman. I can feel it in my gut and I believe Stella might've seen him before she made that call. We've got to find her," Josie said.

"I've got a half-dozen snitches out looking for her. She's hiding . . . maybe with Butch."

"Corsino," Lieutenant Watts shouted from his office.

Josie sighed, slumped in her chair, and rested her forehead on the table. "Tell him I'm dead," she whispered.

Curtis laughed and yelled, "Should I wake her up, boss?"

"Token," Josie mumbled, grinning at the black detective and getting up.

"Affirmative action," Curtis said, pointing at her.

"Look, the bonus-point babies are fighting," Donny said.

"We never needed bonus points to get better stats than you, partner," Curtis said, high-fiving with Josie.

"Close the door," Watts ordered as soon as she entered his office.

She did and sat in the chair in front of his desk and waited.

"Whatever you decide, the captain is thinking about transferring you to the admin office next DP. It would be for your own good," he said quickly before she could interrupt. "Of course, a promotion would come with the move. He'll probably transfer your partner, Curtis, and his partner to different squads, too, and assign eight new detectives in Hollywood."

"Hollywood finally gets a full squad," Josie said sarcastically.

"This isn't a laughing matter. It's obvious this particular division is a breeding ground for corruption. There are too many temptations in Hollywood and it's too easy to cut corners."

Josie knew she should be upset, angry, even a little insulted but was surprised how calm she felt at that moment.

"Lieutenant, I understand Captain Clark can move me or any detective anywhere he wants in his division," she said and saw Watts visibly relax. He had expected an argument, but she wasn't going to plead her case. The deployment period ended in two weeks. That was plenty of time to find Kent's killer. If they found the dirty cop, then she would fight, not beg, to stay with what was left of her squad in Hollywood.

"Ah . . . well, good, I'm happy to see you've come to see things our way. It's for the best," he said, stood, and held out his hand. "I'd appreciate if you kept this information to yourself. I'd prefer to break the news to the others myself."

She shook his hand and asked, "Is that all, Lieutenant?"

"Yes, but you're welcome to take a few days off before the transfer if you'd like, get yourself prepared, buy a few new outfits suitable for an office."

"Not necessary," she said and turned as she closed his door again, almost laughing at his bewildered expression.

She immediately told Tomic, Curtis, and Donny what the lieutenant had said. Curtis was ready to storm into Watts's office and confront the man, but she convinced him and the others it wasn't the right time.

"You're right. There's nothing to justify transferring any of us," Josie said. "We're the ones who caught Too Tall and Art; we uncovered the theft at Property division and unfounded the complaint against Tomic. But none of that matters with Kent's murder unsolved. There's still a cloud over our heads."

"So, we're fucked," Tomic said.

"Not if we can prove his killer is some other cop. Moving us then would be punitive and the union should jump in to help."

"Suits wet their collective pants when the union threatens them," Donny said.

"But as long as they can make the case there might be another dirty cop, they can argue it could be any one of us," Curtis said.

Josie told them what Christopher King had said. She believed somebody was using Hollywood division's missing radio off-duty to avoid running into patrol or plainclothes units. The killer could monitor every call for service as he dealt with Kent on the roof of the Paradise. As soon as the emergency operator put out Stella's information, the killer would've heard it and had plenty of time to retreat before the black-and-whites arrived.

"I think the real question is how much did Stella actually see," Josie said.

"There's only one way to know for sure. We gotta track her down," Curtis said.

"Find her before the killer does," Donny added.

Tomic left the room and came back a few minutes later with Billie's informant package.

"Don't get your hopes up," he said. "If Stella doesn't want to be found, we aren't going to find her."

"She's abandoned Billie to rot on the street. That's not going to help," Josie said pointing at the package.

"All Billie's best contacts came from Stella. Stella never talked to me, but Billie blabbed about practically everyone her little Mexican knew or did business with," Tomic said.

"Split up the names and we'll help you look for her," Curtis offered and gave Donny a stare that warned, don't you dare argue about this.

Tomic wrote down several names and places and reluctantly gave the list to Curtis. He and Josie both knew Curtis would hold on to those names and use them to put together his own investigations at some point. However, if they didn't find Stella and get her to talk, they would probably be forced out of Hollywood and that information would be worthless to all of them.

Her partner did keep the best contacts for himself. He knew a half-dozen places where Billie had told him Stella routinely went for drugs. There were two crash pads Billie had used in the last year, but Tomic was certain Stella was the one who had introduced her to both those locations.

With a fifty-dollar incentive, one of the drug dealers off Hollywood Boulevard admitted selling four balloons of Mexican brown heroin to Stella two days earlier. He said she looked nervous, a little jumpy, but otherwise seemed normal for a hype or needle junkie, not sick or injured in any way. Stella didn't give him any information on where she was staying, but he agreed to call if she returned—for another promised fifty-dollar reward.

"If she's buying here, I'm guessing she's staying somewhere nearby," Josie said after they got back in Tomic's car.

"One of her prior crash pads is on Franklin near Cahuenga Boulevard, that one-story dump just north of the church," Tomic said. "Let's try there. It's close enough."

The building was an abandoned coffee shop with boarded up windows surrounded by an unmarked asphalt parking lot scarred by large cracks and potholes. It was dark, but the streetlight and the church security lights next door provided enough illumination to see the property. Weeds grew in every crevice, flourished anywhere there should've been grass, and nearly covered the front of the building. A blanket of cobwebs hung from the corners of the padlocked door and sheets of plywood had been nailed over all the windows.

"Home sweet home. How do you suppose they get inside?" Josie asked.

"The roof. Billie said there's a ladder stashed under the dumpster out back."

He parked in front of the church and they walked across the lot to the rear of the building. A ladder was leaning against the wall close to the dumpster. Out of habit, Josie lifted the lid of the large trash container to check it and was immediately sorry. It smelled like a septic tank . . . worse. She coughed, and her stomach tightened, but she managed not to throw up the hamburger and Cabernet she was tasting for the second time.

They climbed up to the roof and she could see the trap door had been left open, but no light or noise was coming from inside. She stood directly over the opening.

Tomic took his flashlight out of his jacket pocket, but she stopped him before he could shine it into the hole.

"Let's just go down. Whoever's in there might be sleeping or passed out," Josie whispered.

He nodded and followed her down a steel ladder inside the building. It was cold, and Josie could smell burning charcoal. At least they were smart enough to leave the trap door open for some ventilation, she thought. Most of the time in crash pads during the winter, the occupants light a charcoal fire and try to make the room airtight for warmth. The only way they're found again is when the smell of rotting corpses seeps through the cracks and overwhelms the neighborhood.

A couple of candles on the floor and the glow from a portable barbeque created enough light for Josie to see most of the large room. Several booths were still intact, and she could make out what looked like three bodies curled up on separate padded benches. Tomic checked behind the counter and in the kitchen. No one else was there.

A young boy and an older woman slept in one of the booths on either side of a post where at one time there should've been a table. Stella was asleep a few feet away in a corner booth. She didn't have a blanket like the other two but was bundled in a wool coat over a heavy knit sweater, a knit cap that covered her ears, a scarf, wool gloves, and boots. The charcoal fire had been placed between the two booths and a few feet from the candles.

"Stella," Josie said loudly enough to wake the older woman. She sat up, looked at her boy who was snoring softly, and laid back on the bench. This was not her concern.

The little Mexican woman groaned and turned onto her back, but her eyes were still closed. Josie moved closer and shook her shoulder. Startled, Stella sat up with a knife in her right hand.

"What? What the fuck?" she mumbled, waving the knife and trying to focus on her assailant.

Josie and Tomic took a step back and unholstered their weapons, "Drop the knife, Stella," Josie ordered. "It's Detective Corsino and Tomic."

She rested the knife on her leg until Josie told her again, louder, to drop it on the floor. She did and Tomic picked it up.

"Why are you here? Leave me alone," she mumbled, slumping against the back of the booth. "I'm sick."

"No, you're not," Tomic said. "Take a hit so you can talk to us."

"You mean so you can arrest my ass."

"We don't want to arrest you," Josie said. "We need to ask you some questions . . . here or at Hollywood station."

Stella rubbed her eyes and fumbled in a backpack she'd been using as a pillow. She pulled out a cheap plastic makeup bag where she kept her disposable needle, spoon with a piece of dried cotton stuck in the bowl, a thin leather strap, and a small rolled-up balloon the size of a pea. She slipped off her coat, rolled up the sweater sleeve, and tightened the strap around her upper left arm. Leaning over one of the candles, she heated the spoon containing a few drops of water from a bottle on the floor mixed with the brown powdered heroin from the balloon, stuck the needle into the now saturated cotton, and drew in the liquid. She injected the drug into a well-used vein on her inner arm.

Her expression softened. In seconds, her life had morphed from the depths of hopelessness and misery to soul-numbing pleasure. There should be some moral and legal dilemma here, Josie thought, but it was a little late to feel guilt. The deed was done. Stella got what she wanted, and Josie would too.

~ EIGHTEEN ~

While they were under the influence of heroin, most addicts were eager to talk about everything except maybe their dealer's name, but Stella was different. She became sullen and quiet. Josie figured Ashley's death might've had something to do with her hostile attitude, so after several uncooperative grunts to questions, she decided to bring up the subject that was certain to get a response—Billie's dead baby.

"I went to the morgue today to see Ashley," Josie said, lying. "Did you know no one's claimed that little girl's body?"

Stella looked up. The hard stare melted. This was something she wanted to talk about. "I'm all she's got," she said softly, rubbing her left arm. She was fighting the need to nod off.

"No, you're not, I'll claim her if I have to. She's not going to be buried without a name . . . in a hole with a bunch of bums and criminals," Josie said. The offer was a ploy to get Stella to talk but Josie knew it wasn't just that.

Dry-eyed, Stella stared at her for several seconds as if she were attempting to decipher any signs of deceit.

"Will you take me to see her?" Stella asked.

"Yes," Josie said. "If you help us, I'll let you come with me." She caught herself before admitting the cremation might've already taken place.

Tomic found a couple more pieces of candle and placed them on the back of the booth. The additional light made it easier to see Stella's face. He knew it was impossible to interrogate someone without reading body language and seeing the eyes.

"What do you want from me?"

"I listened to the 911 tape; I know it was you who made the call about Kent."

Stella shifted her weight on the bench, looked up at the ceiling. Everything in her nature was opposed to giving the police information and Josie could sense she was fighting the urge to go silent again.

"Yeah, so what," she said with one last attempt at bravado.

"So, what did you see?" Tomic demanded. He was standing behind Josie and getting impatient with her kinder gentler approach.

Stella looked directly at Josie and said, "All of it . . . me and Butch was there."

"On the roof . . . you saw Kent killed?" Josie asked, glancing back over her shoulder at Tomic.

Stella took a deep breath, exhaled, and leaned against what was left of the padded booth. She slowly began her story. That night, Kent was in his best party mood because the next day he planned to give Tomic the name of his drug supplier, a dirty cop. Later, he and Butch could take the cocaine they'd stolen and drive up north to sell it. If his scheme worked, the supplier would be so busy trying to stay out of jail, he wouldn't have time to worry about them. Kent smoked several rocks that night to celebrate and Butch had sold enough of the coke to buy himself and Stella a couple hits of rare China white, the best heroin she'd had in years. She remembered Kent had been freebasing for nearly an hour before she passed out near a heating vent where it was warm with Butch curled up like a puppy beside her.

Shouting and loud noises woke her. It was dark, but she could make out Kent and another man standing near the roof door. She couldn't hear what they were saying, but the man kept punching

Kent and yelling, "Where is it! Give it up, fag!" He began hitting him with a baseball bat until Kent fell on the ground and didn't move. His hands were behind his back and he didn't defend himself, but Stella could hear him moaning and crying for help.

"He's making these sick weird noises like a dog or something," she said.

"Did you hear a police radio?" Josie asked.

"When?"

"While the man was beating Kent."

"Yeah . . . Butch got scared, said he was a pig . . . sorry, a cop."

"You didn't recognize him?" Tomic asked.

"Nah, I don't know no cops . . . except you two . . . anyway, I never seen his face," Stella said, looking down.

Josie didn't believe she hadn't recognized the man, but pointing a finger at anyone, even a dirty cop was a step too far for someone like her.

"Where's Butch?" Josie asked.

"Took off as soon as he could . . . never seen him that scared."

"Where is he now?" Josie repeated.

"Said he wasn't never coming back to Hollywood . . . wanted me to go but I couldn't . . . you know . . . the baby," she said. Her voice was barely audible, and Josie couldn't understand the last few words.

"So he dumped you, took the coke, and split," Tomic said.

"It's not like that," Stella said, shaking her head. "You don't understand nothing."

"I understand you're sleeping in this pigsty and he's somewhere sitting on kilos of cocaine worth a small fortune."

Stella pulled her coat closer around her neck and got quiet.

"Do you know where he's gone?" Josie asked again. Stella shook her head and Josie said, "If that cop finds him before we do, you know Butch is a dead man, right?"

"I know cops protect each other," she whispered.

"We arrested Detective Gilbert. He got fired. We'll get this guy too, with or without you, but if you help, we might be able to catch him before he kills Butch."

Stella stared blankly at her and Josie knew the conversation was done. They agreed to meet around eleven the next morning in front of the church on the adjoining property. Josie would drive her downtown and arrange for a viewing of the baby's body at the morgue. It wasn't as big a deal as Josie made it sound but she wanted Stella to feel indebted to her and Tomic. More importantly, she wanted to follow the little hype after the viewing, knowing that eventually she'd lead them to Butch. When they left the morgue, Josie would have Curtis and Donny waiting to start the surveillance. She was certain it wouldn't take more than a day or two before Stella led them to the skinny blue-haired hype. Her experience told her Stella's refusal to talk about Butch meant she was protecting him and she knew exactly where he and the stolen cocaine would be.

Street people were geniuses at surviving, but not always the most cunning liars. Everything about Stella told Josie she was in a holding pattern, waiting to reconnect with Butch. The two addicts had to know Kent's killer would be searching for them, trying to find the contraband, so they'd split up. Stella had all her belongings and was in a place where someone with cash or savvy wouldn't stay. Money was never a problem for Stella. She always had enough for a place to live, food and clothes, so it was unlikely anyone would look for her at the coffee shop crash pad. This was the sort of place someone like Billie would call home.

The possibilities for where Butch might be hiding were endless. He was a street hustler and among his male clients there had to be several who would be willing to take him home for short periods of time. That would explain why Stella couldn't go with him. Josie hoped if Butch saw Kent's killer and recognized him that he'd stay hidden until she and Tomic could find him and keep him alive long enough to identify their corrupt cop.

~ NINETEEN ~

After Tomic dropped her off at the Hollywood office, Josie found a message taped to her phone. One of the detectives in the Venice squad had left it to let Josie know her husband had called and needed her to be home early to babysit. The call had been taken hours earlier.

If Dolores had been there, she would have reached Josie on the radio and told her to call home, but at this time of night, communications were haphazard at best.

Jake answered the home phone after several rings. She expected him to be upset, but he calmly told her not to worry about it.

"When I didn't hear from you, I figured you didn't get my message. I came home early," he said.

"Where's your mom? Is she okay?"

"She fell . . . missed the bottom step of our stairs and twisted her knee, nothing serious."

"That's not good at her age," Josie said. She was genuinely concerned about her mother-in-law but didn't like the calm detached tone of Jake's voice. He was being much too understanding about her not getting the message. There should have been some recriminations. This was his perfect opportunity to harp on the demands of her current job, the abandonment of her child, and the need to find a better position with regular hours. He was acting so calm and considerate that it was pissing her off.

"They've offered me a promotion in the admin unit. In a few weeks I should be home every night on time. We won't need your mom's help anymore."

The silence on the other end of the line told her the announcement had achieved the desired effect. His condescending, selfless attitude had been intended to make her feel bad. It didn't, but she knew her news would leave him speechless and a bit confused. She'd taken away his reason to feel superior.

"That's great," he said finally. "That will make our lives so much easier."

No, that will make your life easier, she thought, but said, "You'll have to help out for the next two weeks and after that I should be there when David gets home from school."

She could hear the change in his attitude now. He sounded happy. She'd made him believe their lives were about to change dramatically and he would have a wife to come home to every night. None of it was completely true . . . except the job offer, that was real. But if things worked out and she had her way, there would be no transfer. She would stay in Hollywood and hopefully be the new Detective III to replace Behan. She'd have more control over her hours, but it wouldn't be an office job.

Nevertheless, things were going to change. Nonna could go home and rest her twisted knee forever because Josie had already decided to hire a fulltime nanny/housekeeper. One way or another, in two weeks she was going to be a Detective III, and that would give her the means to pay someone to help with David and do the housework, but this time the support would come from an employee who wouldn't try to run her life or interfere in her marriage.

She wanted to share her real intentions with her husband and have him be supportive and happy for her but knew if he didn't believe she was changing assignments, it would push him away and back into the annoying role of resident martyr. It was selfish, but she needed time to concentrate on finding Kent's killer and keeping her squad together.

For the next two weeks, she'd be able to work hard, go home and enjoy his company, have a peaceful family life, and prepare him for that moment when the proverbial "other shoe" would fall.

THE NEXT morning, she got David ready for school and waited until his bus drove away. Jake left early but promised to be home when the boy got back from school. She told him about her plan to hire help and he readily agreed. Even without her promotion, he said they could afford it and seemed relieved his mother wouldn't be needed to babysit any longer. The possibility that Nonna might've been getting on his nerves hadn't occurred to Josie, but she felt better knowing if she failed to find the killer and got transferred to the admin unit, she could survive being miserable at work without the added aggravation of coming home every night to the other Mrs. Corsino.

Dolores was attempting to contact her on the radio as Josie backed out of the driveway and waved at the grumpy neighbor across the street. She wanted to know Josie's ETA at the office.

"I'm on my way. Tell Tomic to wait," Josie answered.

"He's already in the field with the odd couple," Dolores said. The odd couple was her nickname for Curtis and Donny.

"What's up?" Josie asked.

"Don't know, but the boss is with them." The boss was what she called Behan. Dolores had a nickname for Lieutenant Watts, too, but "puppet brain" wasn't something she'd ever use on the radio.

"Homicide?" Josie asked.

"Don't know."

"Location?"

"Hollywood and Normandie."

"Please don't let it be Stella" was the only thought Josie had during what seemed like an endless ride into Hollywood. She got off the freeway at Western and drove east toward Rampart division.

It was easy to find her partner. Emergency lights and traffic congestion were the obvious signs of police activity. She drove past the commotion, parked off the boulevard, and walked back across Normandie to where yellow tape blocked the sidewalk and the westbound traffic for at least a block.

What she saw shouldn't have surprised her, but it did. By all odds, Billie should have been dead years ago and her lifestyle would've killed most people, but she'd persisted. Josie saw her as sister to the cockroach, surviving in the shadows on other people's scraps, exposed to diseases bred in filth and garbage that would have wiped out most of the pampered Purell-addicted population.

"OD'd," Tomic said, as she stood over the body.

Billie was dressed in the same outfit Josie had seen the day before, but a piece of rubber tubing was tied around her left bicep and a disposable hypodermic needle stuck out of her lower arm.

"Hot load," Behan said. He and the odd couple were watching from a few feet away.

"Definitely not Hollywood heroin," Curtis said. "She'd have to shoot up a gallon of that stuff just to get down."

"Last night Stella told us she and Butch got hold of some China White. Maybe Billie had a taste of that," Tomic said, glancing at Josie.

"Paramedic was saying he's rolled on a couple fentanyl calls . . . both DOA. He thinks this looks like it might be more of the same," Behan said.

"Billie couldn't afford that stuff . . . she was barely getting by feeding her habit with free methadone," Josie said.

"Somebody gave it to her," Curtis said.

Josie knelt beside the body. She took a closer look at the injection site. The needle was still touching Billie's open right hand with the tip inserted in the vein. She died before she could remove it. No other fresh puncture wounds were visible. Her hand was filthy with dirt under the broken nails and caked between the fingers. Body odor mixed with the strong smell of human feces forced Josie to stand and move away.

"There aren't any other fresh injection sites. She hasn't had anything else for a while," Josie said, coughing to clear her lungs.

"We'll treat it like a homicide," Behan said. "Let's see what security videos or witnesses have to say."

Josie filled Behan in about the meeting with Stella and that she had promised to take her to the morgue to see the baby's body.

"If you can find probable cause, arrest her," Behan said. "I can't think why anybody would go to the trouble of intentionally killing this particular whore unless she knew something she shouldn't, and it's no secret everything Billie knew Stella told her."

"I'll take her to see Ashley," Josie said and hesitated before saying, "She'll be down so I could arrest her, but I'd rather not." She knew Behan was right, but she explained how she was counting on Stella to lead them to Butch. Besides, if they kept her under surveillance, she'd have round-the-clock police protection. Behan wasn't convinced but said he trusted Josie and agreed to her plan.

"If she gets away from you, I wouldn't bet on the odds of her staying alive," Behan added. "Seems like Kent and his friends are going down like ducks in a carnival shooting gallery."

Tomic and Josie got to the church parking lot about fifteen minutes early. They decided to wait in the car rather than make the trek onto the roof again. A few minutes after eleven, Tomic got impatient and climbed down into the crash pad. Stella was gone; the mother, young boy, and all their belongings were gone. Josie contacted Curtis on the radio and asked him to check the other places Tomic had given him.

It was nearly two hours later when Tomic decided to call off the search. The little Mexican hype had burrowed into one of her hiding places and both he and Josie knew they weren't going to find her without a snitch or a lot of luck.

When they got back to the office, Josie called the coroner's office. There was a slim possibility Stella had found the courage and the means to get downtown on her own. One of the morgue assistants remembered a woman with an accent calling very early that morning to ask about viewing a baby Jane Doe who was brought in the day Ashley died. He told her the body had been cremated, but she was welcome to come in and claim the remains.

"Mystery solved," Tomic said, after Josie repeated the assistant's story. "She wanted to see a body not an envelope full of crispy critter."

"No Stella, no Butch . . . what now?" Josie asked as her partner tried to shush her. He had answered a phone call and kept waving his hand to get her to stop talking. She was imagining herself sitting at a desk in the admin unit, just steps down the hall from Captain Clark's office. It made her stomach turn. There had to be another way to find Butch, she thought, as Tomic slammed the phone back into the cradle.

"Son of a bitch," he whispered, grinning at Josie. He got up quickly and motioned for her to follow. "Let's go, pretty lady. Our dirtbag dealer wants his fifty-dollar finder fee. Stella's waiting at his place for a drop-off."

"God must have a really weird sense of humor," she mumbled, following him to his car.

As Tomic pulled out of the parking lot, Josie radioed Curtis to tell him they'd located their subject. She asked if he could set up nearby and be ready to help in the surveillance. He immediately agreed and a couple of minutes later said he was in position waiting.

Josie saw Maddy in civilian clothes getting into an orange Volkswagen bug in the Hollywood officers' parking lot as Tomic drove by and she asked him to stop and go back before the young woman drove away. She was end-of-watch and that gave Josie an idea.

"We'll need somebody to get out on foot and Stella's only seen Maddy once when she was really strung out. I don't think she'd remember her."

Tomic stopped the car and said, "Not a good idea, Corsino. Nobody's okayed her working overtime with us."

"I'll get Behan to talk to her lieutenant. We can't get anywhere near Stella. She'd make us in a second."

Tomic wouldn't look at Josie and said, "I'm not working with her."

"Why not? She's a good cop . . ." Josie's voice trailed off. Sometimes it took a second for the obvious to sink into her uncomplicated brain. "Is this because of Vern?" she asked.

"I don't want to work with her," he said, emphatically.

"You said you believed her . . . that she saw him plant dope," Josie said and waited a few seconds until she realized what should have been clear after years of working with this man. Maddy had broken his unwritten rule—always protect your partner. Vern needed to be caught but she shouldn't have been the one to do it. Tomic had no problem with dirty cops going to jail but, in his world, other cops shouldn't be the ones to make it happen.

Curtis broadcast that Stella had just purchased her heroin and was walking southbound in the alley parallel to Western. Without another word, Tomic drove up Wilcox toward Hollywood Boulevard.

"Just for the record," Josie said, buckling her seat belt. "You're full of shit."

"So I've been told."

Josie knew it was pointless to argue. It was more than prejudice with him; it was a creed, his code of conduct. In her opinion, Vern was dirty and needed to go down, and she didn't care who made that happen or how. She also knew it was personal with Tomic. He would never badmouth Maddy, and no one would ever know why he preferred not to work with her. Other coppers might assume it was because she was a woman which would make him look small-minded. Similar bad behavior from older officers certainly hadn't hurt Josie's career.

She could insist he work with Maddy, but she would never do that to her partner . . . the irony of that decision didn't escape her. Maddy was tough, and she would be fine. The real shame was they didn't have the benefit of her talent now when they needed it.

Stella was walking so she hadn't gone very far by the time they arrived in the area. Donny was on foot, too, with a radio and was able to follow her from a distance in the alley. He was the only one of the four of them who hadn't spent any time with Stella. She might've seen him in the office, but the little Mexican rarely got arrested. This was one occasion Josie was grateful Donny preferred paperwork to the street.

"We've gone about a block . . . now she's walking back toward Western," Donny said. His breathing sounded labored. All those hours working at his desk, drinking coffee, hadn't done much for his cardio. After a few minutes, he broadcast that Stella was back on Western and had settled on a bus bench in front of a check-cashing store.

Tomic parked a couple of blocks away and Josie was able to take the point from their car.

"I've got her, Curtis. You can pick up your partner. Sounds like he's about to have a stroke," Josie broadcast.

"That's the most he's moved in a year," Curtis said.

"Funny," Donny said. "Like the rest of you are in better shape."

Nobody responded because he was right. While most uniformed cops had regular hours and spent time running or lifting weights before or after their shift, dope cops never seemed to stop working. Time spent in court, on the street, or building cases didn't allow for a healthy lifestyle. Exercise and decent meals gave way to fast food and a few hours' sleep.

Several buses stopped near Stella's bench, but she didn't move. She hadn't checked the schedule and didn't seem to be watching for any particular bus. Whenever a black-and-white drove by, she looked down and raised her coat collar to hide most of her face. She was still wearing the knit cap pulled down over her ears and hugged the backpack on her lap.

She sat there for ten minutes before a car stopped about twenty feet from the bench. Stella didn't move, staring at the older model Chevy for several seconds before the passenger window rolled down and only then did she jump up, hurry to the rear passenger door, and climb into the back seat.

Josie calmly broadcast exactly what she was seeing. There were two people in the front seat, but the windows were tinted, and she couldn't describe them. The car drove off southbound as Donny's voice immediately came over the radio to say they had the point. Josie and Tomic slid down in their seats not to be seen, but there was so much traffic on the busy street, she doubted that precaution was necessary.

She'd been able to copy the front license plate number and while Tomic concentrated on staying close to the surveillance, she got Dolores to run the plate. It came back in a few minutes "not in file." The only license plates she knew that usually came back "not in file" belonged to law enforcement.

"This guy drives like a maniac," Donny reported, and Josie could hear screeching tires in the background. He inadvertently keyed the microphone again and yelled "Watch it!" Curtis was a good driver, but tailing another car was always dangerous.

"Don't lose him," Josie ordered.

"Can you take the point for a few miles?" Donny asked. "We've had to do some crazy stuff to keep up. I'm pretty sure they didn't make us as cops but better safe."

They weren't that far behind and Tomic quickly got into position to follow the Chevy and Curtis dropped back into traffic. They had taken the Hollywood Freeway to the 110 Freeway southbound. The driver seemed to slow down a little as soon as he transitioned onto the second freeway.

"Something might've made them hinky at first, but he's driving better now," Tomic said. He had relaxed and given the Chevy a lot of room.

It wasn't until the car got off that freeway and onto the Artesia Freeway headed west that Josie realized where they might be going. That freeway ended in a few miles and became Artesia Boulevard; the road would take them through the South Bay beach cities. There was only one reason she could think of that might bring Stella and Butch here, but it seemed so implausible.

She didn't say anything to Tomic and it was he who mentioned it first.

"You remember who lives out here, right?" he asked.

"Yes," she said and keyed the microphone. She gave Curtis the address and directions to Kent's sister Beverly's house and told him to set up there and wait for the Chevy's arrival. Josie wondered how the fragile, seemingly gentle woman could've gotten mixed up in her brother's dirty business.

The car didn't go directly to the house but stopped in Torrance Old Town at a coffee shop next door to an army surplus outlet. It wasn't a big surprise that Butch was the crazy driver. He got out of the car, followed by Stella, and they both went to the front passenger door to assist Beverly. Even with help, she struggled to lift herself out of the cramped space and stood on the sidewalk for a few seconds to regain her balance before using a cane and leading the way into the coffee shop.

Josie left Tomic to watch the front of the place from his car and she walked across the street, through an alley that ran behind the stores, and entered the back door of an upholstery business directly across the street from the coffee shop. The worker in the back room was stapling the cushioned seat onto a chair frame and only stopped long enough to glance at Josie's badge. The owner was an older woman who sat behind her desk in the front room and chatted in a one-sided conversation as Josie tried to focus on the trio across the street.

They sat at a table close to the coffee shop's front window, so it was possible to watch them. Beverly seemed to be doing most of the talking. The little 8x30 monocular Josie had borrowed from Tomic made it easier to see their expressions and no one looked happy to be there. At one point, Stella leaned back and folded her arms, stared defiantly at the table. The blue had disappeared from Butch's shaved head and he'd removed the studs from above his eye and lip, but Josie had no problem recognizing him. He had cleaned up but still looked like a skinny hype.

Beverly's frustration was very apparent and eventually she stopped talking and with some difficulty got out of her chair. She slapped away Butch's hand as he tried to help and nearly took a tumble before regaining her balance.

"Big sister is not pleased with her little wards," Josie thought before thanking the owner who hadn't stopped talking. She jogged back to Tomic's car, filled him in on what she'd seen, then asked Curtis over the radio if he and Donny were set up on Beverly's house.

Two clicks told her they were. She watched Beverly and the others get back into the car and drive in the direction of the house.

"They're coming at you, Curtis. As soon as they get inside we'll door knock and see if she's got any more surprises in there. Can you and Donny cover the back?" Josie asked and got two more clicks.

Butch parked the Chevy in the driveway and this time Beverly allowed him to help her. They walked slowly to the front door and Josie waited until the three of them were inside and the door closed before she and Tomic approached the house.

Within seconds, she and her partner were on the porch. He rang the doorbell and knocked. Beverly opened it immediately with Butch and Stella standing behind her. Their expressions were a mix of surprise and confusion.

The two hypes turned to run until Josie shouted, "Don't bother, we've got officers covering the back."

They stopped and Butch crouched in the middle of the room and stayed in that position while Stella looked back and forth from the front door to the hallway behind her. Beverly tried to help Butch stand again; he was visibly shaken, tears running down the sides of his face.

"I'm dead . . . I'm so fucking dead," he whispered, shaking his head but not looking at anyone.

"We're not going to kill you," Josie said and ordered everyone to sit on the couch while Tomic let Curtis and Donny into the house.

Beverly tried to calm Butch, but it wasn't until Josie sat on the coffee table in front of him and ordered him to "stop acting like a baby" that he finally looked up and stopped crying.

"Why don't you leave me alone?" he pleaded.

"Because you're a thief and dope dealer," Josie said and turned to Beverly. "You want to explain to me what these two misfits are doing in your home?"

"No, I don't . . . but I will," she said and glanced at Butch. "Brian, or Butch, I guess you call him, was very important to my brother. In his way, Clark loved him. Brian came to me and I gave him a safe place to stay."

"Safe from what?" Tomic asked.

"One of you," she said. "He told Stella where he was, so she had to come too. We were afraid he might find her, kill her like Billie."

"Who might find her?" Tomic asked again, louder this time.

"How do we know you're not like him . . . you'll kill all of us," Beverly said. She was frightened and the palsy in her hands grew more intense.

"If we were dirty, you'd probably be dead already," Curtis said. "We want him caught as much as you."

"Please tell them," Beverly said, looking at Butch. "I trust her . . . this has to end." She did look exhausted and much frailer than she had when Josie met her.

Butch hesitated and studied Josie's face as if trying to find proof she wouldn't harm him. It wasn't until Stella whispered, "Tell her," that Butch began to talk. He told them he and Kent faked their fight outside The Carnival. Kent's plan was to steal ten kilos of cocaine from the Raven and blame Butch who was then supposed to disappear and stay hidden until Clark introduced him to Tomic as the snitch who would give up the dirty cop.

"He was gonna tell me a name to give you. Cop goes to jail . . . we could sell his stash and we're rich."

"How did he get his hands on the ten kilos? No dealer's going to trust a guy like Kent with that much dope," Tomic said.

"He accidentally found the stash pad."

"Where."

Butch shrugged and said, "Wouldn't never tell me."

"So what happened to this perfect plan you and the other genius put in motion?" Tomic asked.

The problem, Butch told them was that Clark had to sell some of the stolen coke to his regular customers for traveling money and the Raven found out. He killed Clark trying to make him reveal where he'd hidden the rest. Butch concluded by claiming he was hiding on the roof that night and saw Kent's murderer.

"You recognized him," Josie said.

Butch nodded. "It was Officer Fisher," he said. "I seen him clear as I see you . . . no uniform, just regular clothes . . . and I heard his police radio."

"Vern Fisher," Tomic said. "You're saying you saw him kill Kent."

Butch nodded again. "I ain't lying . . . Billie figured it out. Look what happened to her. That dude's fucking crazy. He killed Lance trying to find me, didn't he?" Tears welled up in his eyes and began streaming down the sides of his face again. He was clearly terrified.

"Bullshit," Tomic said, shaking his head. He might believe an overzealous cop planted a rock in his misguided zeal to make an arrest, but selling drugs meant this was a man he really didn't know. "Where's the rest of the coke?"

"I have it," Beverly said quickly. "I hid it in the garage."

"Why?" Josie asked. She was attempting to absorb the idea that a man she thought was a good cop was just another low-life killer, and Beverly hiding ten kilos of cocaine wasn't an act that fit her image of the straitlaced middle-aged woman. Her reality was way out of kilter.

"I found it in Clark's room after he was killed. It was stupid. I guess in a way I was still trying to protect him . . ."

Beverly described the shopping bag that contained the cocaine and where she'd hidden it in the garage. Going outside to retrieve it was an opportunity for Josie to be alone with Tomic and they could decide what their next move was going to be. If Vern had worked that day, he would have gone end of watch and could be anywhere by now. All they had to connect him to Superman's murder was Butch's word and that was worth nothing without corroboration.

They might be able to prove he planted coke on suspects at some point but that was a long way from killing them.

"I say we book the cocaine and leave the three of them here. Maybe get them some protection until we can get more proof," Josie said.

"What if Vern finds out or already knows Kent had a sister and where she lives?" Tomic asked.

"He didn't tell you he had a sister. Did he? And he really liked and trusted you. I don't think he ever talked about her or this part of his life."

"You're probably right, but if we leave them here we get Behan to arrange a protection detail. We could arrest him and Stella."

"No, bad idea. The most we can arrest them for is under the influence. Misdemeanors just aren't staying in jail. We can't pin the coke on them. Beverly hid it. If Vern is our killer, as soon as they step out of jail, he'll pounce on them. At least here, he can't find them . . . I hope," she said.

They went back inside the house with the cocaine. It was packed inside two large paper grocery bags doubled for extra strength. Beverly had put it in a corner of the garage on the floor in the middle of a trash pile with a few filthy rags on top. Butch couldn't take his eyes off the bag. Josie had to believe he had searched the property for the cocaine. He'd probably noticed the rag bag but didn't bother to look inside because obviously no one would hide drugs worth hundreds of thousands of dollars like that.

Josie explained that she was going to leave Butch and Stella in Beverly's care. If either one or both left the house or returned to Hollywood, they would be arrested.

"Can't you arrest that officer?" Beverly asked.

"Not without proof. Butch's word doesn't cut it," Tomic said.

"I ain't lyin'," Butch whined.

"Nobody said you were, but it's not enough," Josie said.

Curtis agreed to wait at the house with Donny until Behan could arrange a security detail to guard their witnesses while Josie and Tomic booked the cocaine and talked to Behan. They needed to protect Butch and she wanted to get permission to have Internal Affairs surveillance set up on Officer Fisher.

THE RIDE back to Hollywood gave Josie an opportunity to organize her thoughts. Tomic never talked much, but tonight he was silent. She knew he was angry, not with her but with the world. A cop had killed Kent, not to protect and serve but for greed.

Her first question was how Vern had gotten hold of ten kilos of cocaine. She would check property reports, but that was a lot of coke to steal from booked seizures. Maybe he figured out a way to get it from Property division before it was destroyed in their regular burns, or had he stolen it from another dealer? If Vern was Raven, then Kent was delivering several ounces of cocaine every day to his bevy of customers. Where would Vern keep that much cocaine, she wondered. It had to be someplace obvious. Kent wasn't smart enough to find a clever hiding place.

Vern planting drugs on other dealers was making much more sense now. He was eliminating the competition by arresting Abby's dealers and taking over the street, forcing them to do business with him.

Josie figured Abby didn't know the Raven's identity yet, or Gaetano would have dealt with him the way he tried to deal with Marge for her interference in their business. Kent was her only connection to Raven and she probably bailed Butch out of jail hoping he might tell her what Kent couldn't any longer.

Finding Vern's stash pad might be the only way they could tie him to Kent. SID could test the drugs to determine if they came from the same batch Beverly had in her garage. Josie was certain he held the key to deciphering Kent's book of bird names. There had to be a log and that would be another link. He'd been smart enough not to shoot either Kent or Lance McCray, instead, killing them in ways that were difficult to trace back to him.

Cops usually make terrible criminals, but Vern was clever and vicious. He had bested the Testas at least for now and managed to keep his day job in a black-and-white while dealing large quantities of cocaine. Josie glanced at Tomic's somber face and wondered if he might be having a change of heart about never arresting one of his brothers in blue.

~ TWENTY ~

After five or six years on the street, most cops developed what Josie called a reliable shit detector, and they could sense when a version of events didn't smell right. The criminal element wasn't that complicated or clever and tended to be somewhat predictable. She believed Butch had been on the roof of the Paradise and had seen Kent bludgeoned to death, but something about his story was bothering her. It wasn't until Tomic parked outside Hollywood station that she realized what it was.

"You coming or what?" Tomic asked. He was standing outside the car by her open door, but she hadn't moved and still had her seat belt buckled.

"How tall would you say Vern is?" she asked, not moving.

"Couple inches shorter than me, I guess. Why?"

"Not a big guy, probably doesn't weigh more than what . . . hundred and sixty, more or less."

"Maybe, so what. Let's go, Behan's waiting," Tomic said.

"Superman was huge, muscular . . . must've weighed two hundred pounds at least. You think Vern could overpower him, wrap him in duct tape, roll his body in a heavy Persian carpet, and lift him over a three-foot retaining wall on the roof . . . by himself?"

Tomic was quiet for a few seconds and finally said, "I guess not."

"There had to be at least two people to handle Kent."

"He'd been freebasing . . . Vern probably hit him with the bat, so he didn't fight . . ." Tomic said, thinking out loud.

"Maybe, but there's no way he could lift that much weight wrapped in that heavy carpet over a three-foot wall by himself. I think Butch isn't telling us everything. There had to be at least one other person up there that night," Josie said. She got out of the car and started to walk toward the station, but stopped and added, "Unless . . . Butch helped him."

"Nah, Stella was there and she backs up his story," Tomic said.

"True, but it could be one hype lying for another one."

When they got to the back door of Hollywood station, Tomic put his key in the door but paused before opening it.

"They were scared shitless. I don't think he was lying about hiding on the roof," he said.

"Then there's a mystery man or two, but why wouldn't Butch tell us there was another guy?" she asked.

"Haven't got a fucking clue, Corsino, but I think you're right. No way he's getting that body over that wall without help."

Behan was talking with a couple of his homicide detectives in the squad room when they arrived. He waved at them but held up his hand to indicate he needed five more minutes to finish what he was doing. Josie went upstairs to the break room and got a couple cups of coffee from the machine. It was wretched stuff but was hot, kind of had the flavor of coffee, and she needed it.

When she got downstairs again, Tomic was sitting alone at the homicide table with Behan. He had already recounted their surveillance of Stella and what they had learned at Kent's sister's house.

"We're definitely calling Billie's death a homicide. That needle had enough fentanyl to kill half the hypes in Hollywood," Behan said. "Are you saying Vern Fisher is suspect number one for her too?" he asked.

"Butch told us she had figured out that Vern killed Kent, so it makes sense," Tomic said.

"Torrance PD offered to keep a car outside the sister's house. They should be safe if they stay put," Behan said. "Internal Affairs has two teams looking for Vern to put surveillance on him, but he's on days off and they can't seem to locate him."

"There's a big surprise," Tomic mumbled sarcastically. "IA's a prep school for management. None of those guys are real cops."

"The Father Flanagan of Cops town," Josie said. "There's no such thing as a bad cop in Tomic's world." She was still pissed off about his rejection of Maddy and saw the puzzled look on Behan's face but didn't feel like explaining why she thought her partner was a narrowminded knucklehead.

Tomic gave her his "fuck you" look but didn't say anything.

"I'm not going to ask what's going on," Behan said. "I know neither one of you will tell me anyway so the hell with you, work it out yourselves. What about this possible second man on the roof, you think Butch might've been helping Vern?"

"No, I don't think so," Tomic said. "If Vern wanted his stash back and he thought Butch had it or knew where it was, there's no way he'd let him walk away from that roof in one piece unless he spilled his guts about where it was. I'm convinced he and Stella were hiding up there and saw him kill Superman."

"What about you, Corsino?"

"I agree with Tomic. Butch was genuinely scared Vern might find him. We've got the cocaine, but . . . I can't figure out why he won't admit there was another guy."

"Where's the coke now?" Behan asked.

"It's still in the trunk of Tomic's car."

"Get it. Let me take a look at the packaging. Maybe I can tell you where it came from," Behan said.

Tomic retrieved the grocery bag from his car and put it on Behan's desk. It contained ten kilo-sized bricks of cocaine individually wrapped in what looked like white butcher paper. Behan picked them up one at a time and carefully inspected the outside.

“See this red mark here?” he asked, after several minutes of examining each of the packages. He was pointing at what appeared to be a small triangle with the number thirteen in the middle stamped on the paper.

“The distributor’s seal?” Josie asked.

“Every one of these dope families marks their product. Major Violators section should be able to tell us exactly where and who this came from and who seized or booked it,” Behan said. “One thing we know for certain, Vern didn’t buy it. This is mega bucks.”

Tomic agreed to follow up on the cocaine the next morning if Josie would book it at Property division downtown on her way home. Her partner seemed eager to get away. She guessed he was meeting the cheerleader at the Freeway bar and was in urgent need of whatever it was the young woman gave him that made his life tolerable.

She needed a good night’s sleep but knew there was little chance of that happening. Her mind was racing through dozens of scenarios attempting to explain how a patrol cop could get his hands on kilos of what looked to be high quality cocaine. The white powder would be tested in the morning and the purity plus the quantity would tell her exactly how much the ten kilos was worth on the street.

It was a ten-minute stop at Property division to book the cocaine and she was back on the road headed toward home. On the way, she began wondering about the code name that Vern, if he was the Raven, had chosen for himself. Ravens weren’t exactly highly regarded or thought of as the king of birds. Why wouldn’t the guy in charge call himself the eagle or the hawk. Unless he associated that particular bird with something else. Lance McCray’s code name was Nightingale, known for its pretty sound, but ravens were bullies, killing smaller birds. They raided other birds’ nests, stole their eggs . . . She laughed softly and thought, okay so maybe it does make sense.

The house was dark except the den upstairs where she found Jake and David asleep together on one of the loungers. David was snuggled in close to his father, who had his arm around the boy. She turned off the television and covered them with a wool afghan from the back of the couch. Both men in her life were sound sleepers and she knew they would stay in that position until morning. She turned down the light and went to the master bedroom where she set the alarm, undressed, and got into bed. Unlike her husband and son, Josie was a restless sleeper. Most nights she tossed and turned, and in the morning her side of the bed looked as if someone had intentionally torn it apart. Her mind refused to turn off or shut down. After an hour or so, she'd fall asleep but dreams and unresolved problems kept her agitated and moving most of the night. In the morning, she'd feel rested, but the bedding was always a disaster.

This night was different. She couldn't fall asleep. The more she thought about it, the more she was certain Vern had an accomplice. Someone who not only helped him kill Superman, but a person who had a way to steal large quantities of cocaine from Property division. It could've been another cop or a civilian who worked where those drugs were booked and stored, or the worst possible outcome would be another narcotics detective who was familiar with the methods of booking or retrieving large quantities of drugs for testing, court, or eventual destruction.

It was becoming clear to her that Superman and Butch had been working with Vern, but who was the mystery man who helped Vern kill Kent and toss his body over the wall. Also, she couldn't figure out why Butch would be willing to give up Vern for killing Kent, but he was keeping the other man's existence and identity a secret.

Josie did manage to get a few hours' sleep before the alarm woke her. After a quick shower, she dressed and had intended to wake Jake and David, but they were already downstairs in the kitchen. David was ready for school and sitting at the table waiting for his dad to serve his toast and eggs. He jumped up and hugged Josie as soon as she stepped into the room. It might've been her imagination or wishful thinking, but her son seemed happier, less stressed since Nonna's departure.

"I have a few applications on the counter for a fulltime housekeeper/nanny if you want to look at them," Jake said, putting a plate on the table. "Sit down and eat, David, before the bus gets here."

Josie scooted the boy to his place at the table, picked up the paperwork, and sat beside him.

"Did these come from the agency?" she asked.

"Yes, I thought you might want to do a little work on them before we decide," he said, giving her a peck on the cheek and putting another plate in front of her.

She didn't respond because they both knew it was against police department policy to check criminal records for personal reasons. Jake also knew Josie wouldn't hesitate to do it. She wasn't about to leave her kid with a stranger without knowing everything she could possibly learn about the woman. If the LAPD found out and had a problem with her using their official systems, Josie would deal with that when and if it happened. In the meantime, she'd have peace of mind knowing the babysitter wasn't a convicted felon and didn't have a record for child molestation.

They ate breakfast together and Josie waited until the school bus arrived before leaving. She was enjoying her mommy time and her family seemed a lot better off with their new routine. There must be something wrong with me, she thought, as she drove away from the house. I love Jake and David, but I can't seem to give up a job filled with deviants and the dregs of society to make them happy. It was a reoccurring but passing thought.

There was still no sighting of Vern Fisher by the time she arrived at the narcotics office that morning. Internal Affairs investigators had contacted friends, family, and his old partners, but no one seemed to know where the veteran police officer had gone on his days off. Maddy had been interviewed but all she knew was what she'd been told by the watch commander, that her partner had three regular days off and she would be working with another training officer until she completed probation at the end of the week. She said Vern seemed normal and was completing the few remaining pages in her probationary book on the last day they worked together.

"What now?" Curtis asked after Behan had filled them in on the missing cop. Josie and Tomic exchanged looks and she guessed he had been asking himself the same question.

"If he's the dirty cop, doesn't that take our squad off the hook?" Donny asked.

"It should, but we need more than the word of a hype boyfriend," Behan said and added quickly, "Corsino, you and Tomic go back to Torrance and make him tell you who he's protecting. We need to know who the other guy was on the roof."

"Got any idea how we do that, boss?" Tomic asked. His night with the cheerleader hadn't done much for his disposition. He seemed grumpier and hung over.

"Threaten to arrest the little turd as an accessory to murder. Tell him if somebody else didn't help Vern heave Kent's body over the wall, then he must have done it," Behan said impatiently. "Get your mind off your teenage girlfriend and think like a cop."

"Did you guys notice Vern Fisher's serial number?" Curtis asked before Tomic could say something stupid. All of them knew when Tomic had a rough night with the cheerleader he got nasty and Behan had a temper.

"What about it?" Tomic asked, putting on his jacket and glaring at Behan.

"It's only two numbers off Art's," he said.

Donny studied the wall where the search warrants had been taped. It took a second or two, but he found one of the few with Art's name and serial number.

"Yep, Art is two numbers lower. They had to be classmates," Donny said. He tore the paper off the wall and gave it to Behan.

"Pull their personnel packages and see if they ever worked together," Behan ordered. "Curtis, check and see if Art has bailed out."

"No need to check, the jailer told me he bailed the day after you booked him," Curtis said.

"So much for being too scared to be seen in public," Josie said.

"Okay, let's track him down too," Behan said.

Dolores came into the office and told Josie there was a woman on the phone who wanted to talk to her.

"She sounds like a total nervous wreck," Dolores said, pointing to the flashing light on the phone in front of Josie.

Beverly Kent was upset. She told Josie, Butch and Stella had left during the night, managing to slip past the officer in a Torrance police car watching the house.

"More good news, boss," Josie said, hanging up the phone. She repeated what Beverly had told her.

"Fuck," Behan shouted. He was frustrated and angry, the color in his face turning nearly as red as his hair. He picked up his coffee mug and seemed about to smash it on the floor but stopped himself and carefully placed it back on his desk. "My first wife gave me that. I'm not about to waste it on those asswipes."

"If all your wives gave you one, you'd have a full set to replace it by now," Curtis said, winking at Josie.

"At least none of mine tried to cut my fucking throat."

"That's Mexican passion, boss," Curtis said dryly. He'd confided in Josie a few days ago his hot-tempered wife had finally decided to divorce him and go back to Guadalajara. She guessed joking about the breakup was his way of coping.

Donny laughed, but Behan stomped out of the office. Josie watched him through the front window as he jogged across Wilcox to the front door of Hollywood station. He had three homicide investigations, Kent, McCray, and Billie, that were connected but going nowhere. His nearly decimated narcotics squad had given his homicide detectives a possible killer and witnesses/accomplices that no one could locate. She didn't blame him for having a temper tantrum.

"I vote we look for Art," Josie announced, turning away from the window. "If he's the mystery man Butch was protecting, our two hypes are probably headed in his direction . . . wherever that might be."

"I've got something to do," Tomic said, obviously still bothered by Behan's remark. He asked Curtis, "Can you and Donny check out the Venice hippie's address? That's where Art seemed to feel safe." He turned to Josie and asked, "You want to go through Art and Vern's personnel packages?"

"No problem," she said. "Get me on the air when you're done with your secret mission and we'll hook up." She tried to stay calm and be understanding but knew her words and tone were snarky. His need to do things on his own was beginning to grate on her. Usually the clandestine activities involved the cheerleader, but even that was getting old.

He didn't respond and walked out of the office. It was as if he hadn't heard her comment.

Curtis shrugged and said, "Man's gotta do whata man's gotta do. Want to come with us?"

She didn't. Looking at the personnel packages was a good idea. It was Tomic's behavior she didn't like.

Josie went across the street to the Hollywood station, and, to avoid questions, she asked Behan to request Vern's divisional package from the patrol captain. It was routine for detective supervisors to examine patrol officers' packages if they were being considered for a loan to one of the detective tables.

She sat in an empty homicide interview room behind Behan's desk and went through the thick folder, taking notes on each of Vern's assignments. She found several commendations but three of them caught her attention. Starting ten years ago, while assigned to Wilshire patrol, Vern and Art had been recognized for arrests they'd made while working as partners. They were just off probation and caught several street dealers selling marijuana near one of the elementary schools. A large quantity of weed had been recovered in bushes near the arrests and Vern reported that he had seen the dealers go into the bushes before each sale.

It took nearly half an hour to go through the package. She brought her notes back to the narcotics office and compared the places where Vern worked to those in Art's personnel package. Josie was grateful Dolores was always slow following up on administrative work. She still hadn't sent Art's package downtown where it should have gone as soon as he resigned. The secretary was the only person in West Bureau, besides Lieutenant Watts, who knew Art was no longer a cop. Apparently nobody bothered to tell Behan or anyone in what remained of the Hollywood squad. Dolores explained to Josie that Art had resigned in lieu of termination. Internal Affairs had recommended he be sent to a board of rights and fired the same day he bailed out of jail. The fact that he resigned wasn't a big surprise, but what Josie couldn't believe was no one in charge had bothered to mention it to her or the rest of his squad.

There were two other divisions where Josie found Art and Vern briefly worked patrol at the same time. Art spent most of his career in the administration building downtown at the Office of Special Services (OSS) and came to Hollywood narcotics about a year after Vern was promoted to training officer in patrol.

Why a meticulous guy like Art would want a grubby assignment like street enforcement in Hollywood narcotics was always a mystery to her. His personality and demeanor didn't fit the assignment. He was like a bookkeeper digging trenches for sewer lines. Why would he do it?

She quickly read through his rating reports while he was in OSS, all outstanding. It was unusual, but when he got promoted to detective, Art went directly to Narcotics division without the usual route of first being assigned to one of the divisional tables. Josie figured it had to be a perk of working for the deputy chief who oversaw Narcotics.

A lot of her questions were answered when she read his last year of rating reports in OSS. One of his primary jobs had been to organize the monthly burn for Narcotics division, arrange for the transportation of drugs from Property division to the burn site where they could be destroyed. According to his performance review, he excelled in that particular duty, even devising better, safer methods to dispose of the controlled substances.

"I'll bet," she said out loud and thought, you figured out a way to get kilos of cocaine out of there, didn't you . . . you little slime ball.

She took the package across the street to Behan who was still sitting at his desk. He had calmed down and she could smell the reason why on his breath. The volumes containing the California Penal Code were on his bookcase in perfect order, but Josie and a couple of his senior homicide detectives knew he kept a pint of whiskey behind them. She also understood it would be much easier to talk to him now. He was always sharper and more reasonable when he wasn't completely sober.

"He figured out how to steal it and Vern knew how to sell it," Behan said, after she showed him the rating reports from OSS.

"I think they needed Kent and Butch to build their customer list . . . a lot of those buyers, I'm guessing, came from Abby's clientele," Josie said.

"The bird thing is stupid, like something Art would come up with, so he's probably still got the ledger with the real names," Behan said and hesitated as if he suddenly had a thought before adding, "You and Tomic should ask Too Tall if he knows where Art might be."

"Good idea, I'll go to his place now," she said, closing the folder and getting up to leave.

"Whoa, not so fast, where's your partner? You're not going there alone."

"He's MIA. It's okay, I'm comfortable meeting Gilbert by myself."

"I'm not fucking comfortable, Corsino, and I'm the one that counts."

"So, come with me, boss."

"Fuck," he said, closing he eyes and making a noise that sounded like a growl. "I can't wait for the day when you, your asshole partner, and his overactive dick are no longer my problem."

"Why are you mad at me? I'm not screwing the cheerleader," she said, trying not to smile.

"Because you're one of them . . . screwed-up dope cops . . . nothing but fucked-up headaches," he mumbled, putting on his jacket and leading the way out of the squad room. One of the homicide detectives gave Josie a wink behind Behan's back. She was definitely one of them.

They had nearly reached the doorway when Marge walked into the squad room almost bumping into Behan. The redhead's demeanor changed quickly. The tenseness, the military rigidness thawed. He seemed to relax, even smiled.

"You look great," he said, touching the tall blonde's arm. "How are you feeling?"

"Like a fucking human again," Marge said, grinning at Josie.

Josie thought her friend did look much better than the last time she'd seen her. Marge's hair had been trimmed and styled to cover the places on her head that had been shaved. The bruises on her face were fading and hardly noticeable under a layer of light makeup. A small bandage covered the stitches on her neck just below her ear and her left arm was still in a sling. She moved slowly as if her body was sore from the trauma, but overall, she appeared to be healing nicely.

"What are you doing here?" Josie asked. "I thought you'd be off for at least another couple of weeks."

"I was going batshit at home. The captain said I could come in and do paperwork until they put me back full duty."

"Heal faster if you'd stay home," Behan said.

It seemed to Josie her boss's concern for Marge was more than what a supervisor might express, and her suspicions were bolstered when she recognized that sappy puppy-dog expression usually exchanged between a man and woman in public after they'd been intimate. Poor Behan, she thought. He was Catholic, and marriage was the natural culmination of his affairs. He was a serial groom who'd already failed in four attempts. Josie knew Marge well enough to be certain she wouldn't be number five. She'd told Josie on numerous occasions that, for her, sex was like her favorite chocolate ice cream, wonderful for a while but sooner or later she always had to try a different flavor.

"Where are you going?" Marge asked and after Josie explained, she pleaded, "Can I go with you, just for the ride? I promise I won't get involved in anything."

"No," Behan said. "Bad idea."

"I'll sit in the back seat. You won't even know I'm there. Give me a few minutes back in the field," she said, producing the puppy dog look again.

"You glue your ass to that seat and don't move, no matter what happens," Behan demanded, and Marge nodded.

He led the way out of the squad room and the back door of the station with Marge and Josie following.

"Sucker," Josie whispered just loud enough for Marge to hear.

"I meant it unless something happens."

~ TWENTY-ONE ~

The garage behind Too Tall's bungalow was secured with a chain and padlock. His motorcycle was nowhere in sight and there wasn't any response to Behan's pounding on either the front door of the house or the kitchen door off the patio.

Josie suggested they check The Carnival to see if his motorcycle was parked near the stairs leading to Abby Morrison's apartment. If it was there, they could wait until he left and stop him a few blocks away. Technically, he wasn't still working for them, but she didn't want Abby or Guy Testa to think he might be feeding them information.

Behan warned Marge again she wasn't to leave the car no matter what happened. If Marge had any qualms about being this close to the Testas' nest she didn't show it but sat quietly in the back seat.

Josie wondered if Abby had any suspicions about Vern and Art being the brains behind her competition—probably not, because they were still breathing. The Testas might be waiting and plotting for the right place and time to take care of business.

Too Tall's motorcycle wasn't parked behind The Carnival, but what they did see was Tomic's city car tucked away in the alley.

"That can't be good," Marge said.

"What's your partner up to, Corsino?" Behan asked.

Josie didn't answer right away. It was the right question, but she didn't have a clue.

"Hard to say," she muttered, after a few seconds.

"No, it isn't. I'll say it. He's fucked up as usual," Marge said.

"Is there anyone in this damn Hollywood squad, including you, Corsino, that's playing by the rules?" Behan said. He didn't sound angry, maybe disappointed.

"Give him a break. We don't know what he's doing up there," Josie said, but even she could hear the doubt in her voice.

"Come on," Behan said, getting out of the car. "You stay," he ordered, pointing at Marge. "Sonnofabitch, I can't leave you here alone. Come on, but stick like glue to me. Last thing I need is you going after Morrison or her old man."

Marge held up her right hand and said, "Swear I won't kill anybody unless . . ."

"No 'unless' . . . you will stay behind me and keep quiet. You wanted to tag along but that's all you'll do."

Josie didn't say anything and followed him up the metal stairs to the front door of Abby's apartment with Marge trailing a few feet behind. She saw a familiar smirk from Marge and knew staying behind and being quiet weren't any part of her friend's MO. There were probably a dozen reasons they shouldn't barge in on Tomic, but Josie was growing weary of her partner's Lone Ranger approach to investigations and she was willing to deal with the inevitable fallout.

They didn't get an opportunity to knock. The door opened as soon as they were all on the landing.

"Welcome, Josie," Abby said in a cheerful, bit too intimate voice. "Who's the handsome redheaded stranger?" she asked, staring at Behan, but completely ignoring Marge.

"Detective Behan," he said, brushing past her and stepping into the foyer. "Where's Tomic?" he asked and not waiting for an invitation, walked around the wall and into the open living room.

Abby followed and said sarcastically, "Please come in, Detective. Hope you have a warrant."

"Nope."

"Then maybe you'd better get the fuck out until you do or until I invite you in," she said calmly as she went to the bar and poured herself a large glass of gin and tonic. She held up the glass to Josie and asked, "Care for one? I won't ask Sergeant Bailey. Medication and alcohol don't mix. I heard about your unfortunate mishap. Hope you're recovering. We miss you at The Carnival," Abby said sarcastically.

"Fuck you very much; I'm doing fine and hope to be back soon, screwing with you and the degenerate that spawned you."

Josie shook her head and nudged Marge into the master bedroom where Behan was standing over Tomic, who had apparently passed out on the unmade bed. She wanted a confrontation with Abby as much as Marge did, but this wasn't the right time. Behan called for Josie to help him get her partner on his feet.

"What did you give him?" Josie asked Abby, who had followed them into the room.

Behan had managed to get Tomic in a sitting position on the edge of the king-sized bed where he was holding his head and claimed the room was spinning. Alcoholic vertigo, Josie thought, and believed he looked worse than he had when he left the narcotics office.

"Nothing," Abby said. She was leaning against a white oak dresser, watching. "Came in, raided my bar, and passed out."

"And that was okay with you?"

Abby snickered, spitting a little of her drink. "Not really, but I'm fond of Larry and he's obviously going through a bad patch."

"Fond of?" Behan asked.

"We used to be very close," she said, grinning at Marge and emphasizing the word "very." "Don't worry, he never spilled any deep dark police secrets . . . it was sex, just sex . . . finished years ago."

Josie looked at the overweight, badly dressed, middle-aged woman with the Nonna-styled bouffant hair and tried to picture Tomic having sex with her. What is wrong with this guy, she thought. Not only is he sleeping with the enemy, but he's jeopardized his career and exposed his wife to who knows what diseases from this weirdo. If it was true, Josie was done with him and she knew for certain Behan had to initiate a personnel investigation. If Tomic survived the process, he might spend the rest of his time in the police department sitting in some back room counting paper clips. Trust and credibility are a big part of police work. Tomic had damaged both.

"She's lying," Tomic moaned.

"There's a revelation," Marge muttered.

Josie and Behan then managed to get him off the bed, down the stairs, and stuffed into the back seat of the car. Apparently it hadn't taken much of Abby's liquor to finish the job he'd begun with the cheerleader last night, but the stupor seemed to be wearing off and he was able to communicate.

Marge had followed them to the car but not before she stopped on the landing to have a few private words with Abby. The screen door slammed closed as she slowly worked her way down the stairs and got in to the back seat with Tomic.

"Lying about what?" Behan asked. He was disgusted.

"Everything," Tomic said, attempting a smile at Marge and adding, "Good to see you out and about."

"You didn't sleep with her?" Marge asked.

"I've never been that drunk," Tomic said, his voice growing a little stronger. "She's been my snitch for years."

"You were on her bed," Josie said.

"I . . . don't know how I got there . . . I remember her giving me something, whiskey, to drink . . . we talked. I got really tired, dizzy, but . . . that's all I remember."

"One drink, that's all you had?"

"One, I swear," Tomic said, holding up his right hand. "I don't think I even finished that."

"Why did you go there by yourself?" Behan asked, still not convinced.

"I thought I could get her to tell me more about Art. I lied and said we were looking for him to sign some resignation paperwork or he wouldn't get his retirement check."

"So what did she say?" Josie asked. She still wasn't buying his story.

"Can't remember. My head hurts so bad . . . no wait," he said, groaning and leaning a little closer to Marge, "I think it was her might've been asking me about Art."

Behan sighed and said, "Okay, we'll go with your version of events for now. I'll have one of my guys drop you at Central receiving. They can take blood and urine, see if she put anything in that drink. I'll get somebody to take your city car back to the office."

Tomic didn't hesitate. He wanted the tests and, more importantly, he wanted a prescription for medication that would make him feel better.

They went back to Hollywood station and while Behan was arranging Tomic's transportation for medical treatment and a ride home, Josie went with Marge upstairs to the Vice office. Behan had refused to let her ride in the car any longer. He mumbled something about having a block of TNT in the back seat.

"What did you say to Abby?" Josie asked as soon as Marge sat behind her desk and stopped groaning. She was attempting to find a comfortable position in the department-issued oak antique.

"Nothing."

"Okay . . ." Josie was quiet for a few seconds, then said, "You threatened to kill her, didn't you?"

"Of course not, Corsino," she said with the same disinterested tone. "I'm a cop."

"Good," Josie said, nodding several times. "Worse?"

"So much fucking worse."

By the time Behan returned with Josie to Too Tall's bungalow off Melrose, the motorcycle was back, parked in the driveway, and the side door of the garage was open.

Before they got out of the car, Josie asked, "You believe Tomic?"

"Mostly," Behan said. "When she was younger, before she got married, Abby didn't look the way she does now. She was an Italian doll with long brown hair and those big dark eyes. I'm sure that horny bastard partner of yours thought about it even if he didn't do it."

"What happened to her?" Josie asked as they walked up the driveway. She wanted to remind Behan why he'd been married so many times, but knew it was pointless—one horny pot calling the kettle horny.

"Marriage didn't agree with her."

"There's a lot of that going around," she said.

Too Tall came out of the house as they were about to enter the garage. He didn't say anything, but went back inside, leaving the kitchen door open.

"Guess that means come in," Behan mumbled, moving toward the house.

Josie took a quick look in the garage. It was empty. She turned and watched for any movement on the street or around the small patio area before entering the house where the big man was in front of the sink opening a bottle of Budweiser. Dressed in full motorcycle gear, leather jacket and heavy boots, the ex-cop looked as if he'd just arrived. Behan was leaning against the wall watching.

"Where's Art?" she asked, feeling as if she'd interrupted a man-to-man moment, but not really caring.

"Like I told Red, don't know."

"You worked with the guy for two years. You must have some idea where he might've gone," Behan said, seeming to pick up on her sense of urgency.

"I was chemically out of it most of the time we were together, but he was tight with my cousin. I do remember that much."

"We think Abby's searching for him too," Josie said.

His puzzled expression told her maybe he was telling the truth.

"She hasn't said anything to me. I did see her and Uncle Guy talking with one of their Vegas thugs last night. They stayed out on the birds' nest overlooking the club, so I couldn't hear what they were saying, but Guy was as mad as I've ever seen him," Too Tall said, pushing past them and sitting near the table.

"If you couldn't hear anything, how'd you know he was from Vegas?" Behan asked.

"Trust me, I know the type. He's a Testa family soldier."

"Maybe they want Art too," Josie said. "She might've drugged Tomic to get him to tell her what he knew."

"How would Tomic know where Art is?" Too Tall asked.

"He doesn't . . . but he might've been out of it enough to give up that hippie's address in Venice," Josie said. "We're aware of Kit now so I doubt Art would go back there, but . . ." Her voice trailed off because she worried that most of the key players in this investigation ended up dead or missing. She hardly knew Kit, but didn't want to see her become another casualty in the turf war between the Testas and Art.

"He wouldn't go there," Too Tall said, finishing his beer. "Have you checked out Eddie Small's house?"

"Why there? Small told me he hates both of you . . . a lot," Josie said.

"No, he hates me, but I'm sure there's something between him and Art. That day you saw us at Eddie's house, I was trying to force the little weasel to confess what they'd been up to before Art stepped in and stopped me from snapping the jerk's scrawny neck."

"I saw," she said.

"Art swore the drugs were making me paranoid. I knew better but smack doesn't exactly keep you focused either, so I let it go."

"How about Vern Fisher in patrol, did Art seem friendly with Vern?" Behan asked.

"Never saw them together . . . Art never talked about him."

All the pieces were finally falling into place in Josie's mind. Art would need Eddie Small's help to move a large quantity of cocaine out of Property division. If Narcotics' Major Violators could identify the kilos recovered from Beverly's garage, they would tell her exactly how much cocaine had been seized and when that evidence should've been destroyed. When she knew the date and time scheduled to destroy the drugs, she could determine who was in charge of overseeing the burn. She was certain Art's name would be on the paperwork and Eddie Small would've been on the roster to work that day.

After he stole the drugs, Art transferred to Hollywood where he could cut the kilos into grams to sell on the street with the help of Superman while Vern systematically eliminated Abby's street dealers by planting dope and arresting them. Josie had to admit Art was a lot smarter than she'd thought. He'd managed to gain the trust of the police department and Abby while he and Vern betrayed both.

As a member of the Hollywood narcotics squad, Art was aware of every search warrant and narcotics task force. Superman had been Tomic's informant, but he was Art and Vern's paper boy and made his cocaine deliveries virtually untouched. No wonder Kent was so cocky, she thought. He could snitch on Abby's dealers and get paid by Tomic, then turn around and sell cocaine to the Testa family's customers knowing he'd never get caught. If he and boyfriend Butch hadn't gotten greedy, the scheme might've gone on much longer with Art and Vern making a ton of money off cocaine everybody believed had been destroyed.

Josie told Behan what she had figured out when they got back into his car, and he agreed, saying he'd come to a similar conclusion. Her growing fear was Abby might've somehow put those same pieces together and that was the reason for a Vegas hit man.

Too Tall had agreed to go back to The Carnival and try to find out what the Testas were planning. The ex-cop had no love for the LAPD, but he liked his cousin and uncle even less. Now that he was off heroin, he realized his easy access to the opiate might've been facilitated by Art and the Testas to keep him from interfering in their business. It wasn't an excuse because he readily admitted his need and desire for the narcotic, but his partner and family had made no effort to help him. In fact, they encouraged his addiction. His motive for helping Josie was nothing but simple revenge.

~ TWENTY-TWO ~

With the information Too Tall had provided, Josie figured their next target should be Eddie Small's house in the Rampart area. She directed Behan to the location where she and Tomic had first encountered the property officer and they parked down the street. There weren't any cars in front of the house or in the driveway. The shades were closed, most of them torn or hanging crooked on the rods. The lawn seemed to be decorated by gophers with mounds of dirt among the weeds. An ancient refrigerator and rusted gas stove had been left on the porch, completing the picture of a home that had been abandoned.

Josie took one of the police radios and got out on foot. From the neighbor's yard, she walked quickly behind the house, ducking under the windows until she found one with a shade damaged enough to give her a decent view of the inside. The window was in the kitchen over the sink. She could see Stella sitting with her arms folded near a coffee table watching Eddie and Vern share what appeared to be a bottle of bourbon. There wasn't much light in the room, but Josie could see apprehension on the face of the Mexican hype as she frequently glanced over at a wall clock behind her. Her impression was the usually stoic Stella was about to cry.

The drinkers were glassy-eyed, and the half-empty bottle told her they'd been at it a while. Eddie still wore a full cast on his leg. It was filthy, and a piece of plaster had broken off the bottom. He moved clumsily from the table to a counter with a metal crutch in one hand and his glass in the other. He was the only one talking, but Josie couldn't make out the words. Vern was sullen and quiet. He sat beside Stella, glaring at her. A large backpack had been stored under his chair.

Josie moved carefully around the exterior of the house, peeking in other windows until she was reasonably certain no one else was inside before retracing her steps to Behan's car.

"My guess is they're waiting for something or someone," Josie said when she was in the passenger seat again. "Vern's sitting on a backpack like he's ready to take off any second; Stella looks like a kid in a house of horrors expecting an axe murderer to jump out of the pantry; and Eddie . . . is Eddie."

"No sign of Art or Butch?" Behan asked.

"They're not there. Maybe Butch took Art to wherever Superman hid the rest of his stash," she said.

"That doesn't bode well for our blue-haired boy or Miss Stella. Once Art gets his hands on the coke, he really doesn't need them anymore."

"His entrepreneur days on the streets of Hollywood are over, that's for sure," Josie said and added quickly, "Let's get the odd couple over here and arrest everybody. Stella will tell us where they've gone."

Behan didn't answer right away. She always relied on his instincts and expertise, but her sixth sense was agreeing with him that once Art had the cocaine, the rest of the players were expendable. From the look on Stella's face, Josie guessed the street-smart addict had already calculated the slim odds of her survival.

"The best idea would probably be to wait until Art gets back but we don't know for sure he's coming here. They might've planned to meet somewhere else once he has the dope. One thing we do know is that between Art and Abby, they're not leaving any witnesses around to testify. Get Curtis on the air, tell him and Donny to meet us here code three," he said.

It took less than five minutes for Curtis and his partner to find the Rampart location. As soon as Curtis parked, he and Donny climbed into the back seat of Behan's car. Behan explained everything he and Josie knew or suspected, but before he could finish, Curtis interrupted.

"Boss, did Tomic get hold of you?" he asked.

Behan shook his head and said, "He's at the hospital, isn't he?"

"He was, but Major Violators finally contacted him about the origin of that coke you recovered at Kent's sister's. They know exactly when the contraband was seized and when it should've been destroyed. It was a huge bust with over a hundred kilos. Better yet, they got Art, Kent, and Eddie's prints all over the ten kilos you found," Curtis said, grinning.

"Art's toast," Donny added. "The lab tested a sample from your ten kilos and it's definitely part of the hundred kilos that should've been destroyed, same batch."

Behan shifted his weight behind the steering wheel and turned to Josie, "It's your deal, Corsino. How do you want to play it?"

"We've got to find Butch. He's our best witness to Kent's murder. Once Art gets his hands on that cocaine, he has no use for Butch . . . in fact, he's a liability." She hesitated just a moment before saying, "Okay, this is what we'll do. Curtis and Donny, you knock on the front door, yell police, and kick it. I'll be out back with Behan to grab Vern when he tries to run," she said.

"What about the other two?" Donny asked.

"Eddie's not going anywhere, and Stella has nowhere to run," she said.

"Maybe you should get a couple of uniforms . . . you know, in case Vern decides he doesn't want to be arrested," Donny said.

"No," Behan said emphatically.

Josie understood immediately. This was their business, their problem. Hollywood narcotics would clean its own house. They didn't need baby cops with faulty memories and an underdeveloped sense of loyalty. Behan would do this his way and when it was over, create enough documentation to prove it was completely in policy. She knew all that and how close they might come to the line, but the memory of Superman's battered body kept her from confronting him and insisting he do it by the book.

"We'll have the shotgun," she said.

"No, you will," Behan said. "If he comes out that back door, wait until he clears the steps, chamber a round so he can hear it, and point that Ithaca center mass. Get close enough for him to look down the barrel."

"What if he decides to shoot it out?" Donny asked.

"Then kill the sonnofabitch," Behan said.

"Do you want me in the back with Corsino, boss, so you can hold Donny's hand on the front porch?" Curtis asked.

"You're a moron," Donny said.

Josie laughed at the dig Curtis directed at his partner, but she understood it was partly aimed in her direction too. Curtis didn't have confidence in her tactical abilities. He'd made that clear on plenty of occasions, and she was certain he wanted to be where he could jump in to save the day after the girl messed up the takedown.

"Get out of my car and give us a couple of minutes to suit up and get around to the back of the house before you start yelling and kicking the door," Behan ordered, ignoring Curtis's comment, but he was very aware of the dynamics in the Hollywood squad. In his way, the boss had just told Curtis he trusted her. Before they could leave, Behan added, "Be ready. Vern might decide to come out the front door when he sees Donny."

Donny mumbled something that included the word "asshole" and slammed his door shut.

"He's really pissed," Josie said when she and Behan were alone.

"Yeah, I know," he said smiling.

THE SHOTGUN was loaded and locked in the truck of Behan's car. Josie put on a protective vest and grabbed a raid jacket, one of several he had crumpled up behind the spare tire. The jacket smelled of marijuana, engine oil, and body odor.

"Might think about tossing these in a washer once in a while," she said, shaking it several times, trying to air it out before slipping it over the vest.

She removed the shotgun and checked to see if a round had been chambered. It hadn't. The department made officers qualify with the shotgun once a year after graduating from the police academy and she always felt comfortable handling and using it. It was a weapon that could inflict substantial damage to the human body, but she figured dead was dead. Handgun or shotgun, if she had to use either one, the target would be center mass. The official line was cops should never shoot to kill, just to stop, but inserting a projectile of hot lead or 00-Buck traveling at least twelve hundred feet per second into a person's chest usually had a predictably deadly outcome.

She never wanted to kill anyone, but the dilemma of whether she could pull the trigger when the time came had been decided in that moral/ethical part of her brain the day she signed papers to become a cop.

"Nobody cares what you smell like, Corsino. You ready?" he asked, closing the trunk.

She nodded, and they headed toward Eddie Small's house through the neighbor's yard. She carried the gun at port arms as she jogged ahead of Behan and took cover behind the same dilapidated car she'd used the first time she and Tomic had been there.

Only seconds passed before she heard the shouting, banging, and kicking at the front door. She stepped out from behind the vehicle, moved closer to the back door, and stood in the driveway, some twenty feet from the steps. The black-iron security screen flung open and Vern leapt from the small landing to the ground between her and the house.

He was carrying the backpack, but Josie could see the holstered semiauto handgun on his waist when he jumped. His adrenaline must have overloaded his brain because he didn't seem to realize at first that she was standing there blocking his path. When he finally focused on the obstacle in front of him, he froze, dropping the backpack. Josie chambered a shotgun round, creating that unnerving sound of metal on metal signifying death was a trigger pull away. In one motion, she stepped closer, pointing the weapon at his heart.

"Hands up!" she ordered.

He didn't move except his head turned slightly, his eyes searching the yard for signs of other officers. Behan came out from behind the car with his semiauto pointed at Vern.

"Don't be stupid, Fisher. She'll kill you," he said calmly. "If she misses, I'll do it."

Vern Fisher slowly raised his arms and stared at the ground. She could see his shoulders slump and his body seem to deflate as she ordered him to drop to his knees. He complied when she told him to lie flat on his stomach with his arms outstretched.

"Officer Fisher, you're under arrest for the murder of Clark Kent," she said, moving closer where she could smell the odor of alcohol from his heavy nervous breathing. Behan holstered his weapon, handcuffed Vern, removed his weapon, and searched the subdued but visibly shaken officer.

As Josie cleared the shotgun, she noticed Curtis standing behind the security screen watching from the house.

"Is Stella okay?" she shouted at him.

"Just scared," he said and walked away.

"Good job, girl. You didn't let the suspect get away, kill your partner, or shoot yourself in the foot. Maybe you're not a tactical imbecile after all," she mumbled to herself.

"Let it go, Corsino," Behan said as he helped the handcuffed man get off the ground and back on his feet. "You did good. That's what matters."

She didn't respond because that wasn't all that mattered. Having Curtis's respect was important to her.

~ TWENTY-THREE ~

Josie had little expectation that Vern Fisher would be willing to talk or give up Art, so she wasn't surprised when he sat stone-faced and silent after Behan brought him into the house. He'd been drinking heavily, which would delay any interrogation about Kent's murder. Behan would have to wait until he was clearheaded and able to understand his rights. The alcohol had probably dulled his senses enough to soften the blow of having forfeited his life as a cop and a free man, but she knew it was a temporary reprieve. Sobriety would be the beginning of a very bad time for Officer Fisher.

It was obvious Eddie wouldn't be any help either. He was not only drunk, but his mental state had deteriorated considerably since the last time Josie had talked with him. She made him sit on the other side of the room because his body odor was as bad as any homeless drunk on skid row. She believed he hadn't changed his clothes or bathed since he broke his leg and he rambled on incoherently about a three-legged rat and a combative, army-trained cockroach that were spying on him.

The only person who might tell them anything useful was Stella, but in the past, everything in her nature had been strongly opposed to cooperating with the police. She was sitting in the kitchen when Josie came into the house and she glanced up for only a second before looking away.

Behan told Curtis and Donny to drive Vern back to Hollywood station and stay with him until one of the homicide teams arrived. Before she could speak to Stella, Behan pulled Josie aside into a bedroom where they could talk and keep an eye on the two arrestees.

"Do you want me to interrogate her?" he asked. "I'm better at this, and if you're right, Butch might not have much time."

"She hates me because of Billie's baby, but I think she cares about Butch . . . he's really all she's got left. We need to convince her he's a dead man if we don't find Art. I think I can do that, boss."

He closed his eyes tight for a second and grimaced before saying, "All right, you try, but if it starts going sideways, I jump in."

She didn't respond and went directly to Stella, moving one of the chairs to sit a few feet from her.

"Art's going to kill Butch if we don't stop him," Josie said. Stella glanced up at her but didn't say anything. Her expression was cold, angry. Josie shrugged and said calmly, "Fine, let him die. You let Superman and Billie and her baby die, why not him." Another look from Stella, this time hatred.

"Wasn't me killed Ashley," Stella whispered.

Josie leaned closer and said, "Nobody killed that baby. She was born sick. You did everything you could. I know that, but if you don't tell us where Butch is, you are letting him die."

Stella crossed her arms and her fingertips dug into her biceps as she rocked like a bobblehead doll on the chair. Snitching was poison to her, but Butch was her friend and loyalty was important. For years, she'd stood by the selfish, ungrateful Billie and not just for the baby's sake. Josie knew all that but could see the struggle in Stella's body language. She wanted to save Butch but couldn't convince herself to talk to the police.

"Never mind, Corsino, she's not going to help. Let's go," Behan said, tapping her shoulder. Josie got up as he added, "Stella can come visit Butch at the morgue, see what a baseball bat can do to pretty boy's face."

Good move, boss, Josie thought. Stella had watched Kent's murder. She'd already seen what a baseball bat could do to a man's face.

"Wait," Stella said, shaking her head. "Said he wouldn't hurt Butch if he took him to the locker." She looked up at the ceiling. "I knew he was lying."

"No more games," Behan ordered. "Tell us now and we might be able to keep him alive."

Stella gave them the address and unit number for Kent's storage locker in south Los Angeles. The facility was located on Figueroa Street on that narrow strip of land between the cities of Torrance and Lomita. The area was technically in LAPD's Southeast division but practically, with its strange configuration, got very little policing from any agency, making it the perfect place for Kent to stash a hundred kilos of cocaine. An added benefit was his sister Beverly's home in Torrance was less than five minutes away.

Another mystery that bothered Josie, but she knew she might never get solved, was where Vern and Art had stored all that contraband before Kent stole it.

"Do we get the locals to descend on the storage locker?" Josie asked when they were in Behan's car headed down the Harbor Freeway. Curtis and his partner had deposited Vern with Hollywood homicide detectives and had already returned to transport Stella and Eddie back to Hollywood.

"I think you and me can handle Art. Let's hope Butch is still alive," he said.

"Uniforms could get there faster."

"No. I'm not sending blue-suiters in there blind. We don't know who's with Art or what kind of fire power he's got. We'll call them if we need them . . . after we sort it out," he said. Behan was quiet for a few seconds then turned to her and asked, "You okay with this, Corsino?"

"Yes, sir," she said giving him a half-hearted salute. "Just tell me and my incredibly smelly raid jacket what you want us to do."

The drive gave them enough time to plan their approach. Stella had been to the facility with Butch one time to retrieve a few kilos after Kent was killed and was able to recall the general location of Kent's locker. All the storage locker doors faced an asphalt driveway and were easily accessible from a road inside the gates. The unit Kent rented was in the back corner at the end of the first row, and there was a gate off the side street that would put them directly behind that unit.

Behan decided to leave the car on the side street and use the back gate. It had an electronic keyboard, but Stella had given them the code. They entered quickly, and Josie looked down a long row of garage-type doors with security lights over every door. If Stella was right, they should've been standing directly behind Kent's locker. There was no activity in this row, and she could see a break in the buildings about halfway to the end.

They jogged toward the opening, but Josie stopped for a moment when she heard a familiar sound, the roar of a large motorcycle that sounded very close. The noise stopped, and she hurried to catch up to Behan, who had disappeared between the buildings.

"What the hell is he doing here?" Behan said, looking around the corner of the building in the direction of Kent's locker. There was enough artificial light to see all the way to the end.

Josie knelt close to the edge of the building and saw Too Tall's motorcycle parked behind the car she'd seen in the driveway at Art's girlfriend's house in Venice. The security lights in front of the unit made the area almost as bright as daylight. A van had been backed up to the storage unit door and Butch was carrying a box to the van. Too Tall came out of the unit, followed by Art and Kit. The two men appeared to be arguing and shouting at each other. Josie couldn't hear what they were saying, but she was disappointed. She had believed Too Tall's story that he had known nothing about the cocaine and was trying to help her. At this moment, he seemed to be very much a part of Art's scheme.

"Looks like the usual suspects are here," she said, moving back a little and standing behind Behan. "There's no way to get close unless we drive up when they're outside, felony stop, get everybody on the ground."

"Maybe the surprise of seeing car headlights come at them at eighty miles an hour will give us an advantage," Behan said, but gave her a look that said, "fat chance," before adding, "Don't see any other options, so let's do it before Butch finishes loading and he's no longer useful."

Josie turned to go back toward the car when she spotted the outline of a man in the moonlight kneeling on the roof of the building across the driveway but closer to Kent's storage locker. He was holding what she realized could be a rifle, but before she could react, she saw a flash from the muzzle and heard the retort of a high-powered weapon and then immediately another. She and Behan both drew their weapons. Art was on the ground. Too Tall had scrambled behind the van with Butch and Kit. Another round went through the front window of the van and the windshield exploded in a shower of glass. She estimated the shooter was only twenty-five to thirty yards away from her and Behan, but he was so focused on his intended targets he hadn't paid any attention to them standing between the buildings.

Using the edge of the wall to steady her hand and thankful for her new night sights on the Beretta, Josie aimed directly at the man's chest, took a deep breath, and pulled the trigger before he could shoot again. The discharge was like thunder echoing in the narrow passage and made her ears ring. The man turned slightly in their direction as she and Behan each fired their weapons one more time. He seemed to freeze in place for a few seconds before slowly crumpling forward on the roof. She kept her sight picture on his body for a few seconds longer, ready to fire again if he moved.

"He's down," Behan said, as he and Josie holstered their guns. "Get to the van. I'll check him."

She ran toward the van and the first thing she encountered was Art's body sprawled on the ground. He had been shot in the head and chest and was lying in a pool of blood and brain matter. She drew her semiauto again and carefully walked behind the van where she found Butch and Kit unharmed, sitting on the ground and handcuffed to the bumper of Art's car. Too Tall was leaning against his bike with blood covering the front of his shirt and leather jacket.

"Don't shoot, Josie," he said calmly, raising his hands just above his waist.

"Where's your weapon?" she asked, pointing her Beretta at him.

He slid off the bike and walked a couple steps toward her and said, "It's on the bike, in the side pocket. I only came here to warn Art."

"I thought you didn't know anything about all this."

"I didn't. But Abby found out and sent her man to kill Art and take the coke. I tried to warn him."

"Lift up your jacket and turn around," she ordered, and he did. She could see he didn't have a gun. "Put your hands down, just keep them where I can see. Are you hurt?" she asked, moving behind him and removing his handgun from the bike's saddlebag.

"I think the second round went through Art and nicked me. I'm okay."

"Thanks for the help," she said, nodding at Butch and Kit.

"No problem, cuffs don't get used much these days. They're scared shitless. Don't think they could walk, let alone run away."

"Why risk your life to help Art?" she asked. "He tried to set you up with his phony diaries."

"I don't know. He's . . . he was a worthless slug, but I just didn't want her to kill him. Maybe I wanted to do it myself." He hesitated a moment before saying, "I'll testify about her operation, names, places and I've got boxes of documentation on how and when payments were made to this shooter and the guys who killed Lance McCray and Billie. They almost killed Marge to satisfy Abby's petty meanness."

"How would you have all that information if you weren't working with her?"

"My uncle and cousin left me alone for a few hours yesterday in her apartment and left The Carnival office door unlocked. I might not be a cop anymore, but I can still search like one. Give me witness protection and I'll give you enough to put her away for a long time."

Police cars and an ambulance with sirens blaring were coming toward them on the long driveway minutes before Behan got there. He'd had to wait until the shooter was pronounced dead by the paramedics and he had the uniform officers from LAPD secure all the entrances to the storage facility. The South Bureau homicide detectives were more than willing to have Hollywood take over the investigation. Since the south end of the city had more than its share of shootings and killings, giving one away was a welcome surprise. The shooting team from Robbery-Homicide division and a deputy DA arrived shortly after the black-and-whites to interview Josie and Behan, who had fired a total of three shots between them, and the gunman had three entry wounds. He was still holding on to the rifle when he died.

"Piece of cake," Behan said to the RHD officer in charge. "Our casings are in the walkway and our lead is in the dead body. We made it real easy for you."

Josie knew it wouldn't be easy. The department and the district attorney would examine the shooting and decide if it was in policy and legal. She knew it was, but even scumbags got the benefit of a review.

The paramedics treated Too Tall for a superficial graze wound to his chest that bled a lot but wasn't life-threatening. He was eager to ride his bike back to Hollywood, but Behan had it towed and told the big man he'd have to travel in the car with him and Josie.

Most of the cocaine had already been loaded into the rented van. A couple boxes of jewelry and several handguns wrapped in canvas tarp were in there too. Butch admitted that he and Kent were part-time burglars and occasionally, Vern would take something valuable when he found himself alone inside a vacant house after a radio call.

Butch was frightened but happy, too, when Josie assured him Stella hadn't been harmed. He told her his street smarts had alerted him to the possibility Art might not want him around after he recovered his stolen cocaine. He said he took his time finding the storage unit, pretending he couldn't remember which door or number it was and loading the truck very slowly until he could find an opportunity to escape. His survival instincts might have given them just enough time to save his life. He was grateful and agreed to provide them with a statement about Kent's murder identifying both Art and Vern as the killers.

Josie was admittedly surprised to find Kit at the storage locker. She never suspected the aging hippie was involved in Art's drug dealing, maybe using marijuana but not selling cocaine. The woman was nearly catatonic when Josie uncuffed her from the bumper of the car.

"Why are you here?" Josie asked, helping her stand.

Kit shook her head but didn't answer.

"You know being here now makes you an accomplice to drug dealing and murder," Josie said, attempting to get some reaction.

"No, no, that's wrong," she stammered. "He told me we were leaving the state, picking up a few things he'd left in storage, driving north. That's all . . . no drugs . . . no killing." She stopped, caught her breath. The tears began streaming down her face; she grabbed her hair with both hands and screamed, a banshee wail from the depths of her misery. Dozens of police officers scattered along the driveway looked up, a few touched the butt of their guns as they scanned for the source of her howl.

The interview was over. Josie had one of the uniformed officers handcuff Kit again and put her in the back seat of his police car. Stupidity wasn't a booking offense, but Josie wasn't completely satisfied Art's girlfriend was as naive as she wanted everyone to believe. Butch and Kit would be taken back to Hollywood station with the three arrestees from Eddie's house and that's where this clusterfuck would get sorted out—at least a twenty-four-hour uninterrupted nightmare of interrogations/interviews, bookings, and homicide, evidence, and vehicle reports.

She wasn't about to let Too Tall out of her sight either, not until she got all the information he'd pilfered from The Carnival and found a safe place for him and his motorcycle to hide from the Testas.

It was nearly sunrise by the time homicide detectives and the shooting team finished their initial, on-scene investigations. Josie sat on the hood of Behan's car watching the coroner scrape pieces of Art's brain and body off the asphalt. She was finishing her fourth, maybe fifth cup of coffee as the sun came up. In a few minutes, she'd find a supervisor who had one of those portable phones and try to call Jake before he left for work. There didn't seem to be any sense in waking him any earlier. Besides, the DA's shooting review team was housed in his office, so he'd hear all the gory details soon enough.

The coffee had done its magic, keeping her awake for a few hours, but the adrenaline was gradually subsiding, and her body was beginning to feel the effects of sleep deprivation. She felt relief, but a little sadness too. They'd arrested Superman's killer, and Too Tall was confident he had enough information and documentation for Behan to close his other homicide cases, but it was difficult to celebrate. Vern and Art were as bad as any criminals she'd arrested in her brief career, worse than most. She understood any tarnish on the badge reflected on the whole department.

"It's a wrap, Corsino," Behan said, sitting next to her. "You look awful."

"Missed my beauty sleep and I really gotta pee, caffeine overload."

"Good shooting last night," he said. "Both your rounds and mine were on target . . . two in the torso, one head shot."

"I didn't aim at his head."

"I know," he said. "Curtis recovered the stolen police radio in Vern's backpack, and the ledger with our feathered customers' real names. Guess he's our Raven."

"Is he admitting that?"

"Who cares. Might've been Art, but Vern's the last bird standing, and he's holding the book. Are you up to going back to the office to finish reports or do you want to get a few hours' sleep first?"

"Give me half an hour to make a call and shower in Hollywood's locker room and I'm good to go."

"Curtis and Donny will book all the evidence and do those reports. We'll do the rest. Lieutenant and captain, maybe the West Bureau chief are on their way in . . . just a heads up," he said, winking at her.

"They'll be a lot of help," she said, sliding off the hood.

That was another reason not to feel great. The end of this investigation meant she'd either be sitting in the narcotics admin office or the Hollywood narcotics squad room as a Detective III. One outcome would make her happy. The other would please her family and just about everybody else in her world.

~ TWENTY-FOUR ~

The half hour Josie had requested to take a shower and make a phone call turned into two hours. She made the mistake of resting for "just a minute" in the Hollywood station cot room. The noisy day-watch officers banging their lockers shut woke her or she probably would have slept longer. A quick shower and she called Jake at work. He had already heard about the shooting and had called the narcotics office where Tomic filled him in on the rest.

Jake was in a good mood. He understood that the end of the Kent murder investigation meant a promotion for her and more stability in his home life. She didn't mention her desire to remain in the Hollywood narcotics squad in Behan's position as a detective supervisor. Why ruin his day before she knew anything for certain?

She'd made her call in the station's report writing room and was just finishing her conversation when Marge walked into the cramped space with cluttered counters, telephones, and a dozen folding chairs that were all empty at the moment. She sat beside Josie and waited for her to hang up.

"Nice work, Corsino," Marge said with not a sign of emotion. She looked tired and pale and Josie figured she probably hadn't slept all night.

"You hear Gilbert's given us enough to arrest Abby? You won't have to kill her after all," Josie said, hoping she was joking.

"I heard. I pretty much hung around the narco office all night listening to the radio. This morning the captain at Organized Crime promised I could be there when she goes down."

"How'd you manage that?"

"I dated him last year . . . we're still kind of friends," she said and shrugged as if it wasn't a big deal. "I want that fat fucker and her psycho Sicilian dad to see my smiling face when they put the cuffs on. Payback's a bitch," she said, hesitated, and stood before adding, "I know you've gotta get back across the street, but I want to say . . . Behan told me you're the one made this happen. I fucking owe you."

"Yeah, you do," Josie said, trying to look serious. "And I expect at least a couple of great meals with bottles of really expensive Cabernet. Go home and get some sleep so you don't have a relapse and miss all the fun."

THE SQUAD room was bustling with activity by the time Josie got back across the street. Detectives from the Major Violators section were helping Curtis and Donny finish the evidence reports for the large volume of cocaine recovered. It would be put back on Property division's schedule to be destroyed a second time after Vern's and Eddie's trials. Butch and Stella were being interviewed on tape by homicide detectives, and Behan, with the assistance of detectives from Organized Crime, was sorting through the box of files Too Tall had confiscated from Abby's office. A comprehensive statement had been provided by Too Tall, and he'd been removed to a safe house guarded by district attorney investigators.

"We've got a team watching Abby Morrison until we're ready to pick her up," Behan said, handing Josie a stack of files as soon as she walked into the office. "I've already gone through some of them. They're dynamite. Our little Testa spawn keeps great records."

"Are we okay looking at these without a warrant?" she asked.

"Too Tall wasn't working for us, so the DA thinks we're okay, but he's running it by Judge Whitehall this morning."

Josie relaxed. Judge Whitehall was a very conservative pro-police jurist whose decisions usually leaned toward law enforcement. Her advice and direction would keep everything strictly within the law.

Curtis was finishing the evidence reports. Josie saw a ziplock baggie containing several smaller baggies each with one rock of cocaine sitting on his desk and she asked where he had recovered the drugs.

"When I searched Vern's locker, he had them hidden in a can of deodorant spray with a false bottom," Curtis said. "Dirtbag had a stash to plant on the competition." He grinned and made a motion as if he were pulling a lever. "Cha-ching, them charges just keep piling on."

Tomic was helping with the reports but he made no attempt to converse with Josie beyond perfunctory responses. He seemed sober and had shaved, showered, and changed his clothes, all signs of having been home with Mrs. Tomic rather than carousing with the cheerleader. If that were true, Josie was happy for him and could have made an effort to mend their partnership but didn't. If they promoted her to Detective III in Hollywood, Josie could supervise him and the others, but she was weary of all the drama that came with being Tomic's confidante and friend.

It was early afternoon before Lieutenant Watts and Captain Clark arrived in the Hollywood office. They congratulated Behan and the squad for a few minutes and then locked themselves in the lieutenant's office.

"It's so nice to be appreciated . . . for a second or two," Curtis said sarcastically.

"Thanks so much, but your squad's been dismantled. Welcome to South Bureau," Donny said.

"Hey, we solved three murders and found evidence stolen from Property division they didn't even know was missing," Josie said. "Not to mention we put a dent in the Testa family's enterprise. That should weigh in our favor."

"Yeah, but all Art's crap is on the other side of that scale," Tomic said.

"We caught him and Vern. That has to count for something."

The room got quiet. Josie knew why. Except for her, they were all veteran cops and had learned the department always overreacted. Their squad would probably pay the price, so the chief of police could tell the city politicians and community activists he had done something, changed the climate of corruption. It didn't matter that one or two bad cops didn't constitute a climate; that was the nature of the LAPD.

The door to the lieutenant's office opened and the captain's voice shouted, "Corsino, come in here a minute."

She exhaled and gave Behan a tight smile.

"Use your head, don't be a smart-ass," he cautioned as she passed his desk and went into Watts's office.

Captain Clark was sitting in the lieutenant's leather chair behind his desk and Watts stood near the file cabinet.

"Time's up, detective," Clark said with a big grin. "Are you going to take the promotion and come to my admin section or stay here as a Detective II with not much chance of promoting anytime soon." He motioned for her to sit on the only other chair in front of the desk, but she remained standing.

"There's a Detective III spot in Hollywood. I think I've earned the right to be considered for that position," she said with a strong confident voice.

Captain Clark looked at Watts and sighed.

"You're not ready to head up a squad," he said.

"I think I've proved I'm more than ready."

"That's my decision, not yours. Take the promotion or stay here as a Detective II and work for Ray Martinez. I'm moving him from Central narcotics to run the Hollywood squad. I won't force you or the others to move, but that's my onetime offer."

She knew Martinez. He was already a D-III and had a good reputation as a hard-charging, knowledgeable cop. Josie couldn't argue that she was more qualified than he was, but knew she'd be a better D-III in Hollywood.

"I'll take the admin promotion," she said and started to leave, but stopped and added, "Thank you for the opportunity."

Josie gently closed the door behind her and glanced at Behan before sitting at her desk.

"Well?" Curtis asked. "Did you tell him what to do with his admin job?"

"I took it," she said, looking at Behan. He nodded his approval.

"In two years, you'll have Watts's job," Tomic said.

"Maybe in four years you'll have Clark's and we'll have a narcotics captain who has a clue," Donny said.

"I can't believe you'd give up the street for a desk job," Curtis said, not looking at her. He picked up his jacket and went into the hallway. She heard his locker open and slam close.

"What's his problem?" Josie asked his partner and Donny shrugged. "You'd think he'd be happy to be rid of me."

"You're buying at Nora's tomorrow night," Donny said, giving her a hug before he left too.

The paperwork was done, and the evidence had been booked. Vern was sitting in a cell at men's jail downtown, arrested for Kent's murder, and Too Tall was safely tucked away for a few days until they obtained an arrest warrant for Abby Morrison.

Tomic congratulated her before he left, but his cold demeanor hadn't changed. He kept his emotional distance. Their bond had been broken, but she had to admit she'd never really understood him or his complicated personality. He was willing to operate too close to that line between acceptable and questionable. She might put a toe in the water now and then, but he'd taken the plunge far too often for her comfort.

Lost in her thoughts, Josie hadn't realized Behan was still in the office. She needed to go home and sleep, tell Jake the news he'd been waiting to hear. While she was standing in Watts's office, the answer to the captain's question was immediately clear, but now she was having second thoughts. Like Curtis, she wanted to stay on the streets; narcotics enforcement was exciting and fun. But there was another part of her that needed to promote. It tormented her that unqualified leaders like Watts and Clark made decisions that affected working cops' lives and their ability to do their jobs. She liked and admired cops and wanted to make it easier for them to work. Most of all, she wanted to be the one making the decisions. The warrior and the chief halves of her brain were in conflict.

"Corsino, are you going home to sleep or are you going to stay here all day staring into space?" Behan asked. He got up from his desk and sat across the table from her. "You made the right decision," he said.

"Did I?"

"Take the promotion and in a year or less find another position. Clark is never going to give you a squad."

"I love working narcotics."

"There's a Detective III spot opening up in Internal Affairs in a few months to supervise a surveillance squad. You'd be perfect, and it would keep you on the street and give you IA experience when you're ready to take the lieutenant's exam."

"Maybe the chief can still be a warrior," she said and thanked him.

"What?"

"Nothing, a little internal dilemma."

"You've got some time before the deployment period ends, so go home and get some sleep. I expect you to work until you leave."

She followed him out to the parking lot and got into the Mustang. As she drove out toward the exit, Curtis was crossing the street coming back from Hollywood station. She stopped in the driveway and he walked closer to her open window.

"I still think you're making a mistake, Corsino," he said, bending over with his hands on his knees. "You could learn a lot more out here, but I'd work with you any day." He straightened up, extended his right hand, shook hers, and walked away.

Josie rolled up the window and watched him go back into the narcotics office.

"That'll do," she said, nodding, and drove toward home.